JUST HOW BIG *IS* ODELIA GREY?

What reviewers are saying…

"I'd like to spend more time with Sue Ann Jaffarian's Odelia… [Odelia] does not hesitate to give justice a small, well-plotted forward shove at every opportunity."—*The New York Times*

"Odelia Grey is definitely a force to be reckoned with."
—*ReviewingTheEvidence.com*

"Odelia Grey is a keeper."—*Library Journal*

"Jaffarian plays the formula with finesse, keeping love problems firmly in the background while giving her heroine room to use her ample wit and grit."—*Kirkus Reviews*

"[Odelia Grey] is an intriguing character, a true counter against stereotype, who demonstrates that life can be good, even in a world where thin is always in."—*Booklist*

"A sharp, snappy mystery novel…This is a fast and furious read that should be fun to see as a series with Odelia as the lead character."—*AmaZe Magazine*

What fellow authors are saying…

"More fun than a lunch pail full of plump paralegals, *The Curse of the Holy Pail* is a tale as bouncy as its bodacious protagonist."
—*Bill Fitzhugh, author of* Highway 61 Resurfaced *and* Pest Control

"[*The Curse of the Holy Pail* is] even better than her first…a major hoot!"—*Thomas B. Sawyer, author of* The Sixteenth Man *and former head writer/producer of* Murder, She Wrote

"Sue Ann Jaffarian does a masterful job. Once you get to know Odelia Grey, you'll love her. I know I do."—*Naomi Hirahara, Edgar-winning author of* Snakeskin Shamisen

"A plus-sized thumbs up. Jaffarian's a new sharpshooter in crime fiction."—*Brian M. Wiprud, author of* Stuffed *and* Pipsqueak, *winner of Lefty Award for Most Humorous Novel*

SUE ANN
JAFFARIAN

AN ODELIA GREY MYSTERY

BOOBY TRAP

MIDNIGHT INK
WOODBURY, MINNESOTA

FIRST EDITION
First Printing, 2009

Book design by Donna Burch
Cover design by Ellen L. Dahl
Editing by Rebecca Zins

Midnight Ink, an imprint of Llewellyn Publications

This is a work of fiction. Names, characters, places, and incidents are either the product of the author's imagination or are used fictitiously, and any resemblance to actual persons, living or dead, business establishments, events, or locales is entirely coincidental.

Library of Congress Cataloging-in-Publication Data
Jaffarian, Sue Ann, 1952–
    Booby trap : an Odelia Grey mystery / Sue Ann Jaffarian.—1st ed.
        p.   cm.
  ISBN 978-0-7387-1350-2
  1. Grey, Odelia (Fictitious character)—Fiction. 2. Overweight women—
Fiction. 3. Serial murderers—Fiction. 4. Legal assistants—Fiction. 5. Women
detectives—California—Fiction. 6. California—Fiction. I. Title.
  PS3610.A359B66 2009
  813'.6—dc22

                                                            2008036629

Midnight Ink
2143 Wooddale Drive, Dept. 978-0-7387-1350-2
Woodbury, MN 55125-2989

www.midnightinkbooks.com

Printed in the United States of America

DEDICATION

For Whitney
Super Agent and Super Friend

Thank you for helping my dreams come true.

ACKNOWLEDGMENTS

There is never enough thanks for the folks who make every Odelia Grey novel possible.

As always, to Whitney Lee, my agent; Diana James, my manager; all the good folks at Llewellyn Worldwide/Midnight Ink, especially Barbara Moore, Rebecca Zins, Marissa Pederson, and Ellen Dahl.

Dr. Stacia Spaulding for proofreading the manuscript when my eyes couldn't look at it one more minute.

Attorney Mark Hardiman for providing some of the legal background needed for this novel. Attorney Salvatore Zimmitti for information and discussion about international smuggling.

Lee Lofland, friend and author of *Police Procedure & Investigation*, who allowed me to pick his brain from time to time.

My many friends and family who cheer me on and keep my feet on the ground, and listen patiently to my constant brainstorming. With special thanks to Miles Holiman, who gave up a Saturday to help me with research.

To the many readers who take time from their lives to tell me how much they enjoy my books. You're the best!

ONE

As soon as I took my first bite, I knew I should have ordered the salad. As soon as I took my second bite, I knew I should never have agreed to lunch.

Sticking a napkin end into my water glass, I proceeded to dab at the small globs of marinara sauce that had dribbled out of my chicken parmigiana sandwich, landing like large blood drops down the front of my baby blue sweater, not once but twice. Once when I took my first bite—the second when my lunch companion made her startling announcement.

"I think my son is the Blond Bomber" was what she'd said.

Yep, I'm sure of it. Positively, absolutely, and without a doubt sure that the elegant and lovely older woman sitting across from me had said those exact words.

"Odelia, did you hear me?"

I kept dabbing at the now rust-colored pattern of stains dotting the blue sky of my bosom and tried to think of something else. Anything else.

Have you ever noticed that small-breasted women almost never have food stains on the front of their clothing? Maybe Shout or Spray 'n Wash should have plump women with big breasts touting their products on TV. Tiny women with big boobies wouldn't work. After all, no one in their right mind would believe they eat anything worth spilling. Yep, plump women with big, drip-catching boobs—*that* would sell the product to me. I might even audition for the part.

"I said, my son might be the Blond Bomber, the serial killer." This was said just a tiny bit louder and with more conviction than the first time. "You know, the one in the news."

"I heard you the first time, Lil."

My response was gentle, not snappish or impatient. I forgot about the stain on my chest and my marketing plan for stain-removing products and looked up at her just so she'd see I wasn't cross.

Lillian Ramsey sat across the table from me, the picture of grace and propriety. She was about seventy years of age, with ramrod posture and impeccable manners. Her hair, a very pale silver blond, was cropped into a soft, wispy hairdo that accented her crystal blue eyes and perfect, yet lined, complexion. Her makeup was flawless, her choice of lipstick perfect. I should look so good at her age. Hell, I'd be happy to look that good at fifty, which was in one year and four months. But who's counting?

Lil looked at me expectantly, her eyes sad, her coral-tinted lips down-turned, waiting for my comment on her shocking statement.

"That's a pretty serious assumption, Lil, for anyone. But for a mother?"

As tears started welling, she lifted her napkin and dabbed at the inside corners of her eyes. "Do you think this was a conclusion I came to easily? It's not a joke."

Her voice was firm, but there were a few cracks here and there. Something told me that once those cracks were allowed to widen, the steadfast emotional dam would break and she'd be engulfed by a tsunami of tears. It was easy to see that Lil was trying hard to hold herself together.

Lillian Ramsey was originally from Teaneck, New Jersey. She had been widowed twice: once when she was young, the second time a few years ago. Her second husband, Cecil Ramsey, had left her extremely comfortable. Brian Eddy, her son from her first marriage, is a doctor, a plastic surgeon living and working in Orange County. Dr. Brian Eddy had developed a technique that allowed such surgeries to be done with less pain and recuperating time, making it perfect for actors needing a quick tuck between projects. While other plastic surgeons might be considered tops in the field, Brian Eddy was the top of the top, the surgeon's surgeon. His boobs were perkier, his noses straighter, his fannies tighter. He was the Orville Redenbacher of implants and liposuction.

But the Blond Bomber?

The Blond Bomber was the nickname given to a serial killer who had been plaguing Southern California on and off for the past year. So far, four women had been murdered. While they were from different economic stations and varied in age, all the murdered women had one thing in common: they were considered blond bombshells—women with killer figures, long light-blond hair, and even longer legs. Except for the physical attributes, the women seemed to have no other connection.

3

None of the victims had been killed by a bomb, but the media, with their need to attach a sensational and catchy name to the monster, had christened him the Blond Bomber, and the public, always eager to be spectators to the ghoulish and grisly side of life, had jumped on board.

The latest murder had occurred just three weeks ago and had been too close to home for my comfort, even though I am hardly a blond bombshell. Now, if the killer was looking to off a short, two-hundred-plus, cranky, middle-aged woman with medium-brown hair and freckles, I was his gal.

His last victim had been a nurse who worked at Hoag Hospital in Newport Beach. She had disappeared following her shift and was found three days later in Laguna Canyon, naked, tied to a tree, and dead. According to the news, the word *whore* had been printed on her torso in black, just like all the others.

My friend Dev Frye, a Newport Beach homicide detective, had been called in to assist on the case since the victim had lived and worked in Newport Beach. This past Tuesday, in celebration of Greg's birthday, Greg and I had invited him over for dinner with a few other friends, and he had arrived late, with a bottle of fine wine in hand, his face haggard and distressed.

"No, Lil, I'm sure it's not a joke. Not to you, not to anyone. But to suspect your own son of such a heinous thing, it's so … so …" Search as I might, I couldn't think of the right word.

"So unspeakable?"

Bingo. "Yes, Lil. So unspeakable."

Lil took a sip of her coffee and dabbed at the corners of her mouth before continuing. "I'm sure Jeffrey Dahmer had a mother.

And Ted Bundy. And Charles Manson. Monsters are born into this world just like everyone else, Odelia."

I nodded, speechless for a change. I studied Lil. We'd met online several years earlier in an Internet game room and soon found ourselves meeting online once or twice a week to play backgammon. Increasingly, the online meetings had less to do with the games and more to do with sharing our lives and exchanging ideas. We finally thought it silly not to meet in person, especially since I lived in Newport Beach and she lived in Laguna Hills, which aren't that far from each other. We started meeting every few months after that for lunch. Lil had even attended my wedding, and even though I now live in Seal Beach, which is a bit further up the coast from Laguna Hills, we still make time for our occasional lunches.

I had yet to meet the talented Dr. Brian Eddy, even though I'd heard quite a bit about him.

"Of course, I know you're right, Lil. But still, it's so creepy and bizarre. How on earth did you come up with such an idea? I mean, do you have any proof?"

She held the napkin up to her nose and sniffed gently. "No, no hard evidence, just a lot of coincidences. And some things I'd rather not talk about right now." She looked around the restaurant. It was a pleasant and airy café near her home—a place frequented by a lot of her neighbors from Leisure World, the retirement community where she resided. "At least not here."

Stealing a glance around the restaurant, I noted many well-heeled elderly couples and pairs of ladies enjoying their lunch, several of whom had smiled and waved when we first came in. At forty-eight, I was easily the youngest person in the place, outside of the restaurant staff.

Glancing discreetly at my watch, I wondered if Lil expected to continue this conversation back at her condominium after lunch. It was almost two o'clock, and Greg and I were meeting our close friends, Zee and Seth Washington, for dinner and a movie tonight. Still, my curiosity was heightened, and I wanted to know more. I also felt that Lil needed to say more but wasn't sure how to begin outside of blurting out her initial suspicion.

I looked down at my forgotten, messy sandwich. Lil had resumed nibbling on her chicken salad, so I followed suit by removing the top piece of the roll and eating the chicken parmigiana sub with a knife and fork. After a few bites in thoughtful silence, I turned my attention back to Lil's hot topic.

"Why are you telling me this, Lil?"

She didn't look up from her salad but instead studied the mixed greens and chopped chicken when she spoke.

"I didn't know what else to do." Her voice was small. When she did finally look up, her eyes were not the eyes of a twice-widowed mother but the confused, wide eyes of a lost child. "I've had my suspicions since the third girl was ..." Her voice drifted off as she went back to examining her meal.

I still clearly remembered the third victim of the Blond Bomber because she had, indeed, been a girl. Her name had been Gabby, Gabrielle Kerr. A precocious sixteen-year-old from Pasadena, she had naturally and prematurely developed like a Playboy Bunny centerfold. It had come out in the investigation that Gabby had been talking to someone new on the Internet several weeks before she disappeared. Like the others, she'd also been found naked and bound to a tree, with the word *whore* etched across her young stomach. She'd also been the only victim under twenty-one. It had happened just three months ago, and it made me wonder if Gabby had been a mistake—if maybe she'd convinced the murderer that she was older than she was before they met. I also wondered if she hadn't been in such a rush to grow up, would she still be alive?

"Why didn't you tell someone sooner?"

"I kept hoping something would turn up to prove me wrong… something that would show me I was just a silly old woman with an overactive imagination."

I had something harsh to say, something that would only make Lil feel worse, but something that had to be said. I chose my words as carefully as I knew how.

"Lil, please don't think I'm being horrible, but if Brian is the Blond Bomber and you've suspected it since that girl Gabby was killed, you might have prevented the death of the last woman—the nurse."

This time when the tears threatened to flow, Lil made no attempt to stop them. In short order they pooled, dripping down her cheeks slowly. She looked stricken.

"I know, Odelia. Often I've wondered if I'm partially to blame, in one way or another. After all, it's always the mother's fault, isn't it?"

There was food for thought—food that didn't drip down the front of a sweater as much as it dripped down the inside of my brain like hot wax. It made me wonder how much of my own quirky behavior could be attributed to my mother abandoning me at sixteen and her emotional abandonment long before that. Still, I hadn't turned to taking innocent lives to act out my issues. At least not yet.

"Oh, Lil, I'm so sorry, but I'm sure you're wrong. Would you like me to contact one of the detectives on the latest murder? He's a friend of mine. His name is Dev Frye, and I'm sure he could put your fears to rest." *Or confirm them*, I thought but didn't dare say.

Holy crap, I thought to myself, *what if Brian Eddy is* the Blond Bomber? *What then?*

Lil sipped some more tea and composed herself. "Thank you, Odelia, that's very nice of you. But I don't want to involve the police just yet. That's why I said something to you." She daintily dabbed the napkin at her mouth. "If I'm wrong, Brian will be mortified and outraged. He might never let me see my grandchildren again." She looked stricken at the thought.

I reached over and patted one of her hands as it rested on the table. "So what are you going to do?"

"I'm so glad you asked that, my dear. I was hoping *you* could help."

TWO

"How's Lil?" Greg called out from the bathroom.

I had just arrived home and was spending the required five to ten minutes greeting Wainwright, Greg's exuberant golden retriever, and Seamus, my crotchety, one-eyed, ragged-eared cat. Even before Greg and I kiss hello, Wainwright has to be petted, scratched behind his ears, and told what a good boy he is, and Seamus has to receive the kitty equivalent. It isn't this way when guests arrive, just with us. We're mommy and daddy, after all, and as all parents know, the kids come first.

Parental duties out of the way, I headed down the hall toward the master suite and bathroom. Greg and I have been married nearly five months. After the wedding, I moved into his customized home in Seal Beach and rented out my townhouse in Newport Beach. I have a longer commute to work now, but with Greg in a wheelchair, there was no way we could have even considered combining our little family into my two-story digs. But even though I gave up my townhouse, I kept my name. Greg didn't mind, though I think his parents were disappointed. But I've been Odelia Patience Grey a very long time, and it didn't seem right or necessary to change that now.

In the bathroom, I found Greg freshly showered and shaving. Greg wears a very becoming Van Dyke–style beard and was maneuvering the blade around the lathered portion of his face with deft moves. I planted a kiss on the top of his freshly shampooed, wet head before pulling my sweater over my own head.

"Why are you changing?" He stopped shaving and glanced my way. "You look nice."

I held up the blue sweater to display the stains down the front. "Curse of the big boobs strikes again. Fortunately, it's washable." I reached under the sink, pulled out a bottle of Spray 'n Wash, and began squirting the sauce drippings like they were bad guys and I was the SWAT team.

Greg grinned. "I, for one, don't consider your big boobs a curse."

To prove his point, he reached out and pulled me to him. Before I could protest or pull away, he mashed his face, lather and all, into my cleavage and made sloppy kissing noises. I must say, one of the good news/bad news things about being short and having a hubby in a wheelchair is that his face is always at your chest level.

I giggled and playfully slapped at the back of his head. Not only was I enjoying his attention, I was happy to get his mind off of my lunch with Lil. I knew I would have to discuss it with him sometime soon, but I wanted to pick the time, like maybe tomorrow, over breakfast, while his nose is buried in the Sunday paper. Not tonight, after he's worked all day at his shop, Ocean Breeze Graphics, and before we were to meet Zee and Seth.

I knew Greg wasn't going to be happy with what I had to say and would only enlist Seth's legal opinion on the matter. And although Seth Washington is a crackerjack attorney, he is also a crackerjack pain in my big fat behind whenever he thinks I'm sticking my nose into something I shouldn't. He and Greg would be hounding me all night about it. Zee, on the other hand, was always a wild card. Sometimes she took my side, sometimes she didn't. All I wanted from our evening together was a tasty, preferably non-drippy meal, good company, and a fun movie.

The stain remover might have taken care of the marinara sauce, but I was still wishing I had skipped lunch. I wanted to rewind the day back to before I'd ordered the messy sub, and definitely back to before hearing Lil's words *I think my son is the Blond Bomber.* Just hearing those words made me feel involved, no matter what my decision.

"We're doing Chinese tonight, sweetheart." Greg returned to his shaving. "That okay with you?"

"Sure," I mumbled, still lost in my thoughts about the Blond Bomber.

Should I talk to Dev Frye about it? Did I have a legal obligation to go to the police? Could I live with myself if another woman was killed and the murderer turns out to be Brian Eddy? These were questions I did not want to discuss tonight over Mongolian beef and Kung Pao chicken.

Who knows? Maybe my fortune cookie tonight will say something helpful, like *Relax, he didn't do it.*

Then again, it might also say *He who hesitates is lost.*

You are a decisive individual was the sage advice offered up by my fortune cookie Saturday night. It should have read *You are a procrastinating nincompoop.*

We were spending a couple of hours at a small, grassy park located next to the Seal Beach pier and overlooking the beach. Dogs weren't allowed at the park, but every now and then the local police would turn a blind eye when it came to Greg and Wainwright, especially if it wasn't the busy tourist season. I was staked out under a small tree in a folding beach chair, reading the latest Chuck Zito mystery novel, while Greg played Frisbee with Wainwright. It was a gorgeous April day, slightly warm, with a gentle breeze coming off the ocean. Lots of folks were around enjoying a relaxing Sunday, including two young boys who came here regularly. Greg and Wainwright were well known at the beach, and now so was I. Greg and the boys were throwing the round disk back and forth while Wainwright ran between them, trying to nab it or scoop up a wild throw. Sometimes he succeeded, then he would change the throwing game into a game of catch-me-if-you-can. There was nothing Wainwright liked more than to play Frisbee on the beach. If kids were involved, all the better. I think he'd even give up an occasional meal to do it, if he had to.

I hadn't said anything to Greg yet about my conversation with Lillian Ramsey. There were several opportunities over breakfast, including one moment when Greg asked if I was okay. He'd said I seemed preoccupied. That had been the perfect moment, and I had let it slide by, sloughing off his question as if slicked with softened butter.

"How's the book?" Greg asked, rolling up to where I sat. He was hot but full of life and energy. His blue eyes studied me with concern.

"Very good."

"Yeah? Seems it would be much better if you'd turn the pages. You've been staring into space for the past ten minutes."

"Have I?"

I looked past Greg and watched Wainwright rolling around with the two boys. The big yellow dog looked pooped but happy. I put down the book and rummaged around in the large thermal bag sitting next to me. Pulling out a cold soda, I handed it to Greg. He took it silently, his eyes never leaving my face. I tried to ignore him as I pulled out a jumbo Cool Whip container filled with water for the dog.

"Wainwright," I called, "come here, boy." I snapped the lid off the plastic container and placed it down on the ground. The dog bounded over and lapped up the water with gusto.

Greg started to say something, but Silas, one of the boys, came up to us. He handed Greg the Frisbee. "We gotta go. Thanks for letting us play with Wainwright. He's a cool dog."

"Anytime, Silas." Greg gave the boy a wink. "We enjoy it as much as you do."

Silas was eleven years old with shaggy black hair, intelligent brown eyes, and skin kissed by the sun. The boy with him was his younger brother. He sported a buzz cut and equally tanned skin. His name was Billy. Both boys had their tee shirts off.

As the boys scampered off, I got up and started packing up my book and chair, still not meeting Greg's eyes. "It's really getting hot out here. Mind if we go home?"

"Not at all, sweetheart, I was thinking the same thing myself. I brought some work home from the shop that I need to attack this afternoon."

Greg downed the soda in two huge gulps. He took his empty can and the one I had drained earlier and rolled over to a homeless man who sat on a bench near our van. He handed him the cans. The homeless man was very old and was called Pops by everyone who lived in the area. Greg handed him the cans and a five-dollar bill.

"Thanks for watching my van, Pops," Greg said to him. "Great job."

It was a ritual that happened every time we drove the few blocks to the beach instead of walking. Not that the van needed watching—it was the middle of the day, and it was parked in a handicapped space right in front of the park, but Greg and Pops had an understanding. Pops believed in working for his money. So the entire time we were at the beach, Pops never left the bench next to our vehicle. That was his job—that and collecting cans and bottles. Sometimes we would have brunch at a small restaurant across the street before enjoying the park. On those days, Greg would order an omelet with extra crispy hash browns and sliced tomatoes to accompany the five-dollar bill. He told Pops the meal was a well-earned bonus.

How could I not love this man?

Once at home, Wainwright slurped down more water before plopping down on the cool tile floor for a nap. Seamus joined him. Cats love comfort, and Seamus thought there was nothing more comfortable than using a golden retriever as a pillow.

After cleaning up, Greg went into our home office and dug into his work. I went out to our covered patio and plunked myself down on a chaise. For a few minutes, I thought about what I was going to do with the chicken breasts I'd defrosted for dinner, then I tried once again to concentrate on my book. But all I could think about was Lil and her request.

It wasn't too long before Greg was at the open patio door. "Ice cream or Thin Mints?" he asked me with a smile.

"What?"

"Is this a Cherry Garcia problem or a Thin Mint problem you're stewing over?"

I laughed in spite of my worry over Lil. Greg not only loved me, he knew me. Whenever faced with a problem I can't quite resolve, I drown myself in specific comfort foods.

I'm told that most people gain weight when they marry. In the short time I've been married to Greg, I've lost nearly fifteen pounds. I must be happy because there has been a lot less emotional eating in the past five months.

"It's a bucket-o-puddin' kind of problem," I told him with a dead-serious face.

Instantly, Greg dropped his smile, and his face clouded over. "You sure?"

I nodded. Bucket-o-puddin' referred to a large container of pre-made chocolate pudding and was code for a very serious problem.

Greg disappeared and returned with a container of Ben & Jerry's Cherry Garcia ice cream and two spoons. As he stripped the seal off of the container, I joined him at our redwood picnic table.

"Sorry, sweetheart, but we're out of pudding."

As I reached for a spoon, he stopped me. "Before you start, you have to promise to tell me the truth, the whole truth, and nothing but the truth."

"I do."

"*I do* was back in November. Here I'm looking for an *I will*."

I smiled slightly. "I will."

He popped open the container and handed me a spoon. "Would you do the honors of breaking ground?"

"I will." I dug into the smooth virgin ice cream and extracted a large spoonful. Again, how could I not love this man?

By the time the pint was almost empty, I had told him what Lil suspected and what she was asking me to do. Like a slow-moving storm, Greg's face clouded with each word, but he let me talk, not interrupting until I was finished. I did note, however, that he was digging into the ice cream with more urgency as the topic darkened and my possible involvement deepened. After I put down my spoon, Greg pulled the container to him and polished it off in silence. I went into the house and came back out with two large glasses of water with lemon slices.

"Did Lil tell you exactly why she thinks Brian is the Blond Bomber?"

"No, and I didn't want her to. Not until I'm sure I can and will help." I took a drink. "The less I know, the better."

"Wow" was all he said before taking his own big drink of water.

"I'm sorry I didn't tell you sooner." I took another drink. "I had planned to this morning, but I knew you would be upset, and I didn't want to ruin your day."

For several minutes, Greg remained as still as death. He looked at me, his eyes telling me nothing about what was going on inside him. I didn't think it was a good sign.

"Jesus, Odelia." When he spoke, his voice was strong but not angry. "It's barely been six months since the last time you buddied up with danger. Couldn't you have at least waited until we passed our first anniversary?"

He sighed deeply. "When I decided I couldn't live without you, I realized that I would have to live with this penchant of yours to stumble into unsavory situations. I had just hoped that once we married and you moved to Seal Beach, it would at least slow down, not accelerate."

"Geez, it's not like I left a trail of bloody bread crumbs from Newport Beach to here." I started to say more, but he stopped me by raising a hand like a flesh-colored stop sign.

"Let me finish." He ran his hand through his styled, longish hair. "I'm not thrilled about this, to say the least. But I tried ranting and raving once, and it didn't work. So, here's the deal, and it's a three-parter, so please keep your panties on and don't interrupt."

In an uncharacteristic wise move, I kept my mouth shut and heard him out.

"The first part of the deal," he began, taking both of my hands in both of his, "is that whatever you get involved with, I'm your partner on it. I'm your partner in life. I might as well be your partner in crime, so to speak."

My mouth fell open with surprise. "*You* want to help Lil find out if her son is the Blond Bomber?"

"No, I want to help *you*. It's important to me to keep you safe, and if helping you help Lil will do that, I'm in. The second part of the deal is, you do not, under any circumstances, try to find the Blond Bomber. You are only to look for proof that Brian Eddy is *not* the killer, not flush out the real killer. Leave that to the professionals. You understand?"

"Are you kidding? I have no intention of mixing it up with the Blond Bomber."

Greg chuckled. "I know you don't, sweetheart. But you do have a knack for finding trouble you never intended on finding." He paused and locked his eyes onto mine. "The third part of the deal is that you have to promise to always keep me informed."

"Absolutely." And I meant it. After spending the bulk of my forty-eight years alone, it felt great to have a partner—to belong, not *to* someone, but *with* someone. It was no longer Odelia Patience Grey versus the world, but me and Greg in a loving and strong partnership, ready to take on whatever life threw our way—even if that "whatever" was murder and mayhem. We probably should have had that written into our wedding vows.

"So," he said. "What's next? Telling Dev?"

"No, not yet, for exactly the reasons Lil fears."

Greg nodded in understanding.

"What's next," I continued, "is talking to Mike Steele. First thing tomorrow morning."

At this point, Greg threw back his head and laughed out loud. When he stopped laughing, he said, "Too bad I have an important meeting tomorrow. I'd give anything to be there for that. Could you video it somehow?"

THREE

When I lived in Newport Beach, I used to walk most mornings around the Back Bay area with Zee and some of the other members of Reality Check. Originally organized to offer advice and support for women of size fighting it out in a skinny-obsessed world, it now offers support to anyone who feels they don't fit into what society considers *normal*. In addition to plus-size men and women, the group now has members who are little people, who are deaf, and who are in wheelchairs.

Now that I live in Seal Beach, I walk with Wainwright. Greg is not a morning person. Before I moved in, Wainwright's morning exercise consisted of dashing through his doggie door to relieve himself and running laps around the back patio while his master snoozed. These days, he and I walk around the neighborhood and down to the beach. The big, friendly animal is happier than a pig in a mud puddle with this arrangement. Meanwhile, back at Casa de Stevens-Grey, Seamus remains curled up, warm and snug, with Greg. It's a win-win on all fronts. I miss walking with my friends, but to perk me up, Greg bought me an iPod, so now it's me, Wainwright, and a playlist of upbeat rock 'n' roll oldies walking the early morning beat.

This morning, it about broke my heart to see Wainwright standing by the back door, his leash hanging from his mouth. I soothed my guilt with the knowledge that Greg took the dog to work with him every day. The animal is far from neglected.

As Mike Steele is an early bird and his day is usually jampacked, I decided the best time to get his attention would be early in the morning, before the office officially opened.

I am a corporate paralegal at the law firm of Wallace, Boer, Brown and Yates, or "Woobie" as we people in the trenches affectionately call it. Although I technically work for all the attorneys in the firm, my supervising attorney is Michael Steele, a brilliant attorney who considers arrogance a virtue and sarcasm a grace. Steele also had the bad habit of going through secretaries like the Tasmanian Devil. It was a toss-up whether they left because of his obnoxious work habits or because they eventually had an affair with him and decided it wasn't worth the aggravation to stick around when it was over, which was in pretty short order.

Now don't get me wrong: to my knowledge, Steele has never sexually harassed any of these women. That wouldn't be his style. No, he's more of the "woo them with charm and attention" type. Then, after they got to know him, they usually ran screaming from the office. My guess is a lot of the women thought the affair would turn into a commitment or at the very least a cushy job.

Much to everyone's happiness except Steele's, those days seem to be over. For nearly five months, Jill Bernelli has worked as Steele's assistant. She also assists Jolene McHugh, another attorney, and myself. Jill is the domestic partner of Sally Kipman, a former high-school classmate of mine, and is the picture of efficiency and patience. No matter what Steele throws at her, she catches it and throws it back like a catcher destined for the Baseball Hall of Fame. In a short time, Jill has become a favorite with Woobie attorneys and staff alike. And something tells me that even Steele secretly adores her. He may not have a secretary he can bed, but he definitely has a secretary who can match him in both his work and his wit.

I let myself into the office suite at about seven thirty. Woobie opens officially at eight thirty, with most of the staff arriving around nine. In my hands were two large cups of designer coffee, one for me and one as an offering to Steele. The coffee didn't come from one of the ubiquitous chains but rather from a little independent café near the beach that I knew was a favorite brunch hangout for Steele on weekends.

Yes, I'll admit it, the special brew was a bribe, an offering at the altar of knowledge and egotism—an attempt to soothe the bear before I asked him to share his honey.

I found Steele right where I expected to find him—at his desk, his suit jacket already off and carefully hung on the wooden hanger on the back of his door. His fingers were busy on the keyboard of his computer, probably reading and responding to e-mails that had accumulated since last night.

I knocked lightly on his doorjamb. He looked up, surprise registering on his handsome, freshly shaven face.

"Jesus, Grey, a little early for a newlywed like you, isn't it?" His fingers continued to stab at the keyboard while he spoke.

"I need to ask you something, Steele. Got a minute?"

"What? Greg filing for divorce already?" He looked back at the computer screen. "Whatever you do, ask for shared custody of the dog. That'll force Greg to give you anything you want in the settlement."

I stepped into his office and carefully put one of the cups of coffee down on his desk in line with his peripheral vision. As soon as he spotted the familiar logo on the paper cup, he stopped typing and gave me his full attention.

"This must be pretty serious, Grey, for you to come bearing gifts." He picked up the cup, took off the lid, and took a long, appreciative sniff.

"A little half and half, no sugar, right?"

He took a small sip and smiled. "You know me too well."

He took a bigger sip. After he swallowed, he turned in his chair and faced me. I set my own coffee down, shut the door, and took a seat across from him.

"A shut door conference?" Steele narrowed his eyes at me. "You leaving the firm, Grey? Is that what this is all about?"

I honestly couldn't tell if his question held a tone of disappointment or of hope.

"No, I'm not leaving the firm, so you can just keep the cork in the champagne."

It was my turn to take a sip of coffee, but for me it was a stall tactic. I wasn't sure quite how to open the subject of a serial killer.

Steele leaned back in his chair and swiveled slightly. The chair gave off its familiar squeak. For all his obsession with perfection, Steele seems to love that damn squeak. Everyone has tried to get him to oil it. Tina Swanson, our office manager, even sent an office services person down once with a can of WD-40, but Steele banished him back to the copy room with the threat of termination if he ever touched his chair. Personally, I also like the squeak; it's like a bell on a cat. When we hear the squeak, we know Steele's in his office hard at work and not prowling the halls, looking for someone to annoy.

He took a deep drink of coffee and waited.

I also took another drink of coffee. "You won't believe this," I began.

"I believe everything you say, Grey. No one could make up the shit you get into."

He laughed. I didn't.

When I didn't respond on cue, he leaned forward and put his coffee firmly down on his desk. He stared at me, eye to eye.

"Please tell me you haven't gotten yourself involved with another stiff."

"No, at least not technically. I mean, not directly."

"Okay, so how *indirectly* have you gotten yourself involved with yet another corpse?"

"I'm not involved with any corpse," I insisted. "I just need some advice. That's all."

"Uh-huh," he said with a slight snort. "You came into work at seven thirty, armed with my favorite coffee, just for some simple legal advice?"

"Yes." I took a big gulp of coffee to avoid his stare.

"Look me in the eye, Grey, and swear that this simple legal advice has absolutely nothing to do with anyone's death—past, present, or in the future, in any way, shape, or form."

This time, I looked Steele square in the eye. "I can't do that."

He smacked the top of his desk with his left palm. His coffee cup gave a little hop. "I knew it!"

"It's not what you think, Steele."

"Who is it, Grey? Your manicurist? A second cousin twice removed? Who managed to get themselves killed in your screwy little world this time?"

"No one, Steele. I just need some advice about my responsibility in a certain situation."

"*Your* responsibility?" He looked at me, his face serious and full of curiosity. "Did you witness a murder? Plan one? Commit one?"

"No, no, and no."

"An assault?"

"No, and if you'll quit playing twenty questions, I'll tell you."

Steele studied me a few seconds, then picked up his coffee, took a big swallow, and leaned back in his chair again. "I'm all ears."

I took a deep breath. "Someone told me that they think they know who the Blond Bomber is."

Steele catapulted forward in his chair, eyes wide with disbelief, his coffee splashing onto his shirt and desk. If it hadn't been for his big, black lacquered desk standing between us, he and his coffee would have ended up in my lap.

"The Blond Bomber? Are you kidding me?"

"Afraid not. But it's all supposition. She doesn't have any real proof except for coincidences and a gut feeling." I paused. "Anyway, she doesn't want to go to the police, but she told me who she suspects it is."

Steele sat back down and fussed with the coffee spots on his shirt. It was the second time in just a few days that the mention of the Blond Bomber had caused spillage. Fortunately, Steele kept extra shirts in his office.

"My question is, Steele, do I have any legal obligation to say anything to the police?"

"Why don't you ask your pal Dev Frye that question?"

"You know darn well why. If I say anything to Dev, even in a hypothetical way, he'll end up snooping around. And if this man is innocent, just a suspicion could ruin him."

"He's a prominent guy?"

"Very. But does that matter? A suspicion of this type would ruin anyone."

Steele closed his eyes and swiveled in his chair. *Squeak . . . squeak.*

"Have you met this guy?" He asked the question without stopping the swivel or opening his eyes.

"No, I haven't. Does that make a difference?"

"No, it doesn't. But what you have here, Grey, is a sticky problem, not a legal one."

He stopped swiveling and looked at me. "Legally, you have no responsibility to report what you've been told. Under the law, there is no legal responsibility for any private citizen to report knowledge of a crime to the police. A private citizen needs to take affirmative action to assist in the crime either before or during the crime, or be an accessory after the fact, such as concealing evidence or harboring a known fugitive, to share in the responsibility for the crime."

"But morally?" I squirmed a bit in my chair.

"That's where it gets sticky. If you don't do anything and this guy is the killer and kills again, could you live with that?"

It was the same question I'd asked of Lil.

FOUR

"Okay, Lil, I'll help you. I'll try to find out if your son is the Blond Bomber or not."

Lillian Ramsey got up from her chair and threw her slender arms around my neck. "Thank you, Odelia. Thank you so much."

When the hug was over, I asked her to sit back down. It was the following weekend, and we were at Lil's condo in Leisure World, seated at her cheerful dining table set in front of a large picture window that overlooked the golf course.

"But first I need you to understand something." I took both of her delicate hands in mine. She looked at me expectantly. "If I discover that Brian is the Blond Bomber, I will go directly to the police with the information. I will not ask your permission or even stop long enough to tell you first." Lil stared at me and blinked her blue eyes a couple of times. I didn't know if she was in shock or scared or both.

"You won't even tell me?"

"Not until after I've told the police. If I find out that Brian is the killer, I will do whatever is in my power to make sure he doesn't kill again, and I can't risk you interfering. You're his mother. No matter what he's done, you would try to protect him. It would be only natural."

More blinking and staring. Lil removed her hands from mine and sat back in her chair. Her shoulders sagged as she turned her head to look out the window.

"You are right, of course." Her voice was hardly a whisper when she spoke. "If he is the killer, he must be stopped." She turned her head again to look at me. "And if he's not the killer?" This time there was hope in her voice.

"If I find concrete proof that Brian Eddy is not the Blond Bomber, I will immediately tell you that very second. On that, you have my word."

Lil gave me a small smile and refreshed both of our teacups from a floral china pot. "Thank you, Odelia."

I pulled a yellow legal pad and pen from my tote bag and put it on the table beside me. "Why don't we get started? The sooner the better, don't you think?"

Lil nodded and swallowed hard. "You'll want to know why I suspect my own son of such heinous acts."

Truth is, I didn't want to know any of this, but the reality was I had to know to be of help. I studied Lil's lovely face and noted the deep blush creeping into her lined cheeks. Something told me that what she was about to disclose, on a scale of one to ten, was going to be a nine on the doozy scale.

"Odelia," she began, speaking quietly, "have you ever met anyone on the computer—you know, on the Internet?"

"*We* met online, Lil. Remember?"

"I don't mean like us, Odelia."

She paused to take a sip of tea. She sat still for a minute, clutching the dainty cup between both hands. I didn't prod her to continue. It was obvious that whatever she needed to say, it was going to be difficult for her.

Finally, she continued. "I mean romantically. Did you ever meet anyone online and become involved with them?"

I hadn't, but I knew people who had. The stories of online dating had been both good and bad. My friend and co-worker Kelsey Cavendish met her husband, Beau, online, and that seems to have worked out very well. Then I remembered that the news reports had hinted that the Blond Bomber had met all of his victims online.

"Does Brian meet women online?" I knew that Dr. Eddy was married, but I certainly wasn't naïve about married people going online in search of excitement and affairs. Dr. Eddy wouldn't be the first or the last.

Lil nodded slowly. "Yes, he does."

"And he told you this?" I didn't think many men would confess to their mothers that they were playing around online or offline, but especially one that wasn't particularly close to his mother. Lil had told me that her relationship with her son, though intact, was often strained. "I didn't think you two were that close."

"We aren't." Again she paused. This time she held the china cup so hard I was afraid it'd shatter.

"Why don't you put that cup down before it breaks." I reached over and gently extracted it from her hands. She let me and picked up a linen napkin instead and started twisting it slowly.

28

"Have you ever done anything you were ashamed of, but were glad you did it anyway?" She spoke without looking at me.

My first thought was, was there a minimum answer requirement I could get away with? Even though the question was purely rhetorical, it still made me uneasy. How do I screw up? Let me count the ways.

"Are you talking about something you did, Lil? Or something Brian did?"

"Brian ... and I."

I felt my body wanting to squirm but forced it to remain still. In my head, I could see the doozy scale going up to a twelve, possibly even a thirteen.

"As I've mentioned to you before, my son and I are not very close. We used to be, but it all changed after I married Cecil Ramsey. I married my first husband, Brian's father, for love. I married Cecil for security. I don't think Brian has ever forgiven me for that." She took a deep breath before continuing.

"When Brian's father passed away suddenly, I found myself a young widow with a pre-teen son. The two of us struggled to stay afloat, and I often worked two jobs. Shortly after I met Cecil, he proposed. I declined at first, but the more I struggled to raise my son alone, the more I saw the advantages my marrying Cecil would have for Brian. Finally, I accepted. Soon after, Cecil shipped my son off to a very exclusive preparatory school, and from there to a college of Brian's choice. Cecil even paid for Brian's medical school. He lived up to his bargain of providing for my son's future, and I lived up to my part of being the beautiful and gracious wife and hostess."

"You were his trophy wife."

"That's what they call it now, isn't it? And I suppose I was. I was much younger than Cecil, very pretty, educated, and proper. Cecil was very rich and important. I may not have loved Cecil, but I respected him and was a good wife. And though he could often be distant, he was never cruel or thoughtless towards me or Brian. But Cecil made it clear that he had married me, not my son." Lil gave me a small smile. "Actually, as marriages go, it could even be considered a good one."

Cecil Ramsey had never been thoughtless? What do you call separating a mother and child just to have the mother to yourself? It would be interesting to get Brian's side of the story.

"You see Brian and his family fairly often, though, don't you?"

"Oh yes, Brian and Jane, that's my daughter-in-law, have me over for special occasions such as birthdays, anniversaries, and holidays. Jane and I get along very well, and I see my two grand-children often—though now they are quite grown up and off with their friends most of the time."

"If you see Brian often, why do you think you're not close?"

Lil gave that some thought before answering. "It's not that we're estranged physically, but emotionally. He never tells me anything, not even important things. I didn't even know he was going to marry Jane until the ring was on her finger. And I found out about him starting his own practice when I received the announcement in the mail."

She drank some more tea before continuing. "Brian is a dutiful son, Odelia. He makes sure I have whatever I need, even though I can easily afford just about anything. He sees that I'm cared for when I don't feel well, and he even calls me every week to check on me. But it's all mechanical, like it's a job he must do and be done with. When I'm at his home, he is the picture of etiquette but barely speaks to me. Even the weekly calls are often made by Jane, even though she's busy running her own business. She owns Sharp Design, the interior decorating company."

"Your daughter-in-law is Jane Sharp?" In my mind, I let loose with a big *wow*. Sharp Design was one of the most sought-after residential interior design companies in Southern California. Many celebrities lived in Sharp-styled homes. Rumor was, you had to make an appointment with Jane Sharp a year in advance, and even then there was no guarantee she'd accept your business. What a dynamic duo she and Dr. Eddy made. He designed bodies for the rich and famous while his wife designed their habitats.

Lil nodded with pride. "Yes, that's Brian's wife. She built that business practically out of nothing, just her talent and perseverance."

I pushed thoughts of rooms and furniture I couldn't afford out of my mind and went back to concentrating on the issue at hand. Listening to Lil made me think about my relationship with my father. I call Dad every week and make sure I drop by every two weeks, even though I can barely stand my stepmother, Gigi. Sometimes, I'll admit, it does seem like a duty, but the alternative—of not having him around at all—would be painful. Sometimes we spend time alone, just Dad and me, and those times are special. Once we spent two hours at Denny's over coffee, talking about his childhood and the grandparents I never met. The only topic that's taboo is my mother. Greg is also very close to his parents, and we see them regularly. They love me like a daughter, and my father worships the very ground Greg rolls over.

I knew that older people often felt neglected by their adult children, especially when they're busy with careers and families, but that didn't fit Lil. She had a very active life with lots of friends of her own. But maybe she was right. Maybe Brian still hadn't forgiven her for letting Cecil send him away, or maybe she was just being overly sensitive to a naturally reticent demeanor.

"Maybe Brian's just not a sharer." I hoped my words would make her feel better. "I mean, he's a grown man, a busy one—probably thinks it might make him look weak if he told his mother everything. Does his wife complain about him being distant?"

"Sadly, Brian and Jane have grown apart in the past several years. I know this because she's told me, and because I've seen it with my own eyes. They are very polite to each other. Too polite, if you ask me. Like strangers who suddenly find themselves as roommates." Lil hesitated. "Jane confided to me that she thinks he's having an affair."

"Having an affair and being a serial killer are two entirely different things. They're not even in the same solar system, as far as offenses go." I chuckled. "If every man who had an affair turned into a serial killer, no one would be safe outside of their homes and maybe not even in them."

Lil shot me a soft but impatient scowl. "That's not why I think Brian might be the Blond Bomber. It's just part of the background I'm giving you."

"Okay. Well, then, let me ask you: do *you* think Brian is having an affair?"

Just as Lil was going to respond, her doorbell rang. She excused herself to answer it. A few minutes later she returned, followed by a muscular man carrying a small antique table. She directed him to place it against a small section of wall between the dining room and living room, after which he was introduced to me as Paul Milholland, one of Jane Sharp's workers. Paul Milholland appeared to be in his thirties, a bit shy, with sun-bleached sandy hair, a deep tan, and toned body. After Lil thanked him and showed him out, she returned to the table.

"I'm sorry for the interruption."

"That's a lovely table, Lil. Did you recently buy it?"

She smiled. "Actually, it's a gift from Jane and Brian. More from Jane, of course. She saw it at an auction and bought it for me as an early birthday gift." She took a sip of tea. "Paul is her right-hand man, sort of a delivery man, furniture restorer, and carpenter, all rolled into one. You name it, he can do it. He even built the bookcases in my spare room. Been with her for years."

"Sounds like a good man to have around."

Lil nodded. "After Jane's former assistant, Mason Bell, left her to start his own design firm, Paul became indispensable. He really helped bolster Jane, especially after Mason started stealing her clients."

As interesting as this decorator gossip seemed, I wanted to get back to Brian Eddy. I sensed that Lil was using Paul's interruption to stall. Gently, I guided her back to the matter at hand.

"Lil, just before Paul arrived, you told me you thought Brian was having an affair."

Lil got up and went to the new table, caressing its smooth top with a hand. "I know he is."

"Because Jane told you?"

"No." She shook her head and continued to study the top of the table. "I know because he's having it with me."

I could've sworn I heard the doozy meter pop a spring.

FIVE

"Excuse me?"

Lil didn't answer but instead turned to look directly out the window. Her face was as still as a mannequin's. I waited and restrained from verbalizing the *ewww* on the tip of my tongue.

"Not a real affair, of course. Just an online fantasy thing, but very emotional and captivating at the same time." She still didn't look at me. "It has been going on for nearly six months. I should be ashamed. And I am. But I also don't regret it.

"It started one long weekend when I was bored and lonely. I went into several chat rooms that I frequent under my usual screen name of JersyLil, but the conversations were always the same. I tried a couple of new chat rooms, but no one wanted to talk to an old lady."

Lil turned and went into the kitchen. I stayed where I was but could hear her adding water to the tea kettle and setting it on the stove. I gave her space while she spoke.

"Of course, I knew that people used fake identities all the time on the computer," she called from the kitchen. "But I never had, until then. I created a new name, a new identity, and tried it on. It was rather like trying on shoes. Over the course of the weekend, I sampled three names and personalities, and then stuck with the one that received the most attention."

I was afraid to ask.

Still seated at the dining table, I was glad Lil couldn't see me, because I could feel my mouth hanging open like some slack-jawed dolt. I shut my trap when Lil poked her head around the corner into the dining room.

"Did you ever want to be someone else, Odelia? Even for a day or an hour?"

"I wouldn't mind being that guy in Chino who won the lottery last Saturday."

Lil knitted her brows slightly. "That's not what I mean, and you know it."

When the tea kettle started to whistle, Lil disappeared back into the kitchen and came out a couple minutes later with a fresh pot of tea. After setting it on the table to steep, she continued. "I don't mind getting older." Again, she knitted her brows. "But I damn well mind *feeling* old."

"Boy, join the club."

Her serious look melted into a smile. "You have quite a ways to go, dear girl." She fiddled with a thin lemon wedge, squeezing it gently before sliding it into her china cup.

"The nice thing about meeting people on the computer is that they don't have any idea who you really are, so you can be anyone you want. I'm sure a lot of the people I've met are nothing like who they claim to be. I just joined them in their little charade. And it was fun to pretend I was young, vibrant, and beautiful." She paused to look down into her cup. "Even sexually provocative."

I squirmed more. It was bad enough to think of Lil and Brian meeting online, but once Lil took the sharp verbal turn to the sexual realm, I really had a difficult time repressing the *ewww*. I assumed, of course, when she used the word *affair* that something flirtatious had occurred, but Lil had used the *S* word openly. It made me wonder just how sexually provocative her online alter ego had been. And I knew I'd have to know. It was the proverbial elephant in the corner. We both knew it was there, but neither wanted to acknowledge it. Finally and reluctantly, I nudged it into the open.

"Lil, this is difficult for me to ask, but ask I must." I took a sip of tea to loosen my tongue. "Just how sexually provocative were you? Or specifically, how sexually involved did you become with Brian?"

Lil turned her face towards me. Her eyes were wide with the frankness of confession. I braced my brain for the invasion of information and wished there were such a thing as an internal crash helmet.

"To be blunt, I had many sexually explicit encounters over a period of about a year."

"A year? I thought you said six months."

"I have been involved with Brian for about six months, but I've been online under the name of Perfect4u for nearly eleven months now."

Perfect4u. Not as evocative as a lot of the screen names I'd seen online. Ladylike but inviting just the same. At least it wasn't Naykid,

Diddlefest, or some other equally ridiculous or more explicitly vulgar name.

"You said you had many encounters. I assume all of them were online. None of these people asked to meet you? Or even to speak with you on the phone?"

"Most of them did, including Brian, but I always declined, of course. If they became troublesome or too obsessed with meeting me, I'd stop chatting with them." Lil paused. "There was one man who became quite a nuisance, but eventually I shook him off. That was about four months ago. I almost changed my screen name, he became so annoying. Then, there was another man—"

I cut her off gently. "Let's focus on Brian, shall we?" Lil blushed and nodded. "Did he tell you things that made you think he might be the Blond Bomber?"

Lil took a long time to respond. I refilled my teacup and refreshed hers. With all the tea we were drinking, I might have to make several pit stops on my way back to Seal Beach.

"He confessed to me that he had known the women who had been killed through the Internet. Said he even met one of them in person."

Whoa! My mind scampered to gather up the information even as it tried to repel it. Then, just as quickly, my logical side put the brakes on my mental hysteria. Lots of people meet online, and if Brian was using a popular Internet provider and hanging out in regular chat rooms specifically to meet women, even with the millions of folks online, it stands to reason he *might* have come across these women. Especially if he frequented rooms that were geographically specific in their members.

"Did he know the nurse?"

"I don't know. I haven't asked him yet. He just said that he'd met one of the murdered women for coffee. He didn't specify which or when, but it was before the nurse was killed."

A silence hung over us. I stared at Lil until she reluctantly looked me in the eye. "Don't tell me—Perfect4u is a blond bombshell?"

Lil's nod was almost imperceptible, but it was a nod nonetheless. "Was, Odelia. Perfect4u *was* a blond bombshell. I think it's time I put her to rest."

My brain did a quick U-turn and traveled from *ewww* to *hmmm*.

"Not so fast."

SIX

"HE DID WHAT?"

The question came from Greg, who was positioned in front of our patio grill, tongs in one hand, a beer in the other, his mouth dropped to the ground. There was a lot of that happening lately. The sizzle of cooking steaks filled the silence of disbelief that followed his question.

"You heard me." I was in the middle of shuttling place settings, condiments, and salad from the kitchen to the patio table as we talked. "Brian asked Lil to run away with him."

"That's sick!" Greg drained his beer and put the bottle on the table. Knowing instinctively that this was not going to be a one-beer conversation, I twisted the top off another Sam Adams and placed it within his reach.

"But Greg, he didn't know Lil was his mother. He thought—*thinks*—she's some hotsie-totsie sex kitten in her prime."

I was about to say more, but our back gate opened and in trotted Wainwright, towing Silas behind him at the end of his leash.

Sometimes Silas and Billy would drop by and ask to play with Wainwright. Mostly they played in our back patio area, but once in a while Greg would let the boys take Wainwright to a nearby park. Not the one at the beach, but one just a block from the house that did allow dogs. Today, only Silas had come to the door looking for doggie company. Usually our back gate is locked, but in anticipation of Silas and Wainwright's return, Greg had left it unlatched.

"Hey, Silas," Greg greeted him. "Did you two have fun?"

"Yeah, it was awesome. There was a puppy there. A boxer, I think, named Amos. We played with him."

"That's Ted and Sophie's new dog," Greg told him. "They live over on the next street."

I disappeared into the kitchen and came back with the last of the menu items, a couple of piping-hot baked potatoes. I plopped one down on Greg's plate and the other on mine.

"Want to stay for dinner, Silas?" I asked as the boy unleashed Wainwright. "We have plenty."

The boy shook his head. "Thank you. But I have to get home. My grandma is expecting me."

"You can call her," Greg added as he pulled the steaks off the grill.

The boy looked at the meat with hungry eyes but shook his head again. "Thanks, but I can't."

I smiled at him. "Maybe another time you can plan ahead to stay and eat with us. Billy, too." He smiled shyly back.

Silas and Billy lived with their grandmother several blocks away in a run-down two-bedroom home. Greg and I weren't quite sure what the situation was, and the boys never talked about their parents. When they started coming to our house to play with the dog a few months ago, Greg insisted on meeting the grandmother and giving her our address and telephone number. Marylou Smith was her name, and at the time she didn't appear to be in the best of health, but the boys were always polite, clean, and cared for.

As soon as Silas left, Greg locked the back gate. "It's still sick," he said, rolling to the table.

"Huh?"

"The thing with Lil and her son."

"Yes, that. Sorry, I hadn't switched back to that topic yet. Guess I was afraid of getting brain whiplash."

Greg chuckled and positioned himself at the end of the table to my left. He lifted his beer in my direction. I lifted my own bottle of beer, and we clinked them together.

"Here's to us, sweetheart. We may be crazy, but at least we're not sick."

I grinned at my husband. "Well, at least in our eyes we're not."

Working in silence, we each dressed our potatoes. Greg garnished his with butter, shredded cheddar cheese, and fresh ground pepper. I preferred butter and sour cream. But even as I prepared to dig into the fluffy, perfectly cooked innards, I couldn't stop thinking about Lil and her online activities. I was rather glad Silas hadn't stayed for dinner. Otherwise, Greg and I would have had to delay our conversation. Serial killers and online trysts were hardly dinner conversation for a preteen.

"Greg, I know you used to meet women online." He looked up, curious about where I was heading. "Did you ever pretend to them about who you were?"

"You mean, did I ever lie to women about being in a wheelchair?" He paused before answering. "Yes, all the time, at least for a while." He pushed his potato toppings around, concentrating on smooshing them deeper into the hot middle of the spud. Finally, he looked up at me. "It was difficult for me to meet women. I'm sure you realize that, Odelia."

I nodded in understanding and gave him an encouraging smile. Greg had injured himself when he was just a few years older than Silas. It had happened while he and his cousins were performing daredevil actions while crossing a wet and rickety bridge high over a river. The other boys made it; Greg didn't.

"At first," Greg continued, "I told them the truth but couldn't get anywhere. No one would meet me, except for the few hookers I stumbled across in some of the chat rooms. But I was looking for someone nice, a woman I could build a life with." At the end of this remark, he gave me a look so electric with love that it nearly stopped my heart.

"Then I started letting the women I met online assume I was just a regular guy, hoping when they met me they would think I was so terrific, the chair wouldn't matter." He picked up his beer and gave a short snort before taking a drink. "But that didn't work either. In fact, that was a total disaster."

He'd told me a few of those painful experiences. We were both treasures—Greg in his wheelchair, me with my extra poundage—that most people weren't willing to dig beyond the surface to discover. But in the end, we'd magically found each other.

"Finally, I got it through my skull that the type of woman I wanted, the type who'd be able to love and accept me paralyzed from the waist down, would have to be the type who wouldn't shrink at first glance. After that, I started being very open and honest about my situation. And I did meet some wonderful women by being truthful. Maybe not as many, but while the quantity went down, the quality went up. In the end, the truth was the best route. It usually is, don't you think?"

I thought about that as I cut a piece of steak. Greg was right. Even I had discovered that in my sketchy pre-Greg love life. Blind dates where the man was surprised by my physical appearance almost never went well, but those with an idea of the packaging beforehand took the time to get to know me.

"I totally understand why Lil did what she did, Greg, even if I don't agree with it. But in her case, she wasn't looking to meet the love of her life. She just wanted the fantasy of feeling young again and to hear men tell her she was desirable. Throughout history, lots of people have died searching for the fountain of youth. Brian Eddy makes a damn good living off of people searching for it in the modern age. The Internet gave Lil the chance to do that without leaving home, without taking any risks."

Greg finished chewing before he spoke. "Perhaps she didn't take any obvious risks, sweetheart, but now she's in a tight spot because of it. A pickle, as you would say."

He put down his knife and fork and picked up the pepper mill. "So," he said, as he gave it a couple of twists over his steak, "are you going to leave me guessing about the juicy stuff?"

"Juicy stuff?"

"How did Lil finally realize she was getting nasty with her own son?"

"He came out and told her who he was. Not at first, of course. According to Lil, they had been having quite a torrid online relationship when he asked to meet her. When she declined, he told her his real name, hoping that would convince her."

"I can't believe she continued it." Greg shook his head in disbelief. "Especially once she realized who he was."

"Lil claims she cooled it down immediately—didn't even talk online with him for a long time. But her curiosity got the better of her, as well as her desire to know more about her son, and she resumed the relationship, but on a friend-only basis. She says they haven't talked sexually since she found out. She finally told him she was married and didn't feel right about it, but wanted to remain friends. Lil says for the past month they've been more confidants than anything."

"But if the doctor is a competitive guy and thought he was in love, that would have made him even more eager to meet her. And if his own marriage was rocky, as Lil told you, I can see why he continued pursuing her." He paused. "But it still doesn't make him the Blond Bomber, just a lonely, horny guy with a bad marriage."

I took a bite of steak and chewed. "Lil said he admitted knowing a few of the dead women from the Internet. And the night the nurse disappeared, Brian stood her up on a planned online date. Lil said when she became suspicious, she dug up the dates of the last couple of murders and checked them against Brian's schedule. Apparently, he always lets his mother know when he's going to be out of town, and she keeps her old calendars. Each time a woman was found murdered, Dr. Brian Eddy was conveniently out of town."

"And that wouldn't be an alibi rather than evidence?"

"To Lil's thinking, the trip is a cover alibi in case the police find any old e-mails and link Brian to the dead girls."

"And that's her evidence?"

"Yep. It's not totally off the mark. I mean, it does seem coincidental that he would know some of the dead women and would admit that to his online lover. But then again, maybe Brian is trying to appear innocent by being forthcoming. The good doctor is either very cagey or very trusting."

I must admit, it was rather a relief to have Greg working with me on this favor for Lil. I was enjoying brainstorming with him, like we did when our mutual friend Sophie London died. We made a great team.

During the week, Greg had dug up all the information he could on the Blond Bomber and his victims, all four of them to date. Together, we made a detailed list of any common traits and information beyond their physical appearance. I'm sure it's the same thing the police have done, but we were starting from scratch and looking for clues to who didn't do it, instead of who did it. To those lists, we added the information Lil had provided, including Brian's travel data.

According to the sketchy personal information on each victim, the four ranged in age from Gabby, who was sixteen, to Crystal Lee Harper, who died at the age of fifty-three. The information led me to believe that most were active in Internet chatting. All, that is, except the last one, number four, Laurie Luke, the nurse from Newport Beach. There was no mention of the Internet possibly linking her to her killer.

The first victim had been Elaine Epps, twenty-seven, a personal assistant from Long Beach. Crystal Lee Harper was the second victim and a former exotic dancer. The third was the unfortunate Gabby.

Starting with the most recent victim, with the reasoning that the trail would be the freshest, I read every detail on Laurie Luke that Greg produced. According to the information supplied to the press by her sister, Lisa Luke, Laurie was twenty-eight, a dedicated nurse recently engaged to a professional adventure and wildlife photographer, and spent most of her free time out of doors. Based on the photos in the newspapers, Laurie Luke was not just a blond bombshell, she was a knockout. A former Miss Illinois, Laurie was the all-American girl kicked up a notch.

"Something's troubling me." I stopped eating for a moment and hugged myself. It was starting to get chilly. No matter how warm the April days were, evenings near the beach could be cold.

"Just something, as in singular?"

"Actually, everything about this creeps me out. The whole idea that there's someone out there meeting women just for the purpose of killing them is beyond me. But sadly, I know it happens all the time. People are just sick."

Greg took one of my hands in his. "I believe that generally people are good, Odelia. I agree, there are a lot of fruitcakes out there, and some individuals are absolutely evil. But overall, people are kind and good."

"Are you sure your middle name is William and not Pollyanna?"

With a faint smile, he lifted my hand to his lips and gently kissed it. Without letting it go, he stared directly into my eyes. "This is not going to be an easy thing to look into, Odelia. The information is going to be brutal and nasty, and you may find out your friend raised a cold-hearted killer before you're done."

"You don't want me to do it, do you?"

He paused before speaking. "I want you to know you can stop all this right now and no one will think less of you, probably not even Lil. And if she did, she's not your friend. But if you do proceed, I also want you to remember I'm here to listen and to help.

You're not in it alone." He smiled slightly. "And I also know that once you get your teeth into something, you're like a starving dog with a soup bone—you don't let go until you get to the very marrow. So even if you stop everything right now, it will still haunt you until you pick it up and finish the job. It's who you are."

I smiled back at my understanding husband and went back to finishing my meal. Greg did the same.

"So, what is it that's bothering you? You were about to tell me something."

I dug into my brain to grasp the tail of my earlier thought. "What's troubling me is the last victim, Laurie Luke. She doesn't fit except for the fact that she's blond and built." I cut another bite of steak, pausing before popping it into my mouth. "From her sister's comments, she didn't seem the type to chat online socially. She seemed too busy and active for such a pastime. And she was in love and engaged to someone just as active as she was. The information on the other women mentioned that they might have met the killer online in chat rooms, even young Gabby." I chewed and swallowed. "Between her busy schedule as a nurse and her relationship with the photographer, Laurie Luke wouldn't have had much time for Internet pursuits."

Greg paused before taking another swig of beer. "I thought the same thing when I first looked at all the information. Her fiancé was a wildlife photographer. I imagine he traveled a lot. Maybe she did go online when he was out of town and she got lonely. Her sister might not have known that."

"But if she was newly engaged and so in love, why would she agree to meet someone? I saw her fiancé's photo—he's as hot as Laurie was. What a beautiful couple they must have made."

"The guy is hotter than me?" Greg took another gulp of beer and grinned.

I raised my own bottle in a salute. "No one is hotter than you, my darling. You melt the wheels right off your wheelchair."

Greg tilted his head back and laughed out loud. "Let's not sling bullshit while we're eating."

I laughed and poked around my nearly finished salad with my fork, finally spearing a lone cherry tomato. "Seriously, Greg, a woman who's deeply in love doesn't spend time on the computer idly chatting, especially one who is as into exercise and outdoor activities as Laurie seemed to be."

Greg took a few more bites of his dinner before pushing his plate aside. "So, when are you going to talk to her sister?"

It was as if he'd read my mind. As I ate, I was making plans to do just that. "Hopefully tomorrow, while you're playing basketball. That is, if I can track her down."

Greg tossed Wainwright a bit of steak fat. The dog gobbled it up and sat expectantly waiting for more, stopping just short of begging. "I printed out her phone number and address this afternoon for you."

My eyes popped open in surprise.

"You're not the only one who knows their way around computer research, you know." He chuckled and patted me affectionately on my arm.

"I'll call her right after dinner then."

"No need. I called her this afternoon. She's expecting you tomorrow at ten—at her place."

"Just like that, she said yes to having a stranger come over?"

Greg didn't answer right away. Instead, he finished his beer. He was teasing me, knowing I was about to burst. Just when I'd reached my limit and was about to strangle him, he answered. "Not a stranger, sweetheart. She said yes to having Odelia Grey come over."

I stared at him without understanding.

"Did you see the photo of Lisa Luke in the pile of stuff I gave you?"

I shrugged. "I think so, but I was more interested in Laurie."

"Tch tch tch." Greg wagged a finger at me. "Marriage must have dulled your senses. Take another look. Lisa Luke is a big girl—a BBW. I simply told her that Odelia Grey of Reality Check wanted to pay her a visit and see if there was anything she needed."

"And she still said yes?"

"Sweetheart, you and that organization are well known here in Orange County, even among the big girls not involved with it. I just used it to get your foot in the door."

"And what about the others? How are you going to get me through *those* doors?"

"I'm still working on that." His eyes were full of mischief. "By the way, do we have any plans for Monday night?"

I narrowed my eyes in suspicion at him. "Why?"

He shrugged. "I told Gordon Harper we might like to drop by."

"Who's Gordon Harper?"

"The ex-husband of Crystal Lee Harper, the stripper. You know, victim two."

I had created a monster.

SEVEN

LISA LUKE LIVED IN a spacious two-bedroom condo in Newport Beach, the property situated on a hill just off of Pacific Coast Highway. According to the information Greg provided, she and Laurie were joint owners and lived there together. It wasn't far from Hoag Hospital or the beach, which must have suited Laurie Luke's active lifestyle perfectly.

The door was opened almost before my knock was a done deal. Lisa Luke quietly welcomed me, keeping her head down and her eyes fixed on the floor between us as I entered. Before making the trip, I had looked at the only photo of Lisa that had been among the information about her sister. It was a grainy newspaper photo of a plump woman with her head down. She had long blond hair like her sister, but in the photo it had covered most of her face. The sight of Lisa Luke in person shocked me right down to my freshly painted toenails. I stared openly before I remembered my manners, shut my mouth, and smiled.

"Thank you for seeing me, Lisa."

She nodded and, with a slight wave of her hand, directed me into the living room. I took a seat on an upholstered chair and set my tote bag on the carpet next to me.

"Would you like some coffee or something cold to drink, Ms. Grey?" Her voice was quiet and polite.

"Please, call me Odelia. And something cold would be great, Lisa."

"Soft drinks or lemonade?"

"I'd love some lemonade, if it's no trouble."

Lisa shot me the briefest of smiles and went into the kitchen. The condo had an open floor plan, which allowed me to see most of the kitchen from where I sat. Lisa silently busied herself getting ice and glasses while I looked about.

The condominium was decorated in an open, breezy style that suited Newport Beach. The sofa and chairs were covered in matching floral and checked prints of mostly pale green and rose. The wood furniture was a light pine, and there were many healthy plants on display. Framing the patio door were coordinating solid green drapes in a light fabric, and beyond I noticed white wicker furniture and more plants, many flowering. The door was open, letting in the cool ocean breeze.

The dining area was between the kitchen and living room and held a medium table with white painted legs and a light pine table top. There were six matching chairs, all painted white, each boasting a ruffled seat cushion. Four chairs were around the table with two against the wall, standing guard on either side of a baker's rack holding knickknacks and cookbooks. The place was almost too cute and too tidy, like the residents had nothing better to do than to clean. Even the Sunday paper was stacked neatly on the coffee table, not strewn about in sections like at our house. The Luke residence reminded me of a fastidious old woman with young taste.

The television was a flat-screen model hung on the wall across from the sofa. It looked new. Beneath it was a credenza with a large grouping of photographs on top. I got up to study the photos. Many were of Laurie and Lisa, together and apart, during various stages of their lives, including graduations. A few were of Laurie with a young man, probably the photographer. I picked one up.

"Is this Laurie's fiancé?"

Lisa came into the room holding two glasses of lemonade. She glanced at the photo as she passed and quickly hung her head. I didn't know if she was painfully shy or if it was just the effect of her sister's murder, but she had yet to look me in the eye.

"Yes, that's Kirk. Kirk Thomas." She put the glasses down on individual coasters embossed with wildflowers. "He took many of those pictures. He's a professional photographer. Mostly exotic wildlife."

I nodded. "I remember reading that in the newspaper." I picked up another photograph, one of a couple taken many years ago. The woman looked a lot like Lisa. "Are these your parents?"

Lisa looked at the photo in my hand. "Yes." She sat on the sofa and picked up her lemonade, staring into the liquid instead of drinking it.

I had a theory and tested it. "Are your parents deceased, Lisa?" I said the direct words softly to minimize the bluntness of the question.

She quickly popped her head up in my direction, and again I was taken aback by her appearance. "How did you know that?"

"Just a guess. I noticed this was the only photo of them on display. They aren't even present in the graduation photos you have here, just a much older woman."

"That's Grammy, our father's mother. She raised us after our parents were killed in a car accident. She's dead now, too." Her voice trailed off as if it had lost steam.

Suddenly Lisa's shoulders started shaking, and she gulped for air as she hyperventilated. The lemonade in her glass sloshed. Quickly, I went to her side and took the glass from her hand and set it on the table. I bundled her into my arms and held her tight, stroking her long, pretty hair and cooing soothing words into her ear until she began to calm down.

"It's all right, Lisa. It's going to be okay."

She pulled away from me and for the first time looked into my eyes. "You don't understand. It's never going to be okay again."

"What I understand is that you will always feel the pain from the loss of Laurie, and from the loss of your parents and grandmother, but your life will continue, Lisa. You will be happy again, in time."

"My being happy is an impossibility now."

I thought about her comment and made another guess. "Were you and Laurie twins?"

Two things had struck me about Lisa Luke's appearance the moment I set eyes on her. One, she looked remarkably like my deceased friend Sophie London. She was tall and blond and plump, with curves in all the right places. The face was different but the build and sensual beauty were very similar, except that Lisa appeared to be very shy and withdrawn, where Sophie had been gregarious and confident. The other thing that struck me and struck me hard was, except for her build, Lisa was the spitting image of her sister Laurie. It was as if someone had taken Laurie Luke and inflated her.

Lisa shook her head gently. "No, I'm older by two years."

"I take it you two were close."

"Yes, very close. Almost two halves of the same whole. We were all we had in the world. We had no other family, just each other."

An ugly thought occurred to me, and as much as I wanted to push it away, I couldn't. "I imagine when Kirk came into the picture, things changed between you."

Lisa looked at me, confusion about my question filling her intelligent, distraught face. Then the light went on. "You mean, was I jealous?"

"It would be natural."

She thought about it and sniffed back more tears. "I was used to Laurie dating. Men have always buzzed around her like bees to honey. She wasn't just beautiful, she was fun and outgoing, smart and kind. She was gone a lot, while I'm more of a homebody."

"But an engagement is different from dating. Soon she would have married and moved away, leaving you alone."

Lisa nodded. "Yes, I thought about that quite a bit. And she knew it bothered me. She could always tell what I was feeling." Lisa picked up her glass and drank some lemonade. "But Kirk's a doll. Both he and his family welcomed me as much as they did Laurie." The tears started to spill again. "And now I've lost them both."

She put down her glass and excused herself, heading off down a hall to the right of the kitchen. I got up and went back to the photos, picking up and studying one showing Kirk with his arms around both Lisa and Laurie. Both Luke girls looked happy and

54

content, like Nordic bookends on either side of a handsome fairy-tale prince.

I was about to poke around some more when I heard a scratching and slight meow. Looking around, I saw no cat or evidence of one. In our house, Seamus's cat toys were always underfoot, right along with Wainwright's playthings. I walked to the kitchen area and looked around. Not a single food or water dish either. Again I heard a meow and scratching. I looked down the short corridor where Lisa had disappeared, but she wasn't anywhere in sight. To the left of the kitchen/living area was a closed door. The meowing was coming from the other side. I cautiously opened the door and took a peek. Just inside the door was a dark gray fur ball. Two big, round amber eyes stared back at me in a mixture of fright and relief.

I opened the door a little more and bent down to coax the animal to me. "Here, kitty. Come here. I won't hurt you." The animal took a tenuous step in my direction, followed by two scoots back into the room. It wanted to come to me but wasn't quite sure if it should take the chance.

I focused my attention from the cat to the room. The drapes were open and the daylight revealed a nicely decorated but cluttered, large bedroom. The queen-size bed was unmade and the dresser was filled with photographs, cosmetics, and knickknacks. Clothes were scattered everywhere. In the corner was a desk sprinkled with papers, except for the middle where there was an obvious clearing. Perhaps it was the spot where a laptop had resided. I made a mental note to ask Lisa about it. A few more steps just inside the door was a litter box and plastic dishes containing food and water.

The cat mewed again. It appeared to be several months old, somewhere between a kitten and full-grown cat, and half-wild though cared for. Around its neck, it wore a black rolled-leather collar. Again it started for me, then backed away. I took a couple of steps forward and spoke kitty comfort words to it. It was enough for it to stay still until I reached in and scooped it up. As soon as it was in my arms, it snuggled against me and began to purr, starved for attention.

"That's Muffin."

The voice startled me slightly. I hadn't heard Lisa come up behind me. I turned with the kitten still in my arms. "I didn't mean to intrude, but I heard it crying at the door."

"Muffin is ... was ... Laurie's cat. Kirk gave it to her last month."

"Why is the cat shut up? Are you allergic to it?"

Lisa shook her head. She looked at the cat briefly before looking away. "I ... I'm sorry, I just can't bear to look at the thing. It ... it ..." Her words drifted off as she turned and left Laurie's room.

Putting the cat down, I shut the door and followed Lisa back to the living room. She was slumped on the sofa, taking small sips from her lemonade. I took a seat beside her. She looked at me and for the first time seemed to be thinking beyond herself.

"Why did your husband call and ask if you could stop by?"

"I'm here because a friend has an interest in the Blond Bomber, and I wanted to ask you some questions." I took a deep breath. "I'm very sorry if it appears insensitive or intrusive." Intrusive was becoming my middle name.

Silence filled the room while I took a sip from my own glass. I expected Lisa to inquire more about my friend's interest in the Blond Bomber, but she didn't.

"Why did *you* consent to see *me*, Lisa? Greg said you knew who I was—and about Reality Check."

She nodded. "Yes, I've thought several times about going to one of the meetings, especially since they are right here in Newport Beach. Unlike my sister, I have trouble getting out and meeting people, and I thought it might be fun and helpful. Once, I even went to the morning walk around the Back Bay."

I gave her a smile of encouragement.

She looked down at her glass. "But I didn't join the others. I just walked behind them. But they looked like they were having fun."

"It's a nice group, Lisa. You should go, especially now when you need some support."

"That's why I said yes when your husband called. I thought you might be good to talk to about this … this horrible thing." Once again, she started shaking, and once again, I put my arms around her. We sat quietly for several minutes with her cradled against me like a child. Lisa was as lost and frightened as the kitten in the next room.

When Lisa straightened up again, I got up and grabbed a tissue box sitting on the counter between the living room and kitchen area and brought it to her. She mopped her face and blew her nose.

"How is Kirk taking this? He must be devastated."

She was more composed, but her eyes were red and her creamy complexion blotchy. "He's been inconsolable, of course—both he and his family. I haven't even seen them since the funeral, but his mother calls me every few days to see how I'm doing." Muffin scratched at the door again, and Lisa turned her head towards the

57

noise. "I don't think they want to see me any more than I want to see that poor cat. It's just too painful."

"That will change, too, in time."

"I'm not so sure about that." She continued to stare at the door to Laurie's room. "Maybe if I didn't look so much like my sister." She gave a half shrug. "I know Kirk can't look at me without seeing her, and I doubt he ever will."

I thought about the things I wanted and needed to ask Lisa. Although I was here on a mission for Lil, I had also hoped to bring some comfort to Lisa. I decided I would test the waters and see if she was ready to talk. If not, I would have to try another time. My nosiness did have some boundaries of decency and respect.

"Lisa, may I ask something?"

She looked at me and nodded slowly.

"Do you think Laurie met her killer on the Internet?"

The young woman stared at me—but not in surprise. I continued. "One theory is that each of the Blond Bomber victims were contacted first via computer chat rooms. Did Laurie spend time on the computer chatting?"

Lisa placed her lemonade on the coffee table before sitting back and crossing her arms in front of her. "The police asked me the same thing, but as I told them, I didn't think so. She was always on the go, hardly ever home. The police even took her laptop but found nothing. Laurie hardly ever used it." She looked at me. "My sister worked long hours at the hospital. She was a very dedicated nurse. When she wasn't there, she was with Kirk or hiking or exercising. She couldn't sit still for long."

"I read that they believe she was abducted from the hospital parking lot."

Lisa nodded and put her head down. Her long hair covered her face like a curtain. "Yes." Again her shoulders started to shake.

"Lisa, I'm sorry. You don't have to answer me if you don't want to. I realize this must be horrific for you. In fact, maybe I should go."

"No." She looked up at me through the golden hair. "Please don't go. It's difficult, but maybe it's good to talk about it."

It was a long time before she spoke again. I gave her plenty of time to gather her thoughts.

"Laurie worked very late that night. When I got up in the morning and noticed she wasn't home, I thought maybe she'd spent the night with Kirk. But then I remembered he was in Africa on a photo shoot. I called her cell phone but got no answer. The hospital hadn't seen her since the night before. I called several of her girlfriends, but none of them had seen her or heard from her. When she didn't come home or show up at the hospital for her next shift, I called the police."

Lisa looked up at me with glazed eyes. It was apparent she'd told this story before, many times. It came out of her in an almost robotic fashion, in a deadpan narrative.

"The police located her car at the hospital in the employee parking lot. There was nothing remarkable about it. No sign of a struggle or anything like that." She paused and took a deep breath. "Three days later, they found her body in the canyon."

EIGHT

I LOVE THE WAY playing basketball affects Greg. He plays every other Sunday morning, and following the games he's flushed and sweaty and glows with energy. It's as if he's been supercharged with superpowers. And I must admit, some of our best sex has been following this Sunday morning ritual.

Usually I go with him and cheer with the other wives and girlfriends from the sidelines. And sometimes following the game, we go out with some of the other players for brunch. Today, Greg came directly home, dying to know about my meeting with Lisa Luke.

"How'd it go?" he called to me as soon as he was through the door.

Before I could answer, Wainwright barked a couple of times and dashed down the short corridor towards the far side of the house. Greg had originally purchased a run-down one-story duplex with mirroring floor plans and converted them into a charming single-family home with a Spanish hacienda feel. The two bedrooms and bath on the left were remodeled into an extra-large master suite and super bath, and the two bedrooms and bath on the right were remodeled to accommodate his wheelchair. One bedroom served as his home office, the other as a guest room. The two small original living rooms and kitchens were combined into one huge living room, kitchen, and dining area, with the spaces flowing from one to the other without walls and barriers. Off the kitchen and dining area was a covered patio, and beyond that, an extra-large garage accessed from the alley. Every square foot was perfectly designed to assist Greg in living as effortlessly as possible. The home had even been featured in a magazine for the disabled.

It was in the direction of the guest room that the dog had bee-lined. Seamus, on the other hand, had earlier squished his big furry body under the low buffet in the dining room and was sulking. He looked out at the two of us, especially me, with a murderous eye so intense it was almost a solid death threat.

Greg's knowing eye caught on Seamus, then followed Wainwright's path. The dog let out a few yips and whines, and we could hear him pawing at a closed door.

"What's going on?" Greg asked as he wheeled towards the hallway.

"We sort of have company."

Greg cocked an eyebrow in my direction. "And the company is sort of shut up in the guest room?"

I nodded. "It's of the four-legged variety."

"Feline or canine?"

"Feline. Laurie Luke's kitten."

"Permanent or temporary?"

"Not sure yet."

Greg started down the hall. "Let's get a look at the little bugger."

Before I left Lisa, she'd asked for a favor—if I'd take Muffin. She cited that it wasn't fair to the poor creature to be shut up all the time, but she just couldn't bear to be around the cat. It reminded her too much of her sister. I knew Greg wouldn't mind, and I knew Wainwright would love the idea of another playmate. The only sourpuss at the Grey-Stevens homestead would be Seamus. That sealed it—three against one. But I took Muffin with the contingency that we were only fostering the animal until Lisa could get back on track. She was right, it wasn't fair for Muffin to suffer because some monster had killed her owner, but in my heart I hoped that Lisa would, down the line, have giver's remorse and want the cat back for the same reason she was giving it away—it reminded her of her sister. If that time came, we would return it to her.

Once Muffin got over the fright of seeing a big yellow dog loping after her, she settled right in and became part of the family. By that evening, she was curled up asleep in Greg's lap while we watched a movie. The fact that the little animal bonded more with Greg seemed to mollify Seamus a bit. Although he didn't come up on the sofa with us, he at least came out from under the buffet. Baby steps. Or in this case, kitty steps. It was the same when Wainwright and Greg came into my life.

"So, we're still on to visit Gordon Harper tomorrow night?" Greg asked as we got ready for bed.

I paused mid-tooth brushing as I tried to remember who Gordon Harper was.

"Gordon Harper," Greg reminded me. "Crystal Lee Harper's ex-husband."

Of course, victim number two. I spit. "Yes, sure." I rinsed and spit again. "When and where? Do I need to leave work early?"

I patted my mouth dry with a towel, then applied moisturizer to my face and cream to my hands. By the time I climbed into bed, the revised family unit was jostling for position. Greg was sitting up, a book propped in his lap. Wainwright was curled on the scatter rug at the foot of the bed. Seamus, unhappy with Muffin's presence, was standing guard at the end of the bed, trying to keep the newest addition out of his territory. After receiving a few well-placed bats and hisses, Muffin curled up on the outside edge of the bed, against my knees. It was a good thing we had a king-size bed.

"Probably not." Greg looked up from his book. "Gordon said he can't meet us until nine, so why don't you come home and relax a bit? If you don't want to cook, let me know, and I'll pick something up on my way home."

I smiled at him as I picked up my own book from the nightstand. "Sounds good."

I started to read but couldn't keep my mind on the page.

"Greg." He turned to look at me. "If Laurie Luke was someone who didn't chat online, how do you think the Blond Bomber found her?" I put my book back on the nightstand and turned to face him.

Greg put his book face down on his chest. "I can think of several possibilities."

"Me, too. But you first."

He chuckled. "Okay. First, maybe Lisa didn't know her sister chatted online. After all, they didn't spend *all* their time together, and didn't Lisa work days and Laurie nights?"

"Very true."

"And maybe the fact that those other victims were online a lot is just a coincidence. After all, most adults under sixty are online these days."

I thought about it. "I honestly don't think Laurie Luke came across him online. That just doesn't add up in her case. But the coincidence thing could be just the ticket. I'm thinking maybe the Blond Bomber finds his victims another way. We have to find out what else these women had in common."

Greg put his book on the nightstand and turned off his light. "Or, the Blond Bomber just picks his women at random." He scooted down until he was flat and turned towards me.

I turned off my light and did the same. "Another thought I had is maybe he sees them somewhere, fixates on them, and stalks them until he gets them alone." This theory was one that gave me hope that Lil's theory about Brian was wrong. "But if that's the case, then Brian Eddy can't be the Blond Bomber. A busy surgeon wouldn't have time to stalk anyone."

"Good point. Hopefully, more pieces of the puzzle will fall into place tomorrow." Greg kissed me soundly. I turned around, and we fell asleep in the spoon position.

A short time later, I was awakened by a furry tail tickling my nose. Muffin had found her sweet spot—directly under my chin. I fell back to sleep hoping Lisa Luke could find the same peace.

MONDAY MORNING I WAS in the middle of organizing boxes of documents when I received a surprise visitor. It was Zenobia Washington, my oldest and dearest friend, better known as Zee. I first met Zee a billion years ago right here at Woobie. She hasn't worked here in more than fifteen years, but she still knows a lot of the people. Sometimes, I wish she didn't—like now.

This wasn't the first time Zee had popped in to say hello, though usually she calls first to make sure I'm available. But one look at her told me this was not a social call, nor had she dropped by to coax me out to an early lunch or a friendly cup of coffee. The scowl on her cocoa-bean face was set as firmly as the faces on Mount Rushmore and was not nearly as warm. Adding to that was her stance. In spite of her church-going, sweet-potato-pie nature, Zee has this imposing stance that can stop a hardened criminal in his tracks and make him want to call his momma.

Zee and I are about the same size and height, meaning we're both as wide as we are tall. At just past ten thirty, Zee stood in my office doorway dressed in a very stylish copper-colored pant-suit with perfect hair and makeup. An expensive designer handbag dangled from one hand. The other hand was clenched and positioned on one bulky hip. Her pump-clad feet were slightly apart.

If I knew where my momma was, I'd probably pick up the phone.

I thought about lightening up the moment by sticking my tongue out at her, but I was afraid she'd bite it off. I hadn't seen her this angry in a long time, and it worried me.

"Geez, Zee, you look like you're about to go postal." I moved to clear my visitor's chair of files. "Come on in and sit down."

For a moment, she just glared at me, then she stepped inside and sat down. The scowl was still intact, but at least sitting she couldn't keep up the full effect of the stance.

"I need to talk to you, Odelia." The words were said through clenched teeth.

Just as I made a move to shut the door, Steele barged in. "Do you know where Jill is?"

I shook my head. "No, sorry. She's probably making copies or something."

I looked at Zee. Her glare was still fixed on my face. Steele caught it also.

"Damn, Zee, you look like you just caught your husband with a Laker girl."

Zee turned her frosty stare in Steele's direction. "Mr. Steele, you will cease your vulgar comments and leave. And please shut the door behind you. I need to speak with Odelia alone." She turned her piercing eyes back to me.

Steele hesitated, not sure whether he should leave or call security. I picked up my phone and called Jill's desk. When I got no answer, I called the front desk and asked our receptionist to page her to Steele's phone number.

"I'm sure Jill will get right back to you, Steele. Why don't you just mosey along so Zee and I can chat?"

He looked at the work piled on my desk and started to say something, but one glance in Zee's direction and he wisely held his tongue. Quickly, I covered the two steps to the door and attempted to herd him out.

Steele leaned towards me just as I started to shut the door. "I'll bet you one of those disgusting apple fritters you love that your home girl's heard what you're up to."

In a blinding flash, I knew Steele was probably right. Somehow, Zee had found out about the Blond Bomber. I stole a glance in her direction. Yep, that could be it. My involvement in yet another potentially dangerous undertaking would drive her nuts. Then again, Steele could be wrong. It happened. Not often, but it did once-in-a-blue-moon happen.

I sat down and looked Zee straight in the face, sure I'd never see that apple fritter.

NINE

"So Zee's pretty pissed off at you right now, huh?" Greg asked the question while we were heading north on the 405 Freeway. We were on our way to our meeting with Gordon Harper.

"Not me, darling hubby, *us*. Zee is pissed off at *us*." I smiled to myself. As much as it killed me to see Zee so upset, it was rather funny to see her face when I told her that Greg and I had teamed up for this mission. "She was sure you'd lost your mind. The verdict was in about *my* mind a long time ago."

It seems that Lisa Luke took my advice and decided the day after our meeting to get involved with Reality Check.

Me and my big mouth.

At six AM on Monday, she'd showed up at the Back Bay to join the Reality Check walkers. And being the charming hostess that she is, Zee took Lisa under her wing and chatted with her during the entire walk. And Lisa, not realizing my past history with dead bodies, talked about our meeting and my questions about her sister and the Blond Bomber. It was all Zee needed to fuel the disbelief and outrage that brought her to my office a few hours later. The fact that I wasn't looking for the Blond Bomber but was looking for proof that someone *wasn't* the Blond Bomber didn't comfort her one whit. She left an hour later, threatening to lock both me and Greg up in a mental institution and throw away the key, but at least I had extracted a promise from her not to get involved or to call Dev Frye about it.

Greg chuckled. "Did you tell her that I was along for the ride to protect you?"

"I did, and it didn't matter. I'm sure Seth will be calling and yelling at you tomorrow about it."

Greg started to say something but hesitated.

"What?" I turned in my seat to look at him.

He kept his eyes on the road when he answered. "He called the office today, just after lunch."

"And?"

"He asked if we needed a lawyer. Said he'd be willing to put us on retainer."

Gordon Harper lived in a luxury high-rise condominium in Marina Del Rey. The view from his living room included the marina, complete with boats and slips. His condo was spacious, elegant, and had the almost too-perfect look of being professionally decorated. It also included a very impressive but small collection of artwork and sculpture. In spite of how well-behaved Wainwright is, I was glad we'd left him home to referee the cats. The Harper residence did not look pet-friendly.

Greg and I sat in Gordon's living room while Gordon retrieved drinks for us—a soda for me, a beer for Greg, and a Scotch for himself—from a nearby wet bar. The drinks were served in crystal barware, including the beer, which was poured into a matching pilsner.

"So, you're here about Crystal Lee?" Gordon Harper's voice was high and squeaky, reminding me of a Kewpie doll, if a Kewpie doll could talk. He dropped himself into a leather chair the color of wet sand. I sat on the accompanying sofa with Greg positioned between us.

Gordon Harper was in his late sixties, powerfully built and a bit portly, but not uncomfortably so. He had a large, bulbous nose and slightly loose jowls. His pate was bald and his face clean-shaven. He wore an expensive white silk shirt, probably Italian. Around his thick neck hung a substantial gold chain, also probably Italian. He looked like he'd be more comfortable taking meetings in a half-moon leather booth in the back of a dark restaurant instead of a lovely condo with a water view.

To be blunt, Gordon Harper looked like a bulldog who'd done well for himself after escaping the pound. Too bad he sounded like Fifi the wonder poodle.

"Yes, we are," I responded. "We'd like to ask you some questions about her, if you don't mind."

"May I ask why?" His yippy, high voice was distracting coming from such a powerful body. He focused on Greg. "All you told me on the phone was that it might prevent another death. I'm all for that, naturally, but the police haven't been able to find the guy. What makes you two so special?"

I cleared my throat—something I usually do before telling a fib. "I'm friends with the sister of the last victim. I ... we ... my husband and I want to look into anything that might be common to the victims. My friend is quite anxious to know what might have led the killer to her sister."

"Besides the obvious physical attributes?"

"Yes. It would help her a great deal to know how this happened."

Greg chimed in. "And it might also prevent another killing if we knew how the creep picked his victims."

Gordon nodded. "True, but I'm sure the police are looking into that as well."

I put my soda down on the glass coffee table and got down to business. "But we'd like to know, and the police aren't likely to share anything with us about the case."

Gordon chuckled as if I'd just told a joke that only he understood. He studied us each in turn before speaking. "Okay, what's the harm? What would you like to know?"

Greg and I shared a look of relief. It's not easy prying into people's business, and something told me Gordon Harper had a lot of things worth prying into. Supposedly, he was retired from the insurance business, but no amount of research could turn up what kind of insurance or any company. I would have liked to put a background check request out to my pal Willie about him, but I didn't have the time or the contact. After my marriage to Greg, Willie, better known as William Proctor, on-the-run white collar criminal extraordinaire, had disappeared from my life as easily as he had appeared.

Greg threw out the first question. "Was Crystal Lee active on the Internet just before she died?"

"Absolutely." Gordon smiled as he spoke, his fleshy lips parting in pride. "That's how she made her money. She hawked memorabilia from her days as a stripper. She also made custom erotic costumes, mostly inspired by vintage burlesque queens such as Betty Rowland and Lois de Fee." He laughed; it came out as a high-pitched giggle. "She did most of her advertising on the web. Most of her clients were drag queens, closet and otherwise."

The information Greg had gathered mentioned that Crystal Lee Harper had been a specialty costume maker, but it hadn't said anything about vintage burlesque or drag queens. "Did the police check out her clients?"

"Every last one of them that I know of. After her murder, they went through all her sales and order records." He took a hit from his Scotch. "It was very sad. She was killed just as her business hit its stride." His voice was filled with obvious pride.

"What happened to the business and her clients?" I watched him closely when he paused before answering.

"Seventh Veil Costuming is still thriving. I was a silent partner and decided after she was gone to keep it open."

"A silent partner?" I glanced at Greg as he asked the question. His mind was going exactly where mine was headed. "So you provided the start-up cash? Were you two already divorced by then?"

Gordon gave Greg a closed-lip smile. "Yes, we were. We'd been married only a few years, and the prenup allowed for a cash settlement for future living expenses and financial and business advice to start a new business. Crystal Lee wasn't a stupid woman. She knew I'd never allow her to grab my personal assets in a divorce, and she knew she'd be too old to go back to the pole if we split up." He laughed his high-pitched squeal. "Who knew that putting gauze and sequins on fags would be so lucrative?"

I made a mental note to check out Seventh Veil tomorrow. "Mr. Harper, I noted in the information on Crystal Lee's murder that only your name was mentioned. Did she have any family?"

He shrugged. "None that I know of. She never talked of any, and no one came forward when she died." His small, beady eyes turned sad. He got up and disappeared into the next room. When he returned, he was holding two silver-framed photos, which he handed to Greg. I leaned forward to study them with him.

One photo was of a younger, trimmer Gordon Harper sitting and giving the camera a shit-eating grin. On either side of him stood a naked woman, naked except for beaded bikini bottoms and nipple tassels. A brunette was to his left, a blond on his right. Both women were stunning and cupping their considerable breasts, holding them up and out towards the camera on either side of Gordon's head. The other photo showed just the blond, dressed in a skimpy harem outfit, in a very provocative pose.

I noticed my husband paying way too much attention to detail and gently took the photos from him. I handed them back to Gordon. "She was very beautiful."

"Crystal Lee was a great broad and a lot of fun. And she was smart. Never got into the booze and drugs like most of the other girls. That brunette in the photo? That's Joy. She died a few months after that picture was taken from a heroin overdose." He shook his head slightly at the memory.

"But Crystal Lee was different. She knew how to use her assets to get what she wanted. According to her, she was on the streets when she was sixteen. Soon some wealthy john noticed her potential. He cleaned her up, bought her a boob job, and put her on stage. She was an instant hit. I owned a few gentlemen clubs back then and bought out her contract. Best thing I ever did. The place was always packed for her shows. She was a real artist, not just some broad wiggling her tits and ass."

"Sounds like you're still an admirer, Mr. Harper. Why did you two divorce?" I picked up my soda and took a few sips while I waited for his answer.

"Crystal Lee and I were great friends and wonderful in the sack together." He winked a guy-thing wink at Greg. "She'd been my mistress for a number of years when my first wife died. Shortly after, we thought, why not get married? The marriage was a disaster from the start. The only time we weren't fighting was between the sheets. We finally divorced to save our friendship."

"So when Crystal Lee was murdered, you two were business partners and friends, correct?" I didn't like the way Gordon's eyes caressed my chest following my question and neither did Greg. His hands, resting in his lap, clenched and unclenched several times.

"That's right. She went back to being my mistress. She got the money she needed, and I retained fucking privileges." His eyes were still on my chest.

"So, who are you fucking now?" The question, in a tone of barely restrained anger, came from Greg and caused me to whip my head towards him in surprise.

Gordon Harper threw back his powerful head and laughed out loud, except that it came out like a series of short, asthmatic, squeaky wheezes. When he was done, he drained his Scotch glass.

"Well, sport, you might be in a chair, but your balls sure ain't paralyzed."

TEN

We were back home, finally settling in for the night. It had been a long day, and the visit with Gordon Harper had been tense. So had been the ride home.

Gordon never did disclose who he was … um … boinking at present, because I had moved the questioning along to a new topic to ease the tension between the two men.

"Mr. Harper, do you know who did Crystal Lee's breast surgery?"

"The first one? No. It was before I met her."

"She had more than one?"

"Yes, the last one was a repair job. Something about leaking silicone. She had a new type of implant put in and asked the doc to tighten them up while he was in the neighborhood." He grinned. "I paid for that job. Expensive as hell, but worth it. Best tits in the world. Same guy gave her an ass you could bounce a quarter off of and took care of her wrinkles. She had just turned forty at the time, but she had a body and face a twenty-year-old would die for. It was one of the reasons she lasted so long in the business."

"Who was her doctor?" Even before I asked the question, I knew in my gut what the answer would be.

"That Eddy guy. You know, the one all the stars go to." He paused.

Even though I wanted to, I didn't dare glance at Greg for fear of giving something away to our very observant host.

Gordon waved one hand in an arc, indicating the room we were in. "In fact, his wife decorated this place. Classy, huh?" There was a catch in his squeaky voice. "Crystal Lee talked me into having it done."

"I wonder if Laurie Luke's breasts were real?" I snuggled under the covers, nudging Muffin gently out of my sleeping space. As soon as I was still, she settled back down by my legs. The other two animals were already in their spots. When we arrived home, we were pleased to find all three animals accounted for, with no trace of bloodshed or torn fur.

"You going to ask her sister?" Greg was in bed next to me with his nose in his book. He didn't look up when he spoke.

"It's hardly a question one can ask delicately, especially about a dead woman like Laurie. I mean, it was easy to ask Gordon about it. He'd already said Crystal Lee had had a boob job."

Greg kept his nose in his book. "Uh-huh."

"He was quite a boob man, wasn't he?"

This time, Greg looked at me, one eyebrow cocked in displeasure. "Duh! Ya think?"

I giggled and snuggled close. "Thanks for being jealous, Greg. It's much appreciated." I kissed his cheek.

He put his book down. "I'm glad you're amused, Odelia. But honestly, all I could think about on the way home was what might have happened if you'd been alone with the guy."

"Nothing would have happened, Greg. He's an old lech, that's all. I may have a big chest, but I'm hardly his type where other things matter."

The book got deposited on the nightstand. Greg snapped off his lamp. "I'm also convinced he has crime connections." He pulled me close while he talked. "Insurance, my ass. He owned strip joints, a string of them by the sound of it. Probably did some money laundering through them. If Crystal Lee hadn't been killed the way she was, I'd bet he had her killed to get full interest of Seventh Veil Costuming."

"I thought about that, too. But she was killed just like the women before her and just like Laurie Luke." We were silent a few minutes. "Greg, which do you think is more likely—that Crystal Lee met her killer through the Internet or that she met him through her surgery?"

The quiet continued, and for a minute I thought Greg had fallen asleep, so it surprised me when he spoke. "That Brian Eddy connection isn't a good thing, that's for sure."

When I got to the office the next day, I called Brian Eddy's office. I thought it was about time I met the man I had in my snooping sights. His office was located on Hospital Road, across from Hoag Hospital. Just as I hit the last number on the dial pad, I realized that Laurie Luke was last seen at Hoag and that she lived very close to the hospital. It was information that needed to be reviewed and considered with care, but my thoughts were interrupted when my call was answered. When asked why I wanted to see the doctor, I was momentarily stumped. Finally, I told the receptionist I wanted to consult about a breast reduction. I was informed that the earliest Dr. Eddy could see me was in three weeks. Three weeks was not going to work; Lil would be a nervous wreck in three weeks. She was already calling and emailing me several times a day. Another woman could be killed in three weeks. I told the woman on the phone that I would be on vacation at that time, and asked if she could put me on a wait list for any cancellation that might crop up in the meantime. She said it was unlikely, but it did occasionally happen.

"Why do you want to see Dr. Eddy?"

At the sound of the voice, I jumped. My eyes shot towards my office door to confirm what my ears had heard. Sure enough, standing at my door, once again, was Zee Washington. Today she was dressed in light gray trousers and a peridot green silk sweater—a sweater Greg and I had given her on her last birthday. In her hand was the same designer bag, but today her other hand wasn't resting on her hip. There was no evidence of the stance in her demeanor.

"Did you come by to drag me to a mental institution?"

"Tempting, but no." She paused. "I came to apologize, sort of."

"Sort of? Isn't a little bit of an apology like being a little bit pregnant? You either are or you're not?"

"Good point, normally, but in this case, I came to apologize for being so angry at you. It doesn't mean I'm on board with what you're doing or that I no longer think you're insane. It's just…" She paused again but this time looked away.

"Come in and shut the door, Zee. Let's talk about it."

Just as Zee stepped into my office, Mike Steele came around the bend and glanced in. He stopped dead in his tracks.

"Wow, Zee, two days in a row. Make it three and I'll have Tina Swanson hire you as the second-shift word processor."

Suddenly, Zee shifted into the stance. It was so fast I didn't see it happen, like a gunfighter with a legendary quick draw. "I came to apologize to Odelia for my behavior yesterday, Mr. Steele. I promise to be quick about it so it doesn't disrupt your day."

"Are you going to apologize to me, as well?"

"I have no plans to."

"Why not? You were rude to me, too."

"You, Mr. Steele, were inappropriate in your remark to me. Therefore, there is no need to apologize to you for my reply, which was fitting under the circumstance."

Steele started to say something but instead held his tongue and walked away. Zee shut the door and sat down opposite me.

"Sure you don't want a job here, Zee? You don't have to do any real work, just keep Steele in his place."

Zee smiled. "Mike Steele is just a big kid with a smart mouth. I've raised two kids. I know what I'm doing."

After a short pause, we both started to speak at the same time. We stopped, giggled, and I gave Zee the floor.

"Odelia, I'm sorry I stormed in here yesterday ready to take your head off. It's just that these adventures of yours scare the living daylights out of me. You start off well-intentioned, but every time you manage to get injured and close to being killed. It makes me crazy. You know I couldn't bear to lose you."

She reached across the desk and covered one of my hands with one of hers. She may have been apologizing to me, but I was the one who felt guilty.

"I'm sorry I put you in that position, Zee. I don't intend to. I really don't go looking for these problems. They just seem to happen to me."

She patted my hand and withdrew hers. "I know, honey. It's because you have such a good heart and want to help people. People understand that about you, no matter how prickly you try to come off." Zee smiled, and her big chocolate eyes melted into my green ones. I still felt bad for making her feel bad.

"I promise I'll say no from now on, Zee. No matter who tries to get me involved. No more dead people. No more investigations. No more chasing murderers."

Zee laughed her signature creamy laugh. "As much as I'd love to walk away from here with that assurance, I wouldn't want you to make that promise to me. Seth and I spent an hour last night talking this over."

I thought about his call to Greg. "He called Greg yesterday—offered to put us on retainer."

"I know, he told me." Zee laughed again. "But make no mistake, Odelia, Seth doesn't like this any more than I do. He's just more practical about it. He convinced me last night that we need to come to the same conclusion Greg did when he married you—that we need to accept you for who you are and learn to live with what happens to you in order to have you in our lives. You are an important person to us and our family. If we lose you, it would hurt us deeply, but to not love and accept you for the person you are would hurt us more."

I swallowed back tears. "Thank you. I do try to be careful. Honest."

"I know you do, honey. And I'm glad Greg is helping you out. Maybe he can keep you out of harm's way a little better than you do yourself. At least Seth believes that."

I thought about last night and how Greg was ready to take on Gordon Harper just for eyeballing my chest. "He is very protective of me."

She nodded. "That's his job, Odelia, just as it's Wainwright's job to protect him." We smiled at each other for a short while, comfortable with how our long-time relationship had readjusted itself.

Zee broke the silence. "Now, tell me why you want to see Dr. Eddy?"

"I need to ask him some questions. Seems one of the murdered women was his patient." I wanted to share with Zee about Lil and her suspicions but thought it best to keep her out of it.

"He won't talk to you about a patient, Odelia. You know that."

I shifted in my seat, knowing Zee wasn't going to be comfortable with my plan. "I thought I'd get in the door by pretending I wanted some work done." Zee looked at me, but her face was a blank. I continued. "But his earliest appointment is not for three weeks. His receptionist said she'd waitlist me in case there was a cancellation, but only because I told her I was going out of town."

Zee took out her cell phone and flipped it open. "Do you have his office number?" I pushed the yellow sticky note it was scrawled across towards her. She started punching numbers on her phone.

"Good morning," she said into the phone. "Could I please speak with La Tanya Ancrum?" A pause. "Tell her it's Zenobia Washington calling."

Another pause, a longer one. I thumped my fingers on my desk while Zee patiently waited.

"Hi, La Tanya, it's Zee. I'm sorry to bother you at work, but I have a favor to ask. A dear friend needs to see Dr. Eddy sooner than later. Is that possible?" Pause. "Three weeks? Nothing sooner? It's very important, or I wouldn't ask." A long pause. "What time? Wonderful. Thanks a lot, La Tanya. Please give my best to your mother."

Zee shut her phone and got up to leave. "Do you know where his office is?"

"Yes, over by Hoag on Hospital Road."

She checked her watch. "We'd better get a move on, then. Your appointment is in thirty minutes. I'll drive."

I stared at her with an open mouth.

"La Tanya, Dr. Eddy's office manager, grew up in our church." She smiled at me. It was a Mona Lisa–type smile. "I keep telling you, Odelia, never underestimate the power of going to church."

"But you said *we'd* better get moving. There is no *we* in this, Zee. You are not going with me."

"Oh, yes, I am."

"Hell, no, you're not. The last time you insisted on tagging along, you ended up passed out cold in my arms."

"Do you expect to find any dead bodies today?"

"I didn't expect to find one then." I pulled my tote bag out of my bottom desk drawer, shaking my head no the whole time. "But who knows, the day's still young."

I was still shaking my head no during the ride in the elevator and during the walk to the parking garage. When we got to the garage elevator, I punched the button for the fourth level.

"My car's on two," Zee announced as she punched the button for the second floor of the garage.

"I'll call you after the appointment, Zee, I promise."

When we got to the second floor and the door opened, Zee straddled the threshold and wouldn't allow the door to close. We were alone. I wondered if she would have pulled this stunt if others had been in the elevator. For once, I was sorry the elevator wasn't packed.

"What part of *no* don't you understand?" I glared at her, my frustration swelling like bad water retention.

One hand went to her hip. "And what part of *I'm coming with you* don't *you* understand?" She put on her sunglasses and peered at me over the top rim. "You leave without me, Odelia, and I'll call La Tanya and tell her you can't make it. See how far you get trying to make another appointment with Dr. Eddy on your own." She paused. "Three weeks is a long time."

Crap. Crap. Crap.

I stomped out of the elevator, and she let the doors close. She made her way to her car, and I followed with a face so sour lemons seemed sweet by comparison.

"So," I said to Zee's back, "Pastor Hill teaching blackmail from the pulpit these days, or is this a little something you picked up on your own?"

ELEVEN

Dr. Eddy's office was decorated to the nines. Little wonder with his wife being the talented Jane Sharp. It reminded me of an elegant day spa instead of a doctor's office. Everything was a modern mix of cool colors and glass, with interesting sculptures and paintings of the human body, mostly female.

The receptionist, a young woman who looked like she belonged on a runway in Paris, handed me the usual medical history forms to fill out. I sank into a buttery leather chair and got to work. Zee sat in a chair next to me, reading a magazine. Actually, she was doing more fidgeting than reading. I could tell she was about to come unglued with curiosity as to why we were in Brian Eddy's office and why I needed to speak to the god of plastic surgeons. She only knew it had something to do with the Blond Bomber. It was driving her insane that I was keeping my mouth shut and enjoying every delicious moment of her madness. That will teach her to tag along where she's not wanted. I knew that if I told Zee that someone—the man's mother, no less—suspected Dr. Eddy of being the

Blond Bomber, she would have marched me out of there, across her back if need be.

In short order, I found myself led to an examination room by another gorgeous young woman. My guess was that she was in her late twenties or very early thirties. She had long blond hair worn in a French braid, a flawless face, and a pinup girl figure. The name tag on her uniform said *Amber,* but something was out of kilter with the lovely Amber.

I had noticed as I walked through the office that all of Brian Eddy's employees were dressed the same in shapeless pants and tunics the color of raspberry sherbet. Amber wore the same uniform, but I'd bet my next carton of Ben & Jerry's she'd done some tailoring to show off her spectacular figure. In addition, Amber had accessorized her uniform with high heels. Not just ordinary high heels, but upscale hooker shoes. On her feet were quality leather pumps just a shade or two darker than her uniform, with five-inch heels.

My comfort-focused mind thought: *How in the world can she work all day in those?* Followed by: *How inappropriate for a doctor's office.*

As Amber took my blood pressure, I made a mental note to check out the shoes of the other women. Maybe it was all part of Dr. Eddy's glamorous image. But if that were the case, instead of the tunic-style uniforms, he might have picked something from Frederick's of Hollywood to show off his staff's assets.

A few minutes after Amber clickety-clacked her way out of the examination room, Dr. Brian Eddy entered. By now, I was stripped to my waist, wearing a paper poncho that barely covered half of my upper torso. Doctor or not, I felt uncomfortable being half naked in front of this man. I didn't have this problem in front of my usual doctor, but then, Dr. Greenfield was a thousand years old, not the son of a friend, and not a suspected serial killer. On top of that, my breasts were being exposed under false pretense, pressed into service just so I could meet this man. And further on top of that, I was pretty sure my insurance was not going to cover this consultation. Sitting in the cool room with my girls hanging out, I suddenly wished I had rigged a fender bender instead. But even that would have cost me financially. At least this way, I was getting a checkup.

"Good morning, Ms. Grey, I'm Dr. Eddy." He stuck his hand out, and we shook. In his other, he held my chart. He scanned the details and looked up at me. "I see you're here to consult about a breast reduction."

"Um, that's right."

Dr. Eddy bore a striking resemblance to his mother. He had the same crystal blue eyes, slender face, and aristocratic nose. His mouth was different, though. Instead of a full, smiling mouth, Dr. Eddy's mouth was thin lipped and tight, appearing cruel and disapproving. His build was tall and lean, with wide shoulders. Combined with his salt-and-pepper, beautifully styled hair, he was attractive in a country club, appearance-is-everything sort of way. Not at all what I would expect from someone who murdered women as a hobby. But then again, I've never met a serial killer, so what did I know?

"Are you having any back pain?"

"Excuse me?"

"Back pain?" he repeated without emotion. "Most women who seek a breast reduction have severe back pain."

"Um, no. No back pain."

Like a ninny, in using breast reduction as an excuse to get into Dr. Eddy's office, I hadn't thought it through properly. Of course he would ask about back pain. And I probably should have lied and said yes. I had to think fast. I'm good at thinking fast. I'm just not good at thinking fast with clarity and quality.

"Um, I just think they're too big."

The doctor consulted my chart again. "And what does your husband think?"

I blushed as I remembered Greg burying his soapy face in my cleavage. "He thinks they're just fine. But he doesn't have to cart them around all day, does he?"

Without a glimmer of amusement or any kind of emotion, Dr. Eddy quickly turned and placed my chart on a nearby counter. When he turned around, he was putting on surgical gloves.

"If you don't mind, Ms. Grey, I'd like to examine you before I give my opinion on the pros and cons of a reduction."

"ARE YOU GOING TO tell me what's going on with Dr. Eddy, or do I have to beat it out of you like candy from a piñata?"

Geez, Zee was beginning to sound like me. Not good.

I looked across the table at her. "Start beating."

Following my visit with Dr. Eddy, Zee suggested that we go to lunch. At first, all I could think about was heading back to the office and burying myself headfirst into those waiting boxes of documents. Well, that's not true. That was the second thing I thought about. The first thing was to head straight home and bury myself under the covers of our bed, safe and sound. If I'd been driving and alone, I would have tossed a coin: heads—home; tails—the office. But the more I considered it, lunch with Zee would be a nice way to detox from the creepy thought that maybe a serial killer had just touched me.

We were at our favorite Mexican restaurant, Mi Casa on Seventeenth Street in Costa Mesa, which was pretty close to Dr. Eddy's office. We'd just placed our orders and were sipping our drinks—iced tea for me, lemonade for Zee. It was a little past noon, and the usual lunch crowd was just starting to filter in. Before sitting down, I'd called the office from my cell phone and told the receptionist I'd be back immediately after lunch.

Dr. Eddy had been gentle and professional, albeit coldly professional. The whole examination and consultation had taken less than twenty minutes and was very mechanical. My gut told me the doctor was a cold fish and uptight. But it also told me he couldn't be the Blond Bomber. But then my gut also advised me to order the Grande Burrito instead of something light. In about an hour, I would be comatose at my desk—thanks to my gut.

Zee rolled her big browns at me. "Come on, Odelia. Don't you trust me?"

"Of course I trust you. What a silly thing to say. I'd trust you and Seth both with my life, you know that. I'm just not so sure you should trust me with yours, especially since I keep finding myself on the receiving end of violence."

"Did the doctor tell you anything about that murdered patient?"

"No, because I didn't ask." I took a sip of tea. "But he did advise me against having a breast reduction. Said smaller boobs would make me look out of proportion. Said if I wanted smaller ones, to start by losing some weight. After I lost the weight, he said he would be happy to consult with me again."

I power-chomped through a half-dozen tortilla chips.

"That's it?" Zee seemed disappointed. "But what about the murder-victim patient?"

I shrugged and stuffed a few more chips into my mouth to stall. Zee waited, knowing I had to stop chewing sometime. She crossed her arms across her chest and looked at me. It was the stance in a sitting position. She could and would stay like that forever. Usually, I can fight off the stance, but today I was in a weakened state.

I took a drink of tea to wash down the chips. "If I tell you about Dr. Eddy, you have to promise not to go ballistic."

Zee rolled her eyes. "Just when do I go ballistic?"

The waitress brought our food. Zee calmly started her usual food ritual of arranging everything just so in preparation of her first bite. At Mi Casa, the ritual included dumping her sour cream and guacamole onto my plate.

"Geez, I don't know, Zee, like maybe yesterday morning in my office?"

"That wasn't ballistic, that was concern." She snatched her first bite of enchilada off her fork and chewed with annoyance.

I finished the bite of burrito I was working on and swallowed. "I see, then how about you promise me not to get *concerned* over what I'm about to tell you."

She gave me another dose of her sitting-down stance. "I'll get concerned over whatever I please."

"See? That's why I don't want to tell you. I can't have you getting all riled up over something that may not be true. People's lives are involved."

"And you're one of those people, Odelia." She took a drink of lemonade. "You've put more gray hair on my head than both my children combined."

Her words were a two-edged sword, making me feel warm and fuzzy and guilty at the same time. "I'm sorry if I give you so much to worry about, Zee. It's not intentional."

We ate in silence for a few minutes, during which time I made a decision.

"Okay," I began in a whisper. "I'll tell you what's up with Dr. Eddy. But you have to promise not to tell anyone or to get involved any more than taking me to his office."

"Don't worry about me, Odelia. Your job is getting into trouble. My job is praying for your safety."

I was thankful someone was.

While we ate, I filled her in on Lil, Dr. Eddy, Gordon and Crystal Lee Harper, Laurie and Lisa Luke, and even Muffin. When I was done, her mouth hung open like a gaping cave. While she sorted through all the information, I cut off another bite-size piece of my burrito with the edge of my fork and shoveled it into my mouth. I followed that with one last bite before pushing away my half-eaten burrito. My nerves were telling me to devour the whole thing, lock, stock, and guacamole, but my better judgment won out for a change, and I decided to save the rest for lunch the next day.

I hadn't asked Dr. Eddy about Crystal Lee Harper, but I did ask him if he knew Laurie Luke. After all, she did work at the hospital where he saw most of his surgical patients. I had let the question slip out during the hands-on exam of my breasts, hoping he would think it was simply nervous babble. My investigation intent aside, it *was* nervous babble.

The doctor commented about the murder being a tragedy but said he hadn't had the pleasure of knowing Laurie Luke personally. As far as I could tell, his response seemed truthful and sincere.

"His *own mother* thinks he's the Blond Bomber?" Zee had put down her fork and was staring at me.

I nodded, pretty sure she was thinking about her son, Jacob, and whether or not she could ever think such a thing about him.

"His *own mother*," she repeated, struggling to keep her voice quiet. "And what do you think?"

"My intuition is telling me he's not the serial killer, in spite of some of the coincidences. But that's all I have to go on." Our waitress came by with our check, and I asked her to box up the remainder of the burrito. "There's no hard evidence that he is the killer, but there's nothing yet to prove he's not."

"What about motive?"

"Do serial killers need a motive?" I paused. "I mean, it's not like they kill because of vengeance or greed. From what little I know about it from TV or the newspapers, it seems like they have a pattern and choose their victims based on some internal reasoning that makes sense only to them. But then again, I'm getting most of my information from TV, which is hardly known for its accuracy."

"Too bad you can't pick Dev's brain without raising red flags."

I laughed. "Red flags? If I mention anything to Dev Frye about serial killers or the Blond Bomber, he'll have me thrown in jail and guard it himself. There really isn't a nonchalant way for me to ask him about crime in any way without his antennae vibrating."

Zee nodded in agreement.

"By the way, did you notice the woman who took me back to the examining room?"

"You mean the one in the snug uniform and hooker shoes?"

I smiled. Zee seldom missed anything.

"Yes. Did you notice any of the other women in the office dressed like that?" Without waiting for her response, I continued. "Amber—that was her name—was a definite blond bombshell. Don't you think if Brian Eddy was the Blond Bomber, he'd find easier pickings at work instead of combing Southern California for victims?"

"Not really." Zee paused to think it over. "Killing someone so close to home would raise major suspicions. The police would definitely question all the men who knew her, including her boss." She paused. "Do you know if any of the other victims were patients of his besides Crystal Lee?"

"Not yet, but I intend to find out, though I doubt the young girl, Gabby, was."

"But now that you mention it," Zee said once she'd finished eating, "none of the other women in that office that I saw were dressed like that one assistant. I'll ask La Tanya about Amber."

"No, Zee. I don't want you involved."

"What's the harm in asking a simple question? I'm just curious. All the women in that office were drop-dead gorgeous, but only she was dressed in a provocative manner."

I thought about that, happy that Zee had made the same observations I had but not happy with her decision to get involved. If she kept this up, I might be the one putting someone under lock and key for her own good.

"What about La Tanya? Is she gorgeous?"

Zee grinned. "Think Whitney Houston."

"Before or after Bobby Brown?"

"Before."

I raised my eyebrows in a silent, appreciative *wow*.

TWELVE

THE CHAT ROOM WAS hopping with meaningless banter. I looked at the notes to the right-hand side of my keyboard and confirmed that I was in the right place. On the paper were the names of three Internet chat rooms frequented by Perfect4u. The one I was currently in was the one in which she and Knotdead had met and continued to use for their online rendezvous before switching to private instant messages. Lil had told me that Knotdead was the screen name used by Brian Eddy.

Lil had agreed to not go online as Perfect4u anymore and to let me use the screen name to try and ferret out information about her son. She had given me a list with her password and the three chat rooms in which she had played as a twenty-something hottie.

I could tell she wasn't happy that her fantasy life had come to a screeching halt, but in the end Lil realized that her double life wasn't such a good idea. But even though she understood the serious situation her activities had created, I wondered if she would succumb to the call of the tech-age fountain of youth and create a new alter ego to continue cruising the web for excitement. Who knows, thinking the odds were in her favor that something this bizarre would never happen again—besides, she only had one son—maybe she was already playing cyber footsie somewhere under another name.

In an attempt to not throw stones at my friend, I took a moment to honestly examine myself. Internet chat didn't particularly attract me, but what if I could convince someone I was a size four and twenty-two years old? Would I enjoy it? Would I be drawn into the double life out of unhappiness or frustration with the inevitable march of time? Hard to say.

Cupping a mug of hot tea in my hands, I sat in our home office and watched the meaningless chat scroll by, line by line, in an upward-moving waterfall of words. I took note of who was present. Or, more importantly, who was not present. Greg had taken the day shift both Monday and Tuesday, signing on as Perfect4u during the day and keeping the chat room open while he worked. He said Knotdead showed up only once, and that was this morning around ten o'clock. Unfortunately, Greg was away from the computer at the time and didn't see the message, which contained several hellos and several pleas of *talk to me* and professions of love.

Greg was more amused, however, by the numerous other messages sent to Perfect4u, all from men and all obviously acquainted with her in a flirtatious and sexual way, though not in person. He'd told me over dinner tonight that some of the messages had been quite steamy. In fact, at one point, he announced that he had spent a little time conversing as Perfect4u, and the experience had given him some ideas. When my husband winked at me across the meatloaf, I didn't know whether to be thrilled or frightened. Maybe I should be both.

Tonight it was my turn to stand guard as Perfect4u in search of contact with Knotdead. Greg had returned to Ocean Breeze Graphics to finish up a large rush project for an important customer. He was also breaking in a new assistant. Boomer, his faithful and talented right-hand man for many years, had recently gotten married and moved to Colorado with his lovely bride.

Greg had mentored Boomer, a pierced and alternative-looking teen with a minor juvenile record and bad home life, when no one else would give him a chance. But Greg had seen something special under the tattoos and Day-Glo hair. Boomer had turned out to be a talented artist and computer genius who had just needed someone to believe in him.

About fifteen years ago, Greg inherited money from his grandfather. The funds allowed him to buy and remodel the home we live in and to start Ocean Breeze Graphics. Once his business was established, Greg had used some of the money to start a college scholarship program for his employees. Starting out as Greg's delivery boy, Boomer had put himself through college with Greg's assistance. Last year, he approached Greg with a business plan to expand Ocean Breeze outside of California, with him as Greg's partner. Greg was so proud of Boomer and impressed with the plan, it didn't take him long to say yes, especially since one of his largest clients was located in Colorado. Next month, we are all meeting in Denver to launch Mountain Breeze Graphics, with future plans for a Desert Breeze Graphics in Phoenix in another year or so. It was exciting times for all of us, and both Greg and I were so proud of Boomer.

But with Boomer gone from the mother ship, Greg had to spend more time at the shop. His new assistant was another long shot who showed promise under the right tutelage. Chris Fowler was a scrawny high-school dropout referred to Greg for part-time work a few years ago by a client. When hired, Greg insisted that part of working for him would include Chris obtaining his GED, which he did. Last September, with help from Ocean Breeze, he started community college. Though not as gifted as Boomer in the arts department, Chris was proving to be a steady hand with the mechanics of the business and a favorite with both the staff and customers, and, like Boomer, there wasn't a machine in the shop he couldn't fix or maintain.

Boredom with the chat room set in after only ten minutes. Picking up the novel I was currently reading, I buried my nose in it, only glancing from time to time at the ongoing chat. Seamus was curled on the small loveseat in the corner of the room, and Muffin was a ball of gray fur between the keyboard and the screen. Wainwright was with Greg.

After an hour, there was still no sign of Brian Eddy. I stood up and stretched and went to the kitchen to refresh my teacup. Muffin followed me out to the kitchen. She mewed softly and rubbed my ankles. I tossed her a couple of kitty treats while the tea kettle heated. She was so cute that a part of me hoped Lisa Luke would not want her back.

It was just after nine. Greg had said not to expect him home much before eleven. This chat-room surveillance was dull business, but at least I was getting my reading done, a pastime I loved.

When I returned to the computer a few minutes later, there was still no sign of Knotdead, but there were instant messages from two other folks. One said *HI, SEXY! REMEMBER ME?* The other said *SUCK MY DICK*. I deleted both.

I was only interested in whatever Knotdead had to say. But as soon as the messages disappeared, I had a change of heart. If Brian Eddy was not the Blond Bomber, maybe one of these other yahoos, such as the "suck my dick" guy, was the killer instead.

Hmmm. *Now, wait a minute,* I told myself. *You're only supposed to be proving that Brian Eddy is not the killer. At no time are you to go nosing about looking for the real Blond Bomber. But,* said my nosy side, *if you can prove that someone else is the killer, that's the same as proving Dr. Eddy is not the killer. Well, isn't it?*

Still, I really didn't have the appetite to converse with people who wanted me to do intimate things with their virtual body parts. Did Lil play these games? Would she have had a snappy comeback to that message? Would she have put him in his place or encouraged more graphic sex talk? Or would Perfect4u have deleted the vulgar message as well? I wanted to believe that even online under an assumed identity, Lil practiced at least some of the same good taste she did in real life.

The sound of a slight ding roused me from my thoughts about Lil's behavior. It was the announcement that a new instant message had been received. Looking up at the small text box, I saw that it was one of the previous callers, someone named HuckFynn. Cute name. Ol' Huck was the one who'd asked Perfect4u if she'd remembered him.

HOPE I'M NOT BOTHERING YOU, the message said.

I paused, wondering if I should respond. Muffin hopped back up on the desk. I scratched the animal behind her ears and under her heavy collar. She purred in kitty ecstasy.

"What should I do, girl?" I pointed to the screen and said to the cat, "Anyone you remember your mom talking to?"

Muffin yawned and curled up for another snooze. Seamus was still comatose on the loveseat. I was definitely on my own.

I poised my fingers over the keyboard, took a deep breath, and started typing. NO, NO BOTHER AT ALL.

Several seconds lapsed before I received a reply: GOOD. Followed by a repeat of DO YOU REMEMBER ME?

HuckFynn must have been a former online playmate. Or was he someone Lil had simply conversed with? And if so, how long ago? If he had to ask if she remembered him, it couldn't have been too recent. With some care, I pecked out a response. I'M SORRY, BUT I MEET SO MANY PEOPLE ONLINE.

I JUST BET YOU DO.

Conversing online is tricky business. The five words in Huck-Fynn's response could be taken so many ways without knowing the emotion behind them. Was he simply being flirtatious, or was he peeved because Perfect4u didn't recognize him? I wondered if Lil would have instantly known who he was. I wrote down his screen name to remember to ask her.

Again, I put my fingers to work. SORRY. THE NAME'S FAMILIAR, BUT I JUST CAN'T REMEMBER ANY DETAILS.

A long pause followed my message. Just when I thought he'd gone off to sulk, he sent me another message.

UNDERSTANDABLE. IT'S BEEN A FEW MONTHS SINCE WE'VE CHATTED AND, LIKE YOU SAID, YOU MEET A LOT OF PEOPLE ONLINE.

I wondered why Perfect4u and HuckFynn had stopped chatting. Had Lil banished him, or had he lost interest?

WELL, I typed, my message showing up in the small text box, YOU'RE HERE NOW. I paused, grimaced as I added a stupid smiley face, and then hit the send key. On the fly, I decided to take a chance and typed, WHERE HAVE YOU BEEN FOR THE PAST FEW MONTHS? I HOPE I DIDN'T SAY ANYTHING TO UPSET YOU.

He responded, COULDN'T SEE THE POINT AFTER YOU REFUSED TO MEET ME. There was a slight pause. I'M LOOKING FOR MORE THAN JUST A TEASE.

His words made me wonder how long they had been interacting online before HuckFynn moved on.

Another entry showed up. ARE YOU STILL JUST INTO ONLINE CHAT OR ARE YOU READY FOR A REAL-TIME DATE?

I glanced over at the photo Lil had given me for reference. It was a picture of a very pretty, wholesome-looking, twenty-something blond—the photo she'd e-mailed to men when they requested a picture. Who knows where she'd gotten it—probably downloaded it from some poor unsuspecting girl's website. It made me wonder what HuckFynn would say or do if Lil had said yes to the meeting and instead of blondie the dreamgirl, an elderly woman showed up for the date. Or even a forty-something BBW. I was almost tempted to set something up, just to see what would happen.

I'M SORRY, I typed to HuckFynn, BUT MY SITUATION HAS NOT CHANGED. I didn't know what excuse Lil had given to avoid meeting men, but I thought that might cover most anything and everything.

Before I had finished typing and sending my last message to HuckFynn, two new, separate message windows opened. One was from Jinxee, the same creep as before, asking me for another blow job, but this time he'd at least added the word *please*. I added his screen name to my list.

Did some women actually find this endearing? Supposing for a minute that Jinxee was the Blond Bomber, I found it hard to believe that the dead women would have found this line of sweet talk appealing enough to want to set up a meeting. I could see Gabby finding it funny, but grown women? Professional women, such as Laurie Luke? But then, there was no accounting for what turned people on. Maybe women responded to this brand of vulgarity when looking for adventure. But even when I was single, it would have done nothing to cause the pitter-patter of my little heart.

When I read the second of the new messages, my heart didn't pitter-patter, but it did stop short for a beat or two. The second message was a simple hello from Knotdead.

As I was about to type a response, the cordless phone next to me rang, and I saw that the caller was Zee. Quickly, I typed a message to Knotdead: HANG ON, I'M ON THE PHONE.

I NEED TO TALK TO YOU was his reply.

"According to La Tanya," Zee began, cutting to the chase, "Amber has the hots for Dr. Eddy, and the two are having an affair."

"Did La Tanya actually say they were having an affair or that everyone thought they were having one?" While I spoke, I kept my eye on the message screen from Knotdead.

"She told me they're having one right now."

I glanced up at the message screen. Knotdead had written YOU STILL THERE?

Jinxee had also returned, this time asking Perfect4u for more photos, preferably more topless ones. I looked at the photo on the

100

desk next to me. The young woman was fully clad. Had Lil also been sending nude photos of other women to men online? My mind didn't want to go there.

"Did she say how long it's been going on?"

"A few months tops, if that." Zee hesitated. "Do you know anything about Dr. Eddy's marriage?"

"I know he's married to Jane Sharp, the designer." As I spoke, my recent discussion with Lil came to mind. "His mother said their relationship seemed rather distant, and that Jane thought her husband was having an affair."

"Well, La Tanya told me she had lunch with Amber not too long ago, and that Amber told her that Dr. Eddy was going to get a divorce and marry her."

Although I'd never seen a photo of Jane Sharp, the image of the overtly sexy Amber with her hooker shoes flashed in my brain. Amber looked more like Gordon Harper's type than Dr. Eddy's. But you never know.

"Does La Tanya believe her?"

"I asked her the same thing." A pause from Zee's end. "She was uncomfortable discussing it but finally told me she stayed late one night last week and accidentally came upon Dr. Eddy and Amber *in flagrante*."

"Really? Right there in the office?"

"Uh-huh, but here's the odd part. La Tanya said the door to the doctor's office was open a crack. La Tanya peeked in and saw them, but just as she pulled away to leave, she could have sworn she saw Amber catch her eye and wink at her."

"Was this before or after they'd had lunch?"

"A day or two after."

"The cunning little minx. She was making sure La Tanya knew about the affair so there would be no doubt about Amber's influence over the doctor."

"That's what I'm thinking. La Tanya's worked there several years and says Amber's been trouble since she started. She also told me this is the first time she's ever known the doctor to behave inappropriately."

"That she knows of."

While I had been talking to Zee, so many messages lit up my computer screen, the tones sounded like a pinball machine on speed. Perfect4u was a popular gal.

After I said goodbye to Zee, I went back to Knotdead. SORRY, IMPORTANT CALL, I wrote him. ARE YOU STILL THERE?

YES, came the seemingly eager reply. He went on to tell Perfect4u how much he'd missed her and loved her—how his life was empty without her.

I twitched my nose in annoyance, knowing what I knew. He missed her so much, he was doing his own nurse on the side? Counting Perfect4u, he had three women in his life and was cheating on them all. After glancing at the photo again, I had another thought. Amber and the girl in the photo Lil had given me were very similar in appearance. Not exactly, not like Laurie and Lisa Luke, but close enough to be reasonable facsimiles. Maybe the doctor had substituted the willing Amber for the unavailable Perfect4u. It didn't change the fact he was a dog, but it made some sense. Lil told me that she had halted her sexual playtime with Knotdead a few months ago, and Brian Eddy's affair with Amber was a fairly recent thing. Dr. Eddy seemed to have a thing for stacked blonds, just like the Blond Bomber. But then, so did a lot of men.

I'm sure you've found another playmate by now, I wrote him in an attempt to tweak his nose. While waiting for his response, I read and noted the screen names of the other men who were contacting Perfect4u, all looking for companionship and several looking for raw sex talk, apparently Perfect4u's house specialty.

There was another message from HuckFynn saying he was still interested in meeting Perfect4u, offering to take her to dinner at one of the top restaurants in Los Angeles, first class all the way. At least he wasn't asking for something disgusting.

Finally, the next message came from Knotdead. *Truthfully, I have been seeing someone.*

A pause. I waited.

She's a nice woman. Looks a lot like you. Another pause while he typed more. *I was hoping I could love her like I love you, but it's not the same. We don't connect emotionally and spiritually like you and I do. I told her tonight it's over.*

So the ambitious Amber was yesterday's news. But was she really? Was Knotdead just saying that to win over Perfect4u?

But she's real, Perfect4u wrote back via my fingers. *We've only talked online. Even the sex wasn't real between us.*

It was very real to me. Every time I made love to her, I pretended it was you.

I hesitated, at a loss for what to type next.

I'm leaving my wife. His message came quickly on the heels of his last. *Jane has agreed to a divorce. We can be together now.*

I can't. I typed the two words one letter at a time, stalling.

Yes, you can. The typed messages came fast and furious. *At least meet me. Give us a chance to see if we can have in person what we had online. If not, we stay just friends.*

Even with the dryness of the computer, I could feel Knotdead's sincerity. After meeting him, I could see Brian Eddy seated at a laptop, pounding out his heartfelt pain to Perfect4u. As reserved as he was in his professional life, his online demeanor was passionate. His messages were different, more alive and real than the requests for sexual satisfaction from the others. It seemed to me that he might really have deep feelings for Perfect4u.

Another tone. Jinxee was asking again for more naked photos, this time of Perfect4u's butt. I deleted it. HuckFynn wrote a message saying he was heading to bed. He asked if Perfect4u would talk dirty to him before he left. *Like you used to,* he wrote.

I wondered if I could ever look at Lil the same again.

THIRTEEN

EXCEPT FOR THE EARLY morning surfers, the beach was empty during my six o'clock walk. But instead of walking, as I should have been, I was sitting on a bench with a cup of coffee, thinking about my conversations the night before with Zee and Knotdead. Wainwright, unleashed as a treat, was scampering about, running back and forth, chasing seagulls.

I wondered if I should contact Jane Sharp—maybe find out if they were really getting a divorce and why. I could always drum up some pretense of wanting my place redecorated, except that one look at my address and profession and she'd know I couldn't afford her. And I wasn't sure what I could learn from her. I also didn't want to alert her needlessly if the Dr. Eddy/Blond Bomber connection wasn't there. Still, I did want to meet her. Greg was going to try to contact Gabby's family and see if we could set up a time to talk to them. So far, his attempts to reach anyone connected to victim number one, Elaine Epps, had yielded a goose egg.

My gut was still telling me that Brian Eddy was not the Blond Bomber. Last night, after I cooled him down about meeting Perfect4u, we chatted about his marriage and divorce. For all his success, Brian Eddy was a sad and lonely man. So lonely, this highly educated and normally rational man had fallen in love with a personality on the computer, an ideal rather than flesh and blood—fiction, not fact. He had believed everything Perfect4u had told him about herself and about her feelings for him. Even without the fact that he was her son, something she didn't know until much later, Lil had toyed with another human being's feelings for her own amusement, and although I knew Lil was not a mean person by nature, the activity still struck me as being downright irresponsible, even unwittingly hateful. I'm sure not everyone chatting on the Internet is as gullible as Dr. Eddy had been, but I'm sure there are a lot more like him—people who, either from loneliness or despair, or their own belief that most people told the truth, believed everything typed anonymously.

In talking to Brian, I could also see how Lil had decided to stay in contact with him after she found out Knotdead's real identity. He was her son, and he was in pain. No longer his online lover, she had moved herself into the role of confidant and comforter, which only made Knotdead want her more.

I was roused from my thoughts by barks from Wainwright. They were joyful barks, not warnings. I looked around and saw him running for a boy on a bike a few yards away. It was Silas. I waved. Silas got off his bike and walked it over to me.

"Hi, Odelia."

"Good morning, Silas. What in the world are you doing at the beach so early?"

He shrugged. "Sometimes I come down here before school."

"School starts this early?"

"It starts at eight, but I like the beach in the morning."

"Me, too."

"I know. I see you here sometimes." While he spoke, he stroked the dog.

"And you haven't said hello?"

"Usually, you and Wainwright are walking pretty fast." He looked at me, then down at his sneakers. "Can I sit with you?"

I smiled at the boy and scooted over on the bench to make room. He was clean and his hair was brushed, but his school clothes were as worn as his play clothes.

"Does your grandmother know you leave the house this early?"

He shook his head. "She sleeps late. Billy's home getting dressed and eating breakfast. He's a slowpoke." He consulted an oversized kid's watch. "I'll go home and get him, and we'll ride our bikes to school together."

"You take good care of your brother, don't you?"

Silas watched the waves. "When Mom went away, she told me it was my job to look after Billy."

Seems like everyone had a job looking after someone else. Greg and Zee looked after me. Wainwright looked after our family. I looked after Greg, my dad, and Mike Steele. Pops looked after our van, and we looked after him. I wondered who, besides his grandmother, looked after Silas. And who would look after Lisa Luke now that Laurie was gone? Everyone should have someone looking out for them.

"Where are your parents, Silas?"

"Mom went away to a hospital, because she's sick." He looked at me, his young eyes far older than his age. "I haven't seen my dad since Billy was a baby."

"How long has your mother been in the hospital?"

"Two years. She's a druggie." He said it matter-of-factly, as if self-trained to keep the emotion out of his words. "But every time she starts getting better, she gets sick again. We used to live with my aunt, but she got a job working nights, so we came to live here."

"My mother left me when I was a teenager. I haven't seen her since I was sixteen."

He looked up at me, surprised. "Really?"

I nodded. Gently, I put an arm around his young shoulders. Silas stiffened, then relaxed.

"Why do they do that, Odelia? Don't they want us?"

It was the question nagging at my heart for over thirty years, but I gave the boy a hopeful answer. One that people had been giving me since I was sixteen.

"It has nothing to do with us, Silas. Or with them wanting us. Sometimes people just aren't strong enough. Then they turn to drugs, or alcohol, or just leave rather than face their responsibilities."

"You ever want to see your mom again?"

"I'd like to, yes. And maybe one day I will."

Silas turned to look me fully in the face. "Can I ask you something?"

"Sure." I smiled at the boy, a youngster with whom I now shared an emotional connection.

"Are you a cop or PI or something cool like that?"

I did a double take. "No, I'm not. I work in an office. Why?"

"I overheard you and Greg talking when I brought Wainwright home, and it sounded like you were."

A nervous laugh escaped my lips. So, it's true. Little pitchers *do* have big ears. I wondered just how much the boy had heard.

"No, nothing like that. We were just discussing a friend."

Draining the last of my coffee, I got off the bench and tossed the paper cup into a nearby trash can. "I need to get home and get ready for work, and you need to make sure Billy's ready for school."

I called Wainwright to me and was latching the leash to his collar when the cell phone tucked into the pocket of my sweatpants rang. Once I moved to Seal Beach and began walking alone with Wainwright, Greg insisted I always have my cell phone with me for emergencies. Usually, though, the only emergency calls I received in the morning were from Greg, asking me to stop by the bakery on the way back. Besides the cell phone, I also took to carrying a little cash for these morning calls.

Today's emergency involved two cinnamon rolls.

I turned to Silas. "Walk me back, Silas? There's a sticky bun in it for you."

Pops was standing in front of the bakery when we got there. As soon as he saw me, he became agitated.

"The van," the old man said, squinting and pointing at my chest.

"The van?" I was puzzled. He must mean Greg's van. "Not today, Pops. Greg and his van are at home."

"The van," he said again, his bony finger shaking as he again pointed at me.

I smiled. Pops took his job of van watching very seriously. Besides Greg's cinnamon rolls and a couple of pastries for Silas to share with Billy, I bought Pops an egg-and-cheese-filled croissant and a large cup of coffee.

As Silas, Wainwright, and I started towards home, Pops bit into the breakfast sandwich. Even with his mouth full, he kept mumbling about the van.

I HAD JUST SETTLED in at my desk at Woobie when my cell phone rang for the second time that morning. Retrieving it from my purse, I saw it was Dev. Ten minutes later, I was back in my car, racing for Hoag Hospital.

"I got here as fast as I could," I whispered to Dev Frye as I entered the hospital room. In the bed, attached to tubes and monitors, was Lisa Luke. Her eyes were closed, her complexion pasty. She looked dead. Only the beeps of the monitors, one after another in a march of comfort, told me she wasn't. Slumped in a chair next to the bed was a haggard-looking young man. His head was tilted back, his eyes closed. I recognized him from the photos in Lisa's apartment. It was Kirk Thomas, Laurie's fiancé.

Dev took me by the arm, and not very gently. "Let's talk outside."

He took me out of the room and set our course for a quiet corner outfitted with vending machines and sofas. There was a man and an old woman seated on one sofa, so he aimed us at a bank of windows away from them.

He didn't speak for a few minutes. From the set of his jaw, I knew better than to open my mouth. Dev Frye is an imposing man, standing well over six feet tall and built like a tank. When I first met him, his full head of tight curly hair was blond mixed with gray. Now it's mostly gray mixed with blond. His voice is gravelly and deep and belies his sweet, tender nature. We met when he was assigned to investigate the death of my friend Sophie London. In fact, I met Dev Frye and Greg Stevens at the same time, and for a while the three of us were involved in a very polite love triangle.

Dev, a widow, is currently dating a lovely schoolteacher from Irvine named Beverly. The last time I'd see him had been at our home for Greg's birthday. It had been shortly after Laurie Luke's murder—before I'd gotten involved. Now that I was involved, I didn't expect to see so much of Dev's tender nature. Being a cop, he didn't like the fact that I got mixed up in murder investigations from time to time. Being a personal friend, he hated it as much, if not more, than Zee. He was one of the people who looked after me but wished he didn't have to.

Arriving at the windows, he dropped his death grip on my upper arm and gazed out at nothing in particular.

"Would you please tell me," he started, keeping his voice in low gear, "why Lisa Luke, suicide attempt and sister of a murder victim, has your name on her lips as soon as she regains consciousness?"

"*Suicide*? Is she going to be okay?"

"Took a boatload of sleeping pills, but the doc says she'll make a complete recovery. Lucky for her, Laurie's fiancé stopped by the apartment and still has a key."

Tears filled my eyes. "That poor girl. I knew she was distraught over her sister's murder, but I had no idea she'd go this far."

"Which leads me back to my original line of questioning." He cleared his throat. "Why does Lisa Luke even know you? Can't one murder happen in Orange County without your involvement?"

I shifted on my feet as I weighed my words. "I went to Lisa's home in my capacity as one of the leaders of Reality Check." Okay, so it was a lie, but only a partial one. "Lisa is part of the morning walking group." Okay, that was the truth, albeit stretched like a rubber band. I paused and added for effect, "I even have Laurie's cat at my place because it was too painful for Lisa to have it around."

Dev grabbed both of my shoulders and spun me around so that I was forced to look him in the face, or rather the chest. With one hand, he cupped my chin and lifted it upward, forcing me to look him in the eye.

"Tell me the truth. Are you looking into who murdered Laurie Luke?"

"Not exactly."

Dev unhanded me and spun back around towards the window, where he remained quiet for a moment. It crossed my mind to take the opportunity to slink away on my rubber-soled flats, but before I could make up my mind, Dev spun back around in my direction.

"Damn it, Odelia!"

People nearby raised their heads and stared at us. The old woman and young man rose from the sofa and moved to another area.

"Dev, I promise you that I am *not* looking for the Blond Bomber."

"Then what exactly *are* you doing? And why doesn't Greg have better control over you?"

I bristled. "First of all, Greg married me. He doesn't own me and control me like he does his dog." Dev looked down at the index finger I was shaking at him. I hadn't even realized I was doing so. After folding the digit back into my hand, I lowered my arm. "Secondly," I continued, "while I appreciate your concern, it's my business what I'm doing, not yours."

"Not if it involves my case."

"But it doesn't really. I'm just helping out a friend, and talking to Lisa Luke was part of it. And Lisa Luke really is a member of the Reality Check walking group."

"So it's just a coincidence that Lisa's sister was a recent murder victim?"

I looked up at Dev and quickly looked away. No matter how I tried, I knew I wouldn't be able to boldly lie to this man and get away with it—on many levels. He was professionally trained to read people, and he knew me too well. He'd know I was lying in a nanosecond. I also respected him too much to try. But I still didn't think it was a great idea to let him know about Brian Eddy and Lil.

I looked back up at Dev. "No, it's not a coincidence. Part of helping my friend involved talking to Laurie Luke's sister. But," I quickly added, "I assure you that I am *not* looking for the Blond Bomber."

"Who is your friend, and what is the favor?"

"I don't want to say."

"Odeliaaaaa." My name came out of him from his gut, like an earthquake rumble from the center of the earth. "How about I take you in for questioning?"

"You wouldn't!"

He fixed his eyes on mine. Oh yes, he would. I twitched my nose at him.

Dev brought two cups of coffee over to the table. We had moved to the hospital cafeteria. It made me think of a time past when he and I sat in this same room discussing the murder of my friend Sophie London. Dev's wife had been a patient here then. Now, here we were again, once more talking about murder.

"So, what's up?" he asked after taking his first sip. I played with my cup but didn't drink. I was busy trying to figure out what I was going to say without spilling the whole pot of beans.

"A friend of mine has a theory about the Blond Bomber."

"But you said you weren't looking for the Blond Bomber."

"I'm not. She's worried that someone she knows *might* be the killer. She doesn't have any proof that he is, but she doesn't have any proof that he's not. She wants me to find proof that he's not." I fiddled more with my coffee mug. "So, see, I'm not really looking for the Blond Bomber, just proof that this guy is not him."

"And who is this guy?"

"That I can't tell you."

"Can't or won't?"

"Both."

"Odelia." He narrowed his eyes at me. I held firm.

"I mean it, Dev. If I tell you, and the police haul him in and it leaks to the press, it could ruin him. My friend doesn't want that." Dev kept me in his sights. Pushing my muddled brain to perform, I pled my case. "Remember that guy who was first accused of bombing the Olympics in Atlanta?"

"Richard Jewell."

"Yes, that's the man. Turned out he was innocent, but that suspicion hung over him the rest of his life. People don't remember the innocent part, just the suspect part."

Dev took a couple gulps of coffee while he gave the issue some thought. I sipped my own and waited.

"So," he finally said, breaking the silence, "are you willing to tell me why your friend suspects this guy of *possibly* being the serial killer?"

"He knew most of the victims from online chat. I don't know yet if he knew Laurie Luke."

"But you intend to find out."

"That's part of it, yes. Though from talking with Lisa, Laurie didn't strike me as the sort who spent time idly chatting online."

Dev considered me in silence. I squirmed under his gaze, relieved when he finally spoke. "If those women frequented the same chat rooms, it's quite possible a lot of men knew them all."

"And met them in person?"

Dev raised an eyebrow. "You know for a fact that this guy met them?"

"My friend said he told her he did, at least a couple of them."

"Unfortunately, all of the dead women were meeting men online and setting up dates, including the teen. And I'm sure some jokers are out there, claiming they knew them." He drained his coffee. "Just because the papers claim an Internet connection doesn't mean there is one, Odelia. We don't tell the media everything."

"Speaking of Lisa, did she say why she tried to kill herself? Did she leave a note?"

"That was a very clunky and obvious change in subject, even for you." Dev smiled at me for the first time since I'd rushed into

Lisa's hospital room. "And don't think for a minute we're through on the subject of the Blond Bomber, but Lisa did leave a note. She's claiming responsibility for her sister's death."

"Her responsibility? That doesn't make sense."

Dev shrugged. "Apparently, it was Lisa who was chatting online, not Laurie. And Lisa was passing out her sister's photo as her own."

I sank back against my chair. "Oh, no."

"Oh, yes." Dev got up. "You want more coffee?" I shook my head. He refilled his own mug and returned to our table.

"We talked to her a few minutes before she fell asleep. She's sure if she hadn't done that, her sister would still be alive. Said she told men online she worked at Hoag Hospital and thinks the killer stalked the hospital until he matched the photo."

I leaned forward. "Do you believe that?"

He took a sip of coffee and shook his head as he swallowed. "No." He paused and pulled out a pack of gum, fiddling with the wrapper. "There's been another body found in Laguna Canyon, very early this morning, about dawn. It's probably all over the news by now."

"The Blond Bomber?"

Dev looked away, then back to me, then away again, forgetting about the gum in his hand. He was obviously thinking something over. "He wrote something on the body."

"*Whore*, like the others?"

"No. This time it was different." Dev looked back at me. "This time, he wrote *Last one not mine*."

"But what does it mean?" My mind whirred like a roulette wheel until the little ball that was my brain stopped on a possible answer. "Oh my gawd, Dev. Does this mean the Blond Bomber didn't kill Laurie Luke?"

"The killer's definitely trying to tell us something." Dev looked directly at me, eyeball to eyeball. "For reasons I'm not going to disclose, we've always thought the Luke girl was a copycat. Now we're pretty damn sure."

My eyes popped wide open as my brain went into another spinning action and landed on another possibility. I swallowed hard. "This last girl, was she also a nurse?"

"Yeah, in a doctor's office—name's Amber."

The hand clutching my coffee mug started shaking ever so slightly. Dev noticed it immediately.

"Damn it, Odelia, please tell me you have no connection to this girl."

FOURTEEN

THERE WAS NO DOUBT about it: Amber the dead nurse and Amber of Dr. Eddy's office were one and the same. Dev confirmed it after I told him that I just had an appointment with Dr. Brian Eddy, and he had a blond bombshell nurse named Amber.

He had looked at me with frank skepticism. "You simply met this woman during a doctor's appointment?"

I nodded.

Dev unwrapped the gum in his hand and popped it into his mouth. He gave it a few thoughtful chews before speaking again. "Isn't that just too much of a coinkydink?"

I didn't care for the sarcasm in his voice.

"What are you saying, Dev? I went to see a doctor. It just so happens this poor woman was his nurse, and she was memorable, a complete knockout."

"Did you ever meet Laurie Luke?"

"No."

"How about Crystal Lee Harper?"

"No."

"Ah-ha! But you know who Crystal Lee Harper was, don't you?"

"Of course I do. One of the killer's victims. I read the paper and listen to the news just like everyone else, Dev."

With great reluctance, Dev gave up his questioning of me and we went back to Lisa's room. Kirk was awake now, standing in front of the window, looking out. Lisa was still asleep. Dev introduced me and left, but not before ordering me to rethink whatever I was doing or involved with, and to rethink telling him whatever I knew or might know.

With Amber dead, I *was* rethinking everything. Last night Knotdead had told Perfect4u that he had ended his current relationship that same night. He hadn't disclosed who he was seeing, but thanks to La Tanya, I knew that he was involved with Amber, if not possibly others. Had Brian Eddy ended their relationship with murder, or was Amber's death just an unfortunate *coinkydink*? My gut, rocking and rolling now from nerves, was still telling me that Brian Eddy was not the Blond Bomber, but possible evidence to the contrary had now presented itself. Should I tell Dev or wait a little while longer? But what if another woman died? What then?

A thought occurred to me. I stepped out of Lisa's room and hit Dev's speed dial number on my cell phone.

"Dev," I said, as soon as he answered, "do you folks have any idea when Amber was killed?"

"If you two just had a *chance* meeting, why would you care?"

Sigh.

"It could help me prove that my friend's suspicions about the Blond Bomber are wrong." I paused, then added, "And I promise you that if the evidence points to this person as the killer, you will be the very first person I tell."

Now it was Dev's turn to sigh. "It's not exact, of course, but the M.E. thinks she died sometime between eight and midnight."

"Eight and midnight," I repeated. "Hmmm. You can't pin that down a little more?"

"This isn't TV, Odelia, this is real life and a real murder." If Dev wasn't such a gentleman, I'm sure he would have hung up on me, but instead, he just probed. "Does this prove or disprove your friend's theory?"

"I'm not sure yet, but I think it might put her suspicions to rest."

"Good. The sooner you're out of the favor business, the better."

Lisa was awake when I returned to the room. Kirk was back in the chair at the side of her bed, holding her hand. He was dressed in jeans and a white tee shirt with a heavy denim shirt worn open over the tee shirt. His blond hair was unkempt; his face, which sported a few days' growth, was distorted in anguish. I remained at the door, not wanting to intrude.

"Please forgive me, Lisa." Kirk's voice was ragged when he spoke.

"Forgive you?" she asked in a weak voice. "I'm the one who needs forgiving." Lisa closed her eyes for a moment, then opened them to look at him again. "How can you even stand to be near me after what I've done?"

"You did nothing wrong, Lisa. You have to believe that. I'm ..." Kirk stopped when he noticed me at the door.

Lisa looked in my direction and gave me a small smile. "Odelia."

I approached the bed. "How are you feeling, Lisa?"

Kirk released her hand and sat back in his chair. His eyes were hollow, his face like chalk. Losing his fiancée and now nearly her sister had obviously taken their toll.

"Horrible, that's how I feel." Her voice was raspy as she spoke.

"Detective Frye is a friend of mine. He told me you're going to be fine."

"I feel horrible because I'm alive, Odelia. Because I failed ... like I fail at everything." The words came out of her like bile, harsh and bitter.

"Don't say that, Lisa." Kirk was once more holding her hand. Lisa slipped it out of his grasp.

"It's the truth, Kirk. *I'm* the reason Laurie was murdered. *I* should be dead, not her. I'd do anything to trade places."

Lisa looked at me. "I was the one talking to men on the Internet, not Laurie. I gave out her picture instead of my own." She started to sob. "I led that monster to her." She turned her face away, trying to bury it in the pillow.

"Shhh." I plucked a tissue from a small box on the nightstand and gently dabbed at her cheeks. "You did no such thing."

"Please, Lisa," Kirk begged with tears in his own eyes. "Don't talk like that. If anyone's to blame, it's me."

Kirk's last comment caught my attention, and I shot a curious glance at him, which he noticed.

"I mean, I shouldn't have left Laurie alone so much. I should have insisted that she come with me on that last trip."

Kirk got up from the chair and started pacing. I continued to study him. He seemed nervous and agitated. Granted, he'd just found Lisa half dead and was still grieving for Laurie, but to my thinking that should make him sad, not nervous. But then people show grief in different ways.

"But I did, Odelia! It's no one's fault but mine. That should be my grave, not Lisa's."

I sat down in the chair vacated by Kirk and continued to blot at Lisa's tears as if she were a child and I her mother. I offered her another tissue, and she blew her nose. The young woman was devastated. Given her earlier state, Dev probably hadn't told her about the latest murder, or thought it best not to. I wondered how much I should divulge. I wanted to give Lisa some comfort, but until the police knew who did murder Laurie, it still could have been someone Lisa chatted with online.

Like Lil, Lisa had given out someone else's photo and assumed a different identity, and even though it probably hadn't led to Laurie's murder, it still had come back to bite Lisa on the ass emotionally.

A nurse came in to check on Lisa and wasn't happy to find her upset. It was my cue to head back to the office. As much as I wanted to stick close to the grieving woman, I did have a job to do back at Woobie. I also wanted to chat up Kirk a bit and noticed him leaving. He hadn't even said goodbye.

"Lisa, I have to return to my office." I spoke in a hurry, one eye on the departing back of Kirk Thomas. "How about I drop by later today?"

She looked at me with eyes full of despair. "I've caused you enough trouble, Odelia. I don't deserve your kindness."

"Let's put it this way: would you like for me to visit you later?"

She nodded, her eyes downcast.

"Then it's a done deal. I don't know exactly when, but I'll make sure I stop by before I head home tonight. Okay?"

Again, a small nod.

Catching up with Kirk at the elevator, I stood next to him while we waited. He seemed ready to jump out of his skin.

"I'm so glad you stopped by Lisa's this morning, Kirk. You saved her life."

He shook his rugged, handsome head and dug his hands deep into the pockets of his jeans. "Trust me, I'm no hero." Without looking at me, he continued. "I really didn't want to see Lisa. Haven't been able to since Laurie died. I purposely went by the apartment when I thought she'd be at work. I just wanted to get the damn cat."

"I have Muffin." Kirk looked at me, surprised. "Lisa asked me to foster the cat because she couldn't bear to be around it. Reminded her too much of her sister." I paused, not sure I wanted to say my next words. "Would you like her?"

Kirk Thomas stood frozen for a minute, his eyes rolling around in his head as his brain considered my question. He finally returned his focus to me. "If you don't mind keeping the cat for a bit, I'd appreciate it. Lisa left me a voice mail a week ago, saying she couldn't care for it and to come get it. So, that's what I was doing. But I don't really have a decent place for it."

"Muffin can stay with me and my husband as long as you need her to. We have two other animals and they're getting along fine, so it's no trouble at all."

He mumbled a thank-you. Shifting from foot to foot, he punched the down button over and over. I wanted to reach out to stop him. He was making *me* nervous. Something was tormenting this man, and I was beginning to think it wasn't just grief. Honestly, he seemed guilty. Like Lisa, he obviously held himself responsible for Laurie's death.

The elevator came. Two people were inside, one holding a bouquet of flowers. They barely had time to move toward the door when Kirk pushed his way in. I waited until the others were out of the way before entering. As soon as the doors closed, I took my shot at speaking with Kirk.

"Kirk, what did you mean when you told Lisa that you were to blame for Laurie's death?"

The question obviously caught him off guard, and it took him a few heartbeats to respond. He still didn't look at me.

"I'm a wildlife photographer and travel a lot, especially out of the country. Sometimes Laurie came with me. The day she was killed, I was in Africa. She'd wanted to go with me, but I couldn't take her." He swallowed hard, his Adam's apple noticeably moving. "Maybe if I had found a way, none of this would have happened."

The elevator stopped at the lobby, and we both got off. I reached out and touched Kirk's arm before he could dash off. He glanced at me before looking away again. "You and Lisa are not to blame for what happened. Someone else killed Laurie, not one of you."

Kirk's eyes darted about the lobby. This wasn't just a case of guilt. He was afraid of something. No, not afraid—petrified.

"You seem like a nice lady, but you have no idea what you're talking about." He finally let his eyes come to rest on my face briefly. "Do me a favor? Stay close to Lisa. She needs all the friends she can get right now."

Before I could respond, Kirk Thomas headed for the nearest door. Once there, he broke into a run towards the parking lot.

Maybe Kirk *was* responsible for Laurie's death. The way he was behaving made me wonder if he even did it himself. But he'd said he was in Africa when she was murdered, and alibis like that are easy to check and confirm. No, if he said he was in Africa, I had no doubt he was, but I also had no doubt that he knew something about his fiancée's death.

And dollars to donuts, this was one woman I was pretty sure Dr. Brian Eddy didn't kill.

FIFTEEN

On my way back to the office, I called Greg and told him what had happened, including my suspicion that Kirk Thomas was hiding something. Greg, in turn, told me he'd located Gabby's parents. They'd divorced shortly after Gabby's death and gone their separate ways. The father had moved out-of-state, but the mother was still living in Pasadena. He said she would see us tonight around eight thirty.

I made one more personal call—this one to Zee, to find out if she had heard about Amber's death. She had. La Tanya had called her as soon as she'd found out. Zee was shaken and now convinced that Dr. Eddy had something to do with the killings. She wasn't as ready to believe my gut instinct as I was. But, much to my surprise, it seemed someone else was interested in my gut.

Upon returning to the office, I had found plopped in the middle of my messy desk a greasy, sugary apple fritter, though at this moment, it hardly looked yummy. My stomach was knotted with worry and suspicion. Stuck to the pastry bag was a green sticky note in Steele's handwriting. It said, *Re: the news today, you'll need your strength.*

"Ass." I said the word out loud and not without some amusement.

"That's Mr. Ass to you."

My head shot up to find Steele in his usual lurking stance against my doorjamb, hands stuck into his designer suit pockets. How does he sneak up on me so easily? It's unnerving.

He looked at his expensive watch in an exaggerated manner. "Looks like that's going to be your lunch, Grey, not breakfast." When I didn't answer, he added, "Jill told me you came in, then left like a bat out of hell for the hospital. Everything okay?"

I pushed the fritter aside. "Someone I know tried to kill herself."

"From the word *tried*, I'll assume she didn't succeed."

I shook my head. "It was the sister of the last murdered girl. Not today's, but that nurse from Hoag."

Steele stepped inside my office and shut the door, something he seldom did. Usually closed-door conferences were held in his more spacious office, not my cramped and cluttered closet. When Steele sat in the chair across from my desk and settled in comfortably, I really got worried.

"You're in way over your stumpy little head." He crossed one leg over the other as casually as if he were discussing sports scores. "You know that, don't you?"

"I'm always in over my stumpy little head."

He chuckled.

"And the last time my stumpy little head got involved, it saved your Armani-covered ass."

He digested that information, then smiled. "Okay, out with it. It's time to tell me who your friend thinks is the Blond Bomber."

Once I shoved aside the urge to tell my boss to bite me, I considered telling Steele about Brian Eddy.

"Is this covered by attorney-client privilege?" I asked.

"You're not my client."

Yanking open my tote bag, I pulled a dollar out of my wallet and tossed it across the desk. "There's your retainer."

Steele picked up the dollar, folded it as neatly as a clean towel, and shoved it into one of his pockets. He *actually* took it.

"That was an exaggerated gesture, Steele, not a real down payment for your services."

With a jerk of his chin, he indicated the pastry bag. "That heart-stopping brick of grease and dough cost me two dollars. It's only worth a buck, at best. I'll consider your dollar a rebate."

Geez. But still, I really did want his input. Steele had a mind like no other I'd come across. Not even Seth Washington, sharp as he was, could match the quality of Steele's lumpy gray matter.

I took a deep breath, which included the scent of sickly sweet, fried dough. "My friend thinks the killer is …." I paused.

"You waiting for a drum roll, Grey?"

"You just have to promise me, Steele, that you won't run out that door and cause trouble with this information. No matter how good your intentions might be."

He raised an eyebrow in my direction. It was a gesture intended to be as menacing as Zee's stance.

"Okay, okay." I sighed. "Brian Eddy," I blurted. "My friend thinks Brian Eddy might be the Blond Bomber." Then I quickly added, "But I don't."

Steele uncrossed his legs and leaned forward. "Dr. Brian Eddy? Jane Sharp's husband?"

That caught me by surprise. Most people would have said that the other way around. Although Jane Sharp was well-known in Southern California, her celebrity status was not nearly as high as her husband's. Most would connect Jane Sharp with the more famous Brian Eddy, not the doctor with the decorator.

"You know Jane Sharp?"

Steele shrugged slightly. "She decorated my condo. This was back before she became such a hot shot."

I'd been to Steele's condo in Laguna Beach. It was stunning, masculine yet gorgeous, with every detail painstakingly considered. It didn't surprise me to learn he'd had it done professionally.

I studied Steele, thinking about his penchant for bedding just about any woman who crossed his path. Any extremely attractive woman, that is.

"I've never met Jane Sharp or even seen a photo of her. Did you find her attractive?"

Steele shot me a sly smile. "Are you asking me if I've slept with her?"

"I'm asking you what she looks like."

Steele considered his answer before giving it. "She's incredibly beautiful, but very cold and calculating. At least she was when she was doing my place."

"And you were doing her?"

"If you know the answer, Grey, why ask the question?"

Instead of shooting off a smart comeback, I did some quick math in my head. I knew that Steele had purchased his condo in Laguna Beach four, maybe five years ago. So that would have been about the time he'd had the affair with Jane Sharp. I also wondered how many other clients she'd helped launch new digs and if Dr. Eddy had also been having ongoing affairs during this time. Another thought crossed my mind.

"During your affair with Jane Sharp, did she mention anything about her marriage to Dr. Eddy?"

"I never said I had an affair with Jane Sharp."

It was my turn to raise an eyebrow.

Steele chuckled but at least had the decency to look away briefly before turning his attention back to our conversation. "As I recall, I didn't pursue her, she pursued me. It was almost as if the sex came with the decorating services. As soon as the job was over, so were the extra benefits." There was a pause. "Remember my friend Stuart Weinstock?"

"The writer? The one who lives in Carlsbad?"

He gave a slight nod. "Well, it was the same with him. I referred her to him. After she decorated his new home, he sent me several bottles of very expensive wine." Steele grinned. "Guess that makes me a pimp, of sorts."

"Among other things."

"Give me some credit, Grey. I've never referred her to any of my married friends."

"But what about her marriage? Did she ever say anything about it?"

"She didn't seem all that concerned with it." He recrossed his legs and settled back to think. "Once I asked her about it. She claimed her husband didn't care, said they didn't have sex very often. That was about it."

"Did you ever meet Dr. Eddy?"

"Yes." Steele again nodded as he spoke. "Once, at a charity tennis event about two years ago. Seemed like a nice enough guy. Very quiet. Lots of gorgeous women hanging around, wanting to talk to him, but he seemed rather embarrassed by it all, not enjoying it like most men would."

"How did Jane react to all the attention her husband received?"

"Hard to say if she even noticed. Rumor was, while the rest of us were playing tennis, Jane had her own game going on—mostly in the backseat of a Jaguar."

"With a valet parking attendant?"

Steele let out a short, loud laugh. "God, no! Not Jane Sharp. It was the owner of the Jag, some film producer whose wife was drunk at the bar. I believe Jane was decorating their beach house at the time."

I shook my head, thankful I didn't run with the rich and decadent.

Steele started to say something but stopped before the words came out. I watched the struggle in his eyes as he weighed whether or not to tell me what was on his mind.

"Out with it, Steele. I can tell you're about to tell me something that might be important."

He tossed me a crooked smile. "I was just thinking about Jane Sharp."

"And?"

"And, I knew her years ago. Back in college."

"You went to school together?"

"Sort of. I was a few years behind her. I didn't know her personally, but I knew who she was. She's changed a lot in many ways. In others, not so much."

"Meaning?"

"Meaning that back then she wasn't such a knockout. In fact, she was an ugly duckling—but very popular with the guys, if you get my drift."

"She put out?"

"Not indiscriminately. More like she used sex to gain the popularity her looks couldn't get her, like a desperate plan to gain acceptance. She went after only the big-shot jocks and important professors. It was well known that you had to be somebody to get into her panties."

He paused and fiddled with imaginary lint on the leg of his trousers. "Her senior year, Jane had a total mental breakdown."

I gasped slightly, and Steele glanced up at me before continuing.

"She'd fallen in love with one of her playmates, a football player heading for the NFL after graduation. But he dumped her and married the campus beauty queen." He uncrossed his legs and straightened them out in front of him. "Jane created a scene, which included going public about flings with married professors. There was quite a scandal. Rumor was, she ended up being hospitalized with a complete breakdown. She never came back to school that I know of."

"And now she's still hopping from bed to bed?"

"Seems that way. But now she's stunning and accomplished and married to a celebrity surgeon. It's everything she went after in school." Steele scoffed. "Guess it's a case of be careful what you wish for."

"Or that looks and money can't buy happiness."

I wondered if Lil knew about her daughter-in-law's past and present activities and decided probably not. It also made me wonder who started cheating first in the marriage and why. Did Jane do what she did to get her husband's attention, or was she unable to control herself and her husband suffered in silence about it and sought his own comfort?

"Steele, do you think that maybe, just maybe, if Dr. Eddy is the Blond Bomber, that he's murdering his wife over and over with each victim? After all, the bodies had the word *whore* written across them."

"Hmmm. That's a possibility. She certainly fits the physical description, at least now. But why not just kill her instead of other women?"

"Maybe because she's the mother of his children?" It was just a thought, but if Brian Eddy was killing his wife over and over by killing other women, he had to have a reason for not killing her specifically.

I filled Steele in on what I'd learned about Amber and Dr. Eddy, my conversation online with Dr. Eddy, and what Dev had told me about the Luke murder. I also told him why Lisa tried to kill herself and about Kirk Thomas.

Steele sat at attention. "So there are two different murderers roaming the area?"

"That's what the police think now."

My phone rang. It was Jill looking for Steele, letting him know his lunch appointment was waiting for him in the lobby. I relayed Steele's message that he'd be out in a few minutes. Steele got up to leave, but I could tell he wanted to stay and hash out the mound of information.

"Dev wouldn't tell me why they suspected Laurie Luke's murder was a copycat, but the message on the new body seemed to strengthen their suspicions." I fiddled with a pen, doodling on a yellow pad of paper while I talked. "Thing is, even with what you've told me about Jane Sharp and what I know already about Brian Eddy's activities, I still don't think he killed Amber or those other women."

Steele looked at me with interest. "Give me a quick version of why. Then maybe we can talk more about it later, if you'd like."

"Dev said the medical examiner put Amber's death between eight and midnight. I was chatting online with Dr. Eddy from about nine until ten thirty. That wouldn't give him enough time to kill Amber and stash her body in Laguna Canyon, would it?" I paused to do more calculations. "It wouldn't make sense to dump a body at eight—still too many cars and people about at that hour, even in the canyon area. Not dark enough."

Steele gave it some thought. "He could have killed her earlier, stashed the body, and then dumped it after he talked to you. Laguna Canyon isn't that close, but it's not that far away either. And parts of it are very isolated. He could have had a late-night tryst. Depending on where he was when he was online, he could have had time to do it."

My head was beginning to hurt. I leaned my elbows on my desk and rested my chin in my palms. My stomach was still churning, and the smell of the fritter was making it twirl in earnest. I wanted to take a nap and wake up on a beach somewhere with Greg stroking my face.

Steele cleared his throat. I looked up. He was standing at my door, hand on the handle. "I know how you are, Grey. You won't rest until you work this through. I'll help as I can, but there's the firm to consider."

He was right, of course. After all, Woobie was paying me to work for them, not to chase around after possible killers.

"I'll stay late, Steele," I promised. "Don't worry about the work or my billable hours." Then I remembered Gabby's mother. "Crap. I can't stay tonight, but tomorrow I will."

Steele took his hand off my doorknob and turned to face me. "Don't make promises you might not be able to keep, Grey. Besides, right now we have nothing pressing. So work as much as you can, and leave when you must. I'll cover for you, if I have to, with the other attorneys." He pointed a finger in my direction. "But I will still expect you to keep up your billable hours. You can make them up when all this is over."

I nodded in agreement.

"You understand? I'm not giving you time off, I'm just giving you a waiver. Call it a loan of time, payable in full when I say it is."

I nodded again, knowing that one day, when I least expected it, Steele would extract his pound of flesh for this favor. And I knew he couldn't be bought off with an apple fritter.

SIXTEEN

As soon as Steele left my office, I called Zee again to ask a favor I'd forgotten to ask before: if she would visit Lisa Luke. She said she'd make sure she dropped by the hospital. By the time Zee finished fussing with Lisa, she'd forget she was alone in the world. Then I tackled the work I was paid to do.

In between my work for the firm, I researched two companies online. The first was Sharp Design. Its website was slick and beautiful but not flashy. It was pretty clear that Sharp Design catered to the rich and elegant, not to the rich and edgy. Its famous clientele included some movie and TV stars, but not a single rock star.

On the site were a couple of photos of Jane Sharp. She was indeed stunning. A leggy blond in her early forties, with perfect hair and even more perfect clothes, she exuded good taste and exclusivity. It was difficult to believe she had once been a plain Jane. Whatever work she had had done, it had been top-of-the-line.

I had to find a way to meet Jane Sharp. It crossed my mind briefly to have Steele be the go-between, but it sounded as if he hadn't had any contact with her since their affair, and the less I involved him, the better. The fewer people who might fall, even accidentally, within the range of a killer—strike that, *two* killers—the better. Maybe Lil could somehow hook us up without looking too obvious.

The thought of calling Lil had hardly crossed my mind when my cell phone rang, and the caller was none other than Lillian Ramsey herself. As soon as I answered, I could hear the hysteria in her voice.

"Odelia, did you see the news? That poor girl was Brian's nurse! He killed his own nurse! What are we going to do?"

I got up to shut my door before I answered. "Lil, calm down. I did hear about the nurse found this morning, and I know it was Amber from Brian's office, but I have reason to believe Brian didn't kill her."

"You have proof, Odelia?" The hysteria in her voice went down a few notches.

I didn't really have proof. Steele was correct. Given the time of death and my online chat with Knotdead, though very squeaky, Brian Eddy could have had time to kill and dump Amber. But little things just didn't seem right. First of all, when we ended our chat, Dr. Eddy seemed mellow and tired, not someone hopped up to go kill or even to dump an already dead body. I'm no expert, but it seems there would be a certain mindset for something like that. He'd told Perfect4u that he was going to bed, that the day had been exhausting for him. Of course, breaking up with and killing someone could be reason for feeling tuckered out, but the tone in his chat seemed, well, almost defeated, as if I could see his sagging shoulders and sighs through the computer screen.

I didn't know who killed Amber any more than I knew who killed Laurie Luke, but I was still standing firm on my instinct that neither died at the hands of Dr. Brian Eddy.

"Not exactly, Lil, but I do have a feeling about this. No matter how horrible it may look, I'll be very surprised if the Blond Bomber turns out to be your son."

"I pray that's true."

"In fact, I found out something very interesting this morning. You know that other nurse, the one who disappeared from Hoag Hospital?"

"Of course, the poor girl."

"Well, the police believe she may have been killed by someone else, not by the Blond Bomber at all, but set up to look like the serial killer."

"Really?"

"Yes, Lil. But you can't tell anyone that. Okay?" She didn't respond. "Okay, Lil? You'll keep that to yourself for now?"

"Yes, of course, dear. I'm just so relieved to hear your belief that my son isn't a killer, I feel almost lightheaded." A pause. "It will make things so much more comfortable tomorrow."

"Why, what's happening tomorrow?"

"Jane, my daughter-in-law, called. She's coming by for lunch and a chat. It was supposed to be today, but with everything that has happened, she postponed it until one tomorrow afternoon."

I started to ask Lil if I could drop by, then decided against it. Crashing the little party unannounced would be much better for catching people being themselves.

After the call, I went back to my research, this time looking up Seventh Veil Costuming. The company was incorporated in California, and the president was Gordon Harper. The business address was in Los Angeles. A quick MapQuest search informed me the location was near the Los Angeles airport.

The company's website was professional and hi-tech, with samples of sexy costumes, from very understated to the flashiest of flash, where no feather, crystal, or sequin was spared. There were colorful photos with models of both genders wearing the bawdy outfits and even a video trailer showing several being strutted on a stage. The pitch was for custom-made erotic fantasy costumes for all occasions and sizes. The contact information gave an address, telephone number, and e-mail address.

Picking up the phone, I dialed the contact number. After two rings, the phone was answered by a pleasant-voiced woman with an accent. She identified herself as Mrs. Santiago. I told her I was interested in having a special outfit made for my husband's birthday. No, it wasn't for my husband specifically, I informed the woman when she inquired, but for *me* to wear for my husband's pleasure. When she asked if I had anything specifically in mind, I cast a look at the samples on the website and described one of the less flamboyant outfits. The woman then asked when I wanted to come in for a consultation. After informing her I wanted it as soon as possible, Mrs. Santiago set the appointment for one thirty that afternoon.

As soon as my old Toyota Camry was moving north on the 405 Freeway, I called Greg and gave him the updates, including Steele's offer of letting me pursue the matter in exchange for make-up time.

Greg laughed. "Sweetheart, you just made a deal with the devil." After a short pause, he added, "And whatever outfit you get, make sure it's fire-engine red with black feathers." He laughed again, this time longer and louder.

Speeding up the freeway, I tried not to worry about two things. One, that the number of hours I was going to owe Steele and Woobie were piling up rapidly; and two, that I was about to be measured for a stripper outfit.

SEVENTEEN

Seventh Veil Costuming was located in a light industrial area less than three miles from LAX. All of the buildings looked fairly new and housed a variety of businesses, from luggage outlets and building contractors to airport parking services. Seventh Veil was housed in a two-story building made of gray concrete set back from the street to accommodate a couple of customer parking spots in the front. On one side of the building was a large driveway clearance to allow vehicles to reach the back of the building. A chainlink fence separated it from the buildings on either side. There were no windows facing the street except for the frosted glass door front.

I parked and checked my watch. It was 1:10. I had made unusually good time from Orange County. In about three hours, the 405 would be as slow as molasses. The plan was to get in and out of Seventh Veil in time to beat the rush-hour traffic home. I wanted to relax and have a quiet dinner with Greg before meeting Gabby's mother. If I got home in time, I might even cook something nice.

Then I remembered I had promised Lisa I would stop by tonight. So much for feeding Greg a real home-cooked meal.

Just as I was about to pull open the door to Seventh Veil, I heard a voice—a very distinctive, high-pitched voice. Looking around, I didn't see any cars but mine. Edging slowly to the end of the building in the direction of the driveway, I peeked around the corner. The building was shaped in a U formation with short sides and a long middle. The far end of the lot showed a couple of non-descript sedans parked along the fence. I turned the corner and edged down the side. In the center of the lot was a large open area, probably used for deliveries. There were no delivery trucks present, but there were two other vehicles. One was a silver Mercedes sedan and the other a dark green Jeep Wrangler.

At first I didn't see any people, but I again heard the familiar yippy voice. Fifi the wonder poodle was definitely in the yard. I heard another voice. It was male and medium in timbre, but the tone spiked upward with pleas and emotion. I smashed my chunky body closer to the wall to get a better view.

Suddenly, two men came into view. Or rather, one was thrown into my path of vision by the other. Sprawled on the ground near the front of the Jeep was Kirk Thomas, Laurie Luke's fiancé. A very large man dressed in a dark suit grabbed him by the front of his denim shirt and hoisted him roughly to his feet. Once upright, the man threw a one-two punch directly into Kirk's ribs, forcing him backwards against the front of the Jeep. As he slid to the ground, the assailant kicked Kirk in his side and was about to kick him again when a command halted the attack.

"Enough," I heard Gordon Harper say. "He's no good to us dead or too damaged to travel."

He walked slowly into my view, stopping directly in front of Kirk Thomas. The goon placed a foot on Kirk's chest and pulled a gun out from under his jacket, aiming it at Kirk's head. My eyes widened in fear, as if the gun were pointed at my own head. This was definitely not what I expected to find on a simple reconnaissance trip to a costume shop.

"The deal was for three shipments," Gordon said, looking down at Kirk. "Not one, not two, but three."

"No." Kirk's voice was ragged but determined. "No more. Go ahead, kill me. I don't care now." His last words were choked, almost with sobs. "I did what you asked. You didn't have to kill her." He struggled. The other man put more pressure on his chest.

Gordon Harper walked a few steps away and turned around, causing me to duck for cover. When I peeked again, he was facing Kirk once more.

"The broad got herself killed by acting stupid. Don't you do the same."

"I said no." Kirk spat the words at Harper. "So just kill me now and get it over with."

The older man studied the younger one for a moment. "You may not want to save your own skin, sport, but I understand that honey of yours had a sister."

"No!" Kirk protested in a strangled voice. He squirmed under his captor's foot and received a quick kick in his side for his trouble. Kirk let out a cry of pain.

Harper nodded something to his thug-in-waiting. The big man released Kirk and backed away, still holding the gun on him. Kirk struggled to his feet. He was holding his right side.

"You will complete the job, sport. Deliver the third shipment and the goods you lifted from the last one or the girl's dead."

"No."

Harper grinned. "No, don't kill the girl? Or no, you won't do it?"

Kirk hung his head. "Don't kill her. I'll do what you want."

"Good boy."

Kirk looked up. "Then we're finished, Harper. No more."

"Three shipments was the deal, sport. And three full shipments it will be. I keep my end of a bargain." He approached Kirk and poked a fat finger into his chest. "But you ever talk about this, and you and the sis will both wind up tied to trees in the canyon, understand?"

Harper motioned to his goon. In a flash, Kirk dropped to his knees from a blow to his head.

"Now get the hell out of here." Gordon Harper laughed. It sounded like an asthmatic wheeze.

I took that as my cue, too. As quietly as possible, I scooted back to the front of the building and climbed into my car. I'd heard enough to make my brown hair turn gray in spite of its color job. I tried to put the key into the ignition, but my hands shook too much. I had to calm down, but I also had to get the hell out of there. I clutched the steering wheel to stop the shakes.

Trying once more, this time I successfully jammed the keys into the ignition. But before I could turn the engine over, a vehicle approached rapidly from the side driveway. Without time to back up and drive off, I simply ducked and prayed no one noticed me. Fortunately, my car was parked in the spot farthest from the driveway, and neither Kirk Thomas nor Gordon Harper knew what I drove. A vehicle came out of the side driveway and sped onto the street, taking a right. Raising my head slightly, I noted it was the Jeep Wrangler. I was about to follow Kirk's example when I heard another car. Again, I ducked down, lifting my head in time to see the tail end of the Mercedes make a left onto the street. Unlike the Jeep, the Mercedes didn't seem to be in a rush.

With the coast finally clear, I sat upright and took a moment to calm down.

It was pretty clear that Gordon Harper had something to do with Laurie's death. The police believed Laurie's killer was not the Blond Bomber and even the serial killer himself was trying to tell the police that. Given what I had just witnessed, it seemed that Kirk's outpouring of guilt at the hospital that morning was well grounded. But what was he involved with that would get Laurie killed? And was Laurie involved, too? That Gordon Harper was involved in something shady didn't surprise me one bit. Although Kirk's head wasn't stumpy, it was clear that whatever he was involved in, like me, he was in way over his head.

With Gordon Harper off the premises, I thought about my appointment with Mrs. Santiago. I was now a few minutes late and considered calling from the parking lot to cancel. I wanted to hole up somewhere and think about what I had just learned.

Harper either killed or had Laurie Luke killed because of some dealings with Kirk Thomas that went sour. But what about Crystal Lee? Did Harper bump her off, too? He seemed genuinely affected by her death when we spoke to him. I told myself not to lose sight of the fact that Harper was a tough guy, likely a career criminal, who might even kill loved ones to get what he wanted. If he did kill Crystal Lee, was it to gain control of Seventh Veil or for another reason? But what about Gabby Kerr and Elaine Epps? Did they have connections to Gordon Harper as well? Were they killed to teach a lesson to a fiancé, father, or brother? Maybe the Blond Bomber killings weren't the work of a serial killer but were made to look that way, and Laurie's death got screwed up and didn't follow the pattern as it should have. Remembering what Dev said about the writing on Amber's body, my overtaxed brain jumped the track and forged another path. If the Blond Bomber did kill Amber to send a message to the police, then Harper could have tried to make Laurie's death look like the work of the Blond Bomber to send the police on a wild goose chase.

A visit to Seventh Veil might still be helpful, but the questioning would have to travel in a different direction, or even several.

Still sitting in my car, I closed my eyes and rubbed my temples. My head hurt as if I'd been slammed by Harper's thug.

A chime, like a doorbell, sounded as soon as I entered Seventh Veil Costuming. Unlike its no-frills exterior, the small reception area was decorated like an upscale bordello, or at least what I considered an upscale bordello to look like. Gold-flocked wallpaper covered the walls, and the lighting fixtures were festooned with hanging crystals. There were a couple of chairs and a loveseat, all in brocade. Instead of flowers, tall vases on small tables held colorful feathers. On the walls were photographs of women in elaborate but scanty costumes.

The woman who introduced herself to me as Maria Santiago appeared to be in her mid-forties, with an attractive hairdo and simple makeup. Her attire was business casual, her jewelry sparse and tasteful. Around her neck were eyeglasses on a shiny silver chain. She took care of herself but without overdoing it, unlike her surroundings. She held out a hand with short manicured nails for me to shake.

"Ms. Grey, you seem nervous." She held onto my hand and cupped her other hand over it gently.

It was true, my hands were slightly shaking. "It's nothing really." I paused. "There was almost a car accident out front." She looked at me with concern. "Some big silver Mercedes came barreling out of your parking lot and never saw me."

Mrs. Santiago shook her head slightly. "That must have been Mr. Harper, the owner. He stopped by for a minute, which made him late for an appointment." She released my hand. "I must apologize on his behalf."

"Well, no real harm done." With a fake smile, I added, "My husband and I recently met Mr. Harper. That's how I learned about this place. Too bad I didn't realize he was here, I could have arrived earlier and said hello to Gordon."

"I'm afraid Mr. Harper was in a business meeting until right before he left."

Yeah, I thought to myself, still with the plastic smile plastered to my face, *a business meeting that involved brute force and guns.*

"He has an office here?"

"Yes, on the second floor. But he's not here often. He has many other business concerns."

"I'm sure. He told us he took over Seventh Veil after his ex-wife died."

Mrs. Santiago didn't seem to mind my chattiness, but she didn't encourage it either. She responded to my last comment with a slight nod and indicated for me to follow her.

She led me through a door to a room decorated much like the reception area except instead of a loveseat, the furniture consisted of a small conference table and chairs in the same heavy, ornate style. Once out of the reception area, I could hear the hum of sewing machines and light chatter from the back area. As Mrs. Santiago took notes, I went through the motions of explaining the desired fantasy outfit, fire-engine red with black feathers. She showed me several sample books, explaining how elements from different outfits could be combined to make a custom outfit specially suited for my or my husband's tastes. I kept waiting for a good spot to veer the conversation back to Gordon Harper, but that ship had sailed. Mrs. Santiago was all business. Soon she seemed satisfied that she knew exactly what I wanted for my costume, and she even sketched out a crude sample. Then she gave me a cost estimate. I about had a seizure.

Assuring me that they used only the highest quality fabrics and materials, she explained which modifications could be made to lower the price. Crystals, natural feathers, and other baubles were discarded. In the end, I ordered a red bustier with a short black-and-red striped detachable satin train. The bustier and train were edged with fake black feathers and a few sequins. I also ordered matching black stockings and gloves. G-string panties, I was informed, were included with the bustier. Something told me I was going to look like a fire plug on the make.

With great reluctance, I handed her my credit card for the fifty-percent deposit. Originally, I hadn't planned on going through with the actual ordering of an outfit, but as time went by and Mrs. Santiago put more effort into my outfit, and I still hadn't gotten any real information, I just couldn't say sorry and pull out.

Finished with my order, she directed me out of the conference room and into a very large decorated dressing room. Here, there were clothes hangers and a large three-way mirror, as well as a single ornate chair.

"Effie, our fitter, will be in shortly to take your measurements." She indicated the hangers. "You can use those for your clothing."

"You want me to undress?"

She smiled at me in a motherly fashion. "Just down to your panties and bra, Ms. Grey. We can't take an accurate measurement over clothing."

"I'm a standard size 20, or a 2X, whichever you prefer." I sloughed off my suit jacket and showed her the label. "See, size 20WP, women's petite."

"Here at Seventh Veil, we don't follow standard sizes; we use only your personal measurements." When I didn't respond, she added, "You want the garments to fit properly, don't you?"

She was assuming, of course, that I was going to wear them. And I knew that if this outfit came into the house, Greg would cajole me into wearing it at least once.

EIGHTEEN

As soon as Mrs. Santiago left, closing the door of the dressing room behind her, I sank into the chair. Resting my elbows on my knees, I cupped my face with my palms. This would be the second time this week I'd had to strip down in the course of investigating Brian Eddy. At least no one was shooting at me—yet. But if, on the off chance, any shooting did start up, or Gordon Harper returned with his muscle, I'd really rather be fully dressed when I hit the pavement running.

A knock on the door brought me out of my thoughts. When the door opened, a woman poked her head in. A frown crossed her face when she saw I was still dressed.

"Do you need more time?" she asked in an accent thicker than Mrs. Santiago's.

I stood up and sighed. "It's just that I'm a bit modest."

The woman came in and shut the door. "But the costume is not modest." Then she smiled. "Ah, I see. Costume is for husband or boyfriend, huh? To make him happy?"

I nodded. "Yes, my husband."

"Not to worry. Effie understands. We will take off just one piece at a time. I measure, you put it back on. Next piece, same thing. How's that?"

I smiled back at her. If there was trouble, I could make it down the street partially clothed. It was a compromise I could live with.

Effie was about the same age and height as Maria Santiago, but stockier in build. She wore no makeup and her long hair, streaked with gray, was pulled back in a clip. Behind plain glasses were expressive brown eyes the color of rich coffee. Her clothing consisted of stretch pants, a polyester tunic, and dirty white Keds. Around her neck she wore a tape measure.

After depositing my jacket on one of the nearby hangers, I unbuttoned my blue silk blouse and slipped out of it. Keeping my suit trousers on, I turned to face Effie in my bra. She smiled and unwrapped her tape measure.

"Have you worked here long?" I asked as she began measuring, noting the numbers in a small notebook.

"I was one of the first employees, back when Miss Crystal owned it."

"Crystal Lee Harper? The woman who was murdered by the Blond Bomber?"

She nodded but didn't look at me. "Miss Crystal was a saint." Effie stopped scrutinizing my measurements long enough to cross herself. "Gave us living wages and benefits, not like the sweat-shops."

"Are there a lot of employees? Seems kind of quiet to me."

She had me lift my arms up and out. "Now it is slow. Just the usual customers. Halloween and Valentine's Day are the busiest.

151

Then we work longer hours, bring in extra help. But times like now, there are just two of us sewing."

"You and Mrs. Santiago?"

"Mrs. Santiago. That *puta*." She made a spitting sound. "She hasn't picked up a needle in nearly a month, not since she became boss lady. Not that she was that good of a seamstress to begin with."

I may not be bilingual, but living in Southern California all my life did give me an understanding of many Spanish words. *Puta*, I knew, meant whore.

"I thought Gordon Harper ran Seventh Veil?"

"Mr. Harper owns the company." She stopped fussing with her notebook. "You take off pants now."

After slipping my blouse back on, I took off my trousers and hung them neatly on another hanger, taking my time about it.

"Who ran Seventh Veil after Mrs. Harper died?"

"I did. At least until that *puta* fooled with Mr. Harper's head."

Effie directed me to stand on a small, sturdy box. "She slept with him?" I asked as soon as I was aboard.

She shrugged. "Who knows? Maybe, maybe not. But suddenly she becomes boss lady and I'm back to seamstress."

The tape measure went around my full hips, and I cringed. I didn't care what the numbers were, I just didn't want to know them.

"Weren't you angry? If something like that happened to me at my job, I'd be madder than hell. Why didn't you leave?"

Peering over her glasses, Effie gave me a condescending look. "*Estúpida*," she said barely under her breath.

I knew what that meant, too.

Undaunted, I took another path in my questioning. "As I pulled into the parking lot, Mr. Harper was leaving with another man. Does he work here a lot?"

I looked down at Effie as she measured my inseam. "I'm sorry. I'm not usually this nosy. It's just that I babble a lot when I'm nervous." Okay, maybe the one lie and one truth would cancel each other out.

She smiled as she jotted down the number and proceeded to measure a thigh. "Sometimes he uses Miss Crystal's place for business. It's on the second floor. In the back. Part office, part apartment. She worked many long hours."

Finished, Effie stood up and looked directly at me. "Mr. Harper is not always a nice man, but he loved Miss Crystal very much and treats us very well."

"Thank you, Effie, for your patience. I'm sorry if I was so chatty and annoying."

"It isn't easy to stand in front of a stranger in your underwear. *Verdad*?"

True indeed.

I was walking out the front door of Seventh Veil Costuming when the silver Mercedes returned. This time, Gordon Harper saw me. The car stopped directly behind my car, cutting off any possible escape. At least I was fully dressed.

"Mrs. Stevens," he called to me as he hoisted himself out of the passenger's seat. "What a surprise." He walked towards me. When he got close, I held out my hand cordially.

"Hello, Mr. Harper. Nice to see you again." The goon stayed in the car with the engine running.

"You still asking questions about Crystal Lee?" He smiled as he spoke.

"Not this time." I smiled back. "This time I'm a customer." I pulled the receipt out of my tote bag and waved it gently. "After looking at Seventh Veil's website, I decided to have a little something made. It's a surprise for Greg."

Harper took the receipt from my hand and read the description of the garment. He smiled broadly, then scanned my body up and down with his eyes. I felt naked.

"I can just imagine this on you." A short, wheezing laugh followed. "Maybe you'll let us take a few photos for our sample book. All very professional and glamorous, of course. We're trying to expand our appeal to full-figured women."

Professional photos of me in a bustier and feathers? Yeah, right, like *that* was going to happen.

"Hate to disappoint you, Mr. Harper, but I'm way too modest for something like that. And I don't think Greg would like it very much either."

Harper looked at the receipt again. "This says Odelia Grey, not Stevens."

"Grey is my maiden name. I still use it."

"I see. A modern but modest woman." His eyes studied my bosom, taking their own measurement. I was glad Greg wasn't around.

"It was nice seeing you, Mr. Harper. But I must get going if I'm to beat rush hour on the 405." I held out my hand for the receipt. "I'm really looking forward to seeing my new outfit."

He handed me back the paper. "I hope my staff was pleasant and helpful."

"Very. Couldn't have been nicer." I started to get into my car, trying to act naturally. The last thing I needed was for Harper and his sidekick to think I was snooping.

Harper moved to the driver's side of my car, standing between me and the open door. "I'll have Mrs. Santiago take twenty-five percent off your order."

"Thank you, Mr. Harper. It's not necessary, but I never turn down a bargain." I forced myself to smile.

"Then think again about the photo shoot. It'll be free if you model it for *me*."

The change in wording and emphasis caught my attention like a firecracker near my ear. He'd said *me*, not *us*, not *Seventh Veil*. He'd just invited me to model the bustier for him personally. Greg would have killed him. It also made me wonder if Maria Santiago was a *puta*. Maybe she'd snagged her promotion from the horizontal position.

"That's a generous offer, Mr. Harper. I'll think about it."

He nodded and smiled and closed my car door. With a wave of his hand, the Mercedes moved out of my way.

As I pulled out of the parking lot and onto the street, I noticed that once again my hands were shaking. I also noticed they held the steering wheel in a death grip.

"YOU THINK *who* KILLED Laurie Luke?" Greg's surprise came through my cell phone loud and clear.

"Gordon Harper," I repeated. "Or at least I think he had her killed. Something to do with Kirk Thomas reneging on a deal or job, or something like that."

Heading south on the 405 towards Orange County, I filled Greg in on my afternoon at Seventh Veil. He wasn't happy to hear that I'd had another encounter with Gordon Harper, and I was glad I'd left out Harper's proposition from my report.

"Did you buy an outfit?" My husband's interest strayed easily from the matter at hand.

"Yes, Greg, I did."

"Hot damn!"

NINETEEN

ONCE I GOT GREG'S hormones calmed down, I managed to tell him that I was on my way back to Newport Beach to see Lisa Luke at the hospital. I promised I'd call as soon as I was heading home. If all went well, I would have just enough time to scarf down dinner and hit the road to Pasadena to visit Gabby's mother.

It was just three thirty. I'd been up for eight hours but felt like I'd been up and working forty-eight hours straight—at least working for everyone but Woobie. By the end of the day, I would owe Steele and the firm about seven billable hours. I thought about using some of my accrued vacation time, but Greg and I were saving it for something special, like a nice, long vacation somewhere fun and exotic.

Tomorrow, I told myself, I would skip my morning walk and go into the office early. I had to leave in the middle of the day to go to Lil's, but at least I could get in a half day's work before then. And I should make sure I visit Lisa tomorrow, whether she's home or still at the hospital. Using my fingers, I added up the hours I would be out of the office.

Tick-tock. Tick-tock. At this rate, I would be in debt to Steele until I turned sixty.

Lisa looked better physically, but emotionally she was still pretty distraught. Although dry-eyed, her face was splotchy and her eyes red.

I'd thought about bringing her some magazines to read, but generally fashion magazines make women depressed, and Lisa didn't need encouragement in that department. Instead, I stopped by a nearby bookstore and bought a *People* and two light chick-lit novels.

She picked up one of the books and glanced at the title. "I love this author, Odelia. Thank you." Her voice was flat and far away.

I smiled. "You seem much better, Lisa. Are you going home soon?"

"The doctor said he wants to release me tomorrow."

"That's great news."

She shrugged and looked away.

"Lisa, is there something else?"

"It's Kirk." She didn't look at me while she spoke. "He just left. Said he had to go back to Africa tomorrow. Didn't know when he'd be back."

I thought about the scene I'd witnessed earlier. Back to Africa to finish his job for Gordon Harper? Or back to Africa to finish a real assignment?

"Well, I suppose that's where his work is."

"This morning he told me he wasn't going anywhere until next month. Said he'd help me go through Laurie's things." She started to cry again.

"Did the police tell you the news?"

She looked at me, tears running down her face. "What? That they don't think Laurie was killed by the Blond Bomber? Yes, the detectives stopped by and told me that. The one who was here this morning and another. I don't remember his name, started with a Z, I think."

"Detective Zarrabi?" I asked. Lisa nodded. Kami Zarrabi was Dev Frye's partner.

I'd called Dev and left him a voice mail to call me back. I told him I was heading to the hospital and that it was important—that I had information about Laurie Luke's murder.

"So you see, Lisa, you had nothing to do with Laurie's murder."

She didn't say anything or move a muscle. Her mind was definitely somewhere else.

I walked over to the nightstand where there was a large, beautiful bouquet. I took a sniff. "These are gorgeous." Another one stood bright and cheerful on a sill near the window.

"Kirk's family sent me those. The others are from my office."

"When are you returning to work?"

"Probably Monday. I didn't tell them exactly why I was in the hospital, but I think my boss suspects something like this. She told me to take as much time as I needed. She's been terrific through this whole ordeal. In fact, the whole company has been great."

Returning to Lisa's bedside, I sat in the visitor's chair. "Lisa, do you have someone who can stay with you, or maybe someplace you can stay for a few days? I'm concerned about you going home and being alone right now."

"So is the doctor. But I'll be fine."

I wasn't as confident, especially knowing that behind the scenes Gordon Harper was now threatening Lisa's life. It was something I wanted to discuss with Dev. As if by magic, the man himself filled the doorway to Lisa's room.

"How are you doing, Ms. Luke?" Dev nodded a greeting to me as well.

"Better, thank you."

"Lisa may be going home tomorrow," I announced.

Dev looked at her and smiled. He shot me a look laced with curiosity and edged with impatience. I gave him my own bug-eyed look back.

"Would you mind, Ms. Luke, if I stole Odelia away from you for a few minutes?"

"I have to be going anyway," I told Lisa. "Greg and I have an appointment tonight." I jotted my cell phone number down on the back of one of my Woobie cards, along with Zee's number. "Please call either Zee Washington or me as soon as you know you're being released. One of us will pick you up and take you home."

"I don't want to be any trouble, Odelia. I'll be fine. And Zee was here earlier today. She brought me toiletries and makeup."

On the side, Zee was a Golden Rose Cosmetics consultant. She believed the two best ways to cheer up any woman were with prayer and lipstick.

Wagging a finger at her, I said, "You are to call. You are not to go home alone, understand?"

Behind me, I heard Dev chuckle. It sounded like a truck grinding its gears. "Trust me, Ms. Luke, do what Odelia says. It'll be easier for everyone in the long run."

The comment caused Lisa to give us a small smile.

As he had that morning, Dev steered me out of Lisa's room and into the waiting room. This time we found it full. Once again, he offered to buy me a cup of coffee in the cafeteria. We settled in at the same table we'd sat at this morning.

Having opted for iced tea instead of coffee, I unwrapped my straw. "I hope hanging out here doesn't become an everyday event." I stuck the straw into the full glass and stirred the ice and lemon wedge around. "People might talk." I smiled at Dev. He did not smile back. "By the way," I added, "how's Beverly?"

"Bev's fine, thanks." His face was as deadpan as a bowl of oatmeal. "She wants to have you and Greg over for dinner soon." His eyes never left my face. His mouth was tight-lipped and disapproving. "But I don't think that's a good idea."

"Why not?"

"Because I'll probably be in prison for killing you, providing some sicko doesn't get to you first."

My mouth hung open. "And what kind of attitude is that? Especially since I have news about Laurie Luke's murder!"

"That's just it, Odelia. You're not supposed to have news about her murder, or any other murder." His eyes bore into me. "You said you were just checking out a friend's hunch about someone. As I recall, you were just trying to prove this person was not the Blond Bomber." After a slight pause, Dev leaned forward. "Is this friend of your friend's Laurie Luke's killer? Is that what you found out?"

"Not exactly. In fact, I'm pretty sure this guy isn't involved in any murders. But while I was checking out some background information, I stumbled upon the person who just might be Laurie's murderer."

"With all the talented cops and detectives in Orange County, you just happened to have *stumbled* upon Laurie Luke's murderer?"

"Good possibility."

He started to say something, but I held up a hand to halt him.

"Dev, if you make some sarcastic crack about it being a *coinkydink*, I swear I'll kick you under the table until you cry like a girl."

He leaned back in his chair, casually sipped his coffee, and studied me. Slowly a small smile crossed his face. "Okay, tell me what you know. Or think you know."

In detail, I told Dev what I had seen and overheard in the parking lot of Seventh Veil Costuming. As with Greg, I left out the part where Gordon Harper requested a personal show.

"And Lisa Luke told you today that Kirk Thomas was leaving unexpectedly for Africa?"

"Yes. Leaving tomorrow."

Dev and I were both quiet, each of us lost in our own thoughts and theories.

"Dev," I said, breaking the thoughtful silence, "could Kirk Thomas be smuggling furs and things like that for Seventh Veil, for their costumes?"

He gave me a small smile. "Good theory, but my money's on diamonds. And I'll bet it has nothing to do with the costume company."

"Diamonds?" I churned the idea around in my head. "But of course. That's one of the things Africa is known for. Greg and I watched a show about diamond smuggling on the Discovery Channel one night."

Dev nodded. "Gordon Harper is a career criminal, Odelia. He's been into a lot of things. All of them high-end."

Lisa, Laurie, Brian, Jane, Amber, Gordon, Crystal Lee, and Kirk, all wearing diamonds and stripper costumes, spun around in my head like a giant freak show. I closed my eyes and gave my head a shake, as if mixing a martini inside it.

"You okay?"

"Huh?" I opened my eyes and looked at Dev. "Yes, I'm fine. Just too many players and so many possibilities." In my mind, I mentally sorted the information into neat little piles, trying to match up who belonged to what. It was a lot like sorting a pile of freshly laundered socks.

"Dev, do you think Gordon Harper killed Crystal Lee? You know, to take over her business? He became the sole owner when she died."

"Actually, he was a suspect at the time of her death but was quickly ruled out. And according to the reports, he had no connection with the other victims."

"At least none that the police knew of. Maybe someone the victims knew had deals go bad and Harper took it out on the women, as he did with Laurie."

Dev mulled over the possibility. I could almost see the gears in his head moving the information around. "It's unlikely but certainly a possibility, given what you witnessed. I'll talk to the Laguna

Beach Police about it. See what they remember that might not be in the reports."

I moved on to the next pile of thoughts. "Laurie Luke's murder was made to look like it was the Blond Bomber. If Harper has no connection to the other victims, could he have killed her and made it look like the serial killer to throw off the police?"

"That's certainly a possibility."

"Because of Crystal Lee's murder, he would have known enough details about the Blond Bomber to make it look convincing."

Dev shook his head as he took a sip of his coffee. "But he wouldn't have known all the details."

I looked at Dev and waited for further explanation. He again studied me, no doubt wondering how much to tell me.

"The police don't give out all the details, Odelia, especially in open cases, not even to the families of the victims. Lisa Luke's murder mimicked the killings of the Blond Bomber, but not everything matched. Serial killers are often very precise in how they kill. Little things—ceremonies, if you will—can have significance. How they leave the body, what they do to it, the method ... each item of murder, right down to how and why they choose their victims, can mean something to them. It's not one-hundred-percent accurate. There are those that slaughter at will, without a plan, but generally the more precise the killing, the more likely the next one will be the same or very similar."

"So you're telling me that the other Blond Bomber victims were all the same? Even Crystal Lee?"

"Almost like following a manual. Even the latest one, except for the writing. Only the Luke woman's was different, which is why I don't think the other deaths are connected to Harper. The differences aren't huge, but there were enough for us to take notice and consider other possibilities. But so far, until now, we've come up empty-handed." He drained his coffee. "Gordon Harper would have known enough to copy the killings, but not enough to be exact. And if he's using Kirk Thomas to do something dirty, he may have had a motive for killing her."

"Dev, I remember reading that the Blond Bomber victims had all been sexually violated. Had Laurie been also?"

Dev played with his empty coffee mug, obviously uncomfortable. "According to the autopsy, the Luke woman had had recent sex, but she didn't appear to be raped or tortured. But she'd also been given a sedative; the others had not, which could be why there was no sign of a struggle." He stopped fiddling with the heavy mug. "She also died by asphyxiation. The others had been stabbed in the chest. Whoever killed Laurie Luke stabbed her after she was dead to make it look like the serial killer had done it."

I let out a deep breath, not even aware I had been holding it. "Asphyxiation? She suffocated?"

"Yes, Odelia, she was suffocated."

It was my turn to fiddle with my beverage glass. As I poked my lemon slice down to the bottom with my straw, I came to a conclusion.

"Dev, Lisa Luke cannot go home alone. It's too dangerous. Harper may snatch her like he did Laurie."

"That's exactly what I'm thinking."

TWENTY

AT LEAST THIS TIME when I took in a stray, I'd had the good manners to talk to Greg first. I had filled him in earlier about Gordon Harper and his threat to Lisa, so he wasn't surprised when I called and suggested she bunk with us for a while, at least until Dev and his men could do their job and pin Laurie's murder on Harper and remove the threat to Lisa.

After confirming our plans, Dev and I returned to Lisa's room. With Dev's backup, I told her that Greg and I wanted her to stay with us, at least for a couple of days. Dev would talk to her doctor about not releasing her until I could pick her up. I figured I could do that after my visit with Lil.

When Lisa demurred, Dev let out a big, frustrated sigh. After closing the door to her room, he indicated for me to go to her side, knowing what he had to say would be a huge shock. After I positioned myself in the chair next to her bed, Dev filled her in on who we thought might have killed Lisa and why, and how Kirk was involved. Lisa was as still as a mannequin through it all. Finally, she stirred and looked from me to Dev.

"So all that guilt Kirk poured out this morning wasn't just something to make me feel better? He really is connected with Laurie's death?"

"It looks like a good possibility." Dev kept his voice low and tender, but all business. "Kirk is probably involved with something illegal, and his contacts may have killed her to send him a message—to get him to do what they wanted. We don't know exactly what it is, but it involves his trips to Africa. We don't know if your sister was directly involved herself. She could have been."

"No, Laurie would never do anything illegal. It just wasn't her character. She didn't even fudge on her taxes." Lisa paused. "And I always thought Kirk was the same way."

I leaned forward. "Did Laurie or Kirk ever say anything about money—about getting any or maybe having a lot in the future?"

Lisa closed her eyes. I didn't know if she was trying to escape into the black hole of sleep or thinking. Shortly, her eyes opened.

"There was one odd thing back a couple of months ago. Laurie and I were discussing what to do with our condo after she and Kirk married. I offered to take out a loan to buy out her half in a lump sum so that she could have money to put towards a new place for them, but she said not to worry about it. Laurie said that Kirk told her they would have enough money to buy whatever they wanted, so I could take my time buying her out." Lisa gave a short, sad chuckle. "I remember asking her how Kirk was going to manage that, given the Southern California real-estate market. Laurie laughed and said she didn't know, but they were either going to have a great place of their own or be living with me."

There was a short silence again before Lisa turned to me with wide eyes. "But I can't go stay with you, Odelia. If I'm in danger, you might be also. You and your husband."

"Ms. Luke," Dev said, stepping closer, "do you have any family you might be able to stay with, preferably someone outside of California? Although staying with Greg and Odelia would be better than staying in your own home, getting out of town would be the best. At least for a few days."

She shook her head. "Lisa and I had no family, just each other. Not even a stray cousin. Kirk's family had become ours." Her eyes welled with tears. "But it's safe to say that's over now, considering the circumstances."

"Then it's off to our place." I gave her a big smile. "Muffin will be happy to see you."

Lisa didn't return my smile. "Muffin. You know, Odelia, I would really rather you kept her, even after I return home."

After telling Lisa I'd be back the next afternoon to chauffeur her to Seal Beach, Dev and I walked together to the elevator.

He punched the down elevator button for me. "Odelia, inside I'm not happy about Lisa Luke going home with you. As she pointed out, it puts both you and Greg in possible danger."

"But she has no one else, Dev. And no matter where she goes, someone might be in danger."

"True." He ran his hands through his curly hair. "If we weren't so short-handed right now, I'd have an officer go home with her and keep you out of it."

The elevator came. It was empty. Just as I stepped inside, Dev grabbed my arm. "One more thing. Under no circumstances are

168

you to go to Lisa's apartment, with or without her. Harper may have it staked out to grab her."

Yikes! I hadn't thought of that.

"Buy her new clothes, loan her some of yours, I don't care. Just *do not* go to her place. And that's not a suggestion. That's an order."

As much as I hated receiving orders, this time I nodded and said I understood.

"And another thing."

I looked at Dev expectantly, half knowing what was coming next.

"You are not to go messing with Gordon Harper on your own. Stay away from him. He's dangerous and already knows who you are. Hopefully, he doesn't know where you live, and thankfully, you use your maiden name."

It's true Gordon Harper didn't know where I lived. I thought about the order slip I filled out at Seventh Veil and breathed a sigh of relief. I had put down Woobie's address for shipping purposes, not my home address. As for knowing my married name, it was too late, but I opted not to tell Dev. Greg used Ocean Breeze as his address of record, so I was pretty sure our home in Seal Beach would be off Harper's radar, at least for a bit. Besides, if we were careful, there would be no reason for him to know Lisa was with me at all.

"Dev, is there any way we can let leak, through the hospital maybe if anyone inquires, that Lisa is leaving town to visit friends?" He looked at me. The elevator door was beeping to close, but he continued to hold it open. "Just in case. If Harper does try to locate her, it might throw him off the scent."

"I'll do my best."

As I exited the elevator into the main lobby of the hospital, I spied a vaguely familiar face. It took me a moment before I placed it as belonging to Paul Milholland, Jane Sharp's delivery man. He was sitting in the lobby reading a newspaper. When he looked up, I caught his eye and smiled. This was someone I might want to talk to when I had more time. Lil had said he'd been working with Jane a long time. If so, he might have some insight into her relationship with her husband, providing I could get him to talk about his boss.

I walked over to him and extended my hand. "Paul? Right? You work for Jane Sharp."

He looked odd—not bewildered as if he couldn't place me, but almost embarrassed.

I persisted. "I met you at Lillian Ramsey's recently. You were delivering a table to her."

He put down the paper and stood up, still appearing uncomfortable. "That's right. I'm sorry. For a minute, I didn't recognize you." He took my hand and quickly shook it.

"You visiting someone?"

"Uh, no, I'm not." He fidgeted. "Actually, I'm waiting for someone who is visiting a patient here."

I wished I had time to chat right now with Paul while he was killing time waiting for his friend, but I had to head home. Then I remembered Lil saying he'd built her bookcases. Perhaps I could use that as a ruse to get his phone number.

"Paul, Lillian told me you do excellent woodwork on a freelance basis. If you're interested, my husband and I might have some work for you."

He looked surprised but collected himself quickly. "Yes, I can do most anything in the way of furniture repair or built-ins."

"I have to run right now, but do you have a card?"

He dug into his shirt pocket and produced a couple of business cards. They were made of cheap white card stock and simply listed *Paul Milholland, General Handyman*, along with a phone number.

I took the offered cards. "Great. I'll be in touch soon."

TWENTY-ONE

When I got home, there was piping-hot macaroni and cheese, thanks to the microwave, and a nice salad waiting for me. I had called Greg as soon as I left the hospital parking lot and let him know I was on my way. After a quick dinner, we hit the road for Pasadena. I was glad Greg was driving, because I was road weary.

Debra Kerr, Gabby's mother, lived in a condominium in the upscale and lovely area just off of Orange Grove. Unlike Gordon Harper's Marina Del Rey high rise overlooking the harbor, the Kerr condo was in a building only two stories high, surrounded by rolling green lawn and gracious magnolia trees. The address led us to a corner unit on the bottom floor.

After pushing the doorbell twice, a trim, attractive woman with chin-length, honey-colored hair opened the door. She was impeccably dressed and groomed and held a white toy poodle in her arms. After introductions, she let us in. The condo was large and nicely appointed.

"Please call me Debra," she told us after I addressed her as Mrs. Kerr. "I detest being called Mrs." She led us into the living room and indicated for us to sit. She offered refreshments, but we declined. In front of the large picture window was an impressive grand piano. She caught me admiring it.

"Do you play, Odelia?"

"Sadly, no."

"That belonged to my father. Gabrielle played quite well. At least when she took the time to practice." Debra's lips were tight and her voice brittle as she spoke of her daughter.

"Speaking of Gabby," I began.

"Gabrielle, please. Her father gave her that loathsome nickname. I've always hated it."

"We understand that you and Mr. Kerr divorced after Gabrielle's death."

"Gabrielle's father and I were already in the middle of a divorce when ... when Gabrielle was murdered."

"I'm sorry for both, Debra."

"For Gabrielle, yes. We should all be sorry. For such a young, beautiful girl to be killed like that is pure evil." She paused and put the dog down on the carpet. It immediately beelined for Greg and sniffed his legs with fascination.

"We have a dog and two cats at home," he explained with a smile. Greg bent down and scratched the dog behind its curly haired ears. It wiggled with joy.

"Baby." The command from Debra was firm but not sharp. Immediately, the animal returned to sit by its mistress's feet.

I glanced at Greg and then returned my attention to Debra Kerr. "Debra, as my husband explained when he called, we are looking into the deaths of the women linked to the Blond Bomber for personal reasons. Is there anything you can tell us about the night Gabby—excuse me, Gabrielle—disappeared? Or anything about how she was acting? Was she spending a lot of time on the Internet? Things like that."

Debra squared her shoulders and held her head erect. "I remember quite well the day Gabrielle disappeared. My husband and I had had a rather heated discussion. I wanted a divorce, and Harold, my husband, wanted to work things out." She pursed her lips. "Gabrielle was in her room most of the time. When the argument escalated, she slammed her door shut. A while later, she came out and said she was going to Melissa's house. Melissa was a friend from school. It was a Saturday afternoon. I reminded her to be back in time for dinner." Debra paused and took a deep breath. "I never saw my daughter alive again."

"I've seen photos of Gabrielle. In the photos, she looked much older than sixteen. Did she hang out with an older crowd or with kids her own age?"

"My daughter was very attractive, Odelia. Very fit and filled out for her age. But she was still only sixteen."

"I understand, Debra."

"When did Melissa see her last?" Greg asked.

"She never made it to Melissa's home. In fact, my daughter had lied to me that day and, as it turned out, had most days. Melissa was at her grandmother's that afternoon and hadn't even spoken to Gabrielle."

"Do you have any idea where she was going or who she was meeting?"

Debra shook her head slowly. "No." She cleared her throat. "Like her father, my daughter was meeting people behind my back and keeping secrets. It cost him half of everything he had. Unfortunately, it cost Gabrielle her life."

I couldn't tell if Debra Kerr was a naturally frigid woman or if she became that way because of the tragic loss of both her daughter and her marriage. But one thing was sure: the woman was as cold as an iceberg and wound tighter than a bad perm.

Greg pursued his line of questioning. "How far is it from here to Melissa's house?"

"We didn't live here when Gabrielle was alive. I bought this condominium right after her death. We lived over near the border with San Marino then." Debra picked up Baby and put her on her lap. She stroked the little animal with short, nervous strokes. "I couldn't bear to live in that house after everything that had happened."

My heart certainly understood her decision. "I'm sure there were too many memories."

"Oh, I had already planned on moving before losing my daughter. I wasn't about to live in *her* house."

Huh? I looked at Greg. He looked just as puzzled. "*Her* who, Debra?"

Debra Kerr gave off a loud sigh. "This really has nothing to do with Gabrielle. I shouldn't have brought it up. What else would you like to know?"

"If you don't mind, we'd really like to know what happened with the house. Obviously, it was important to you and happened about the same time that Gabrielle disappeared." Greg give me an encouraging nod to continue. "Did the house belong to your in-laws and you didn't want to live there after the divorce? That would be understandable."

Debra remained silent for a few minutes. After another deep sigh, she continued. "The house was ours. Mine and my husband's. But I found out that he'd had an affair with our decorator. That's why I wanted a divorce. I couldn't bear to live in that house with or without him, with reminders of that woman in every nook and corner."

Decorator? A decorator who sleeps with her clients? My brain was jotting down notes inside my skull.

Debra Kerr dropped her head and started to silently weep. It was the first real sign of emotion we'd seen. "First my husband. Then my daughter. I still don't know what I have ever done to deserve this."

"Where is your ex-husband now, Debra?" I asked the question in as soft a voice as I could.

She cleared her throat and looked up at us. Her tears had caused her eye makeup to blotch, but her cold veneer was back like lacy frost on a cold window.

"He's somewhere in Chicago, I believe. His girlfriend dumped him. That's why he was trying to patch up the marriage. Gabrielle was our only child. After she was killed, there was nothing to save and no reason to save it. I moved here, and he moved to Chicago."

I got the feeling Debra wasn't going to be very forthcoming about her daughter's activities, and I didn't have the heart to get tough. I couldn't imagine what it would be like to have a daughter murdered, especially in the manner Gabrielle was killed. I decided to give her one last gentle push, then leave it be if it didn't yield results.

"I'm sorry we've upset you, Debra. But it's important for us to find a link between all the women who were murdered by the Blond Bomber. It's to help a friend."

"Yes, Odelia, that's why I agreed to help. I wouldn't want anyone else to go through something like this if it could be avoided."

She paused and put a hand to her mouth, appearing to be thinking it over. We waited, hoping she would decide to talk more about her daughter's disappearance.

A moment later, Debra took her hand down. She straightened her shoulders and held her head erect. She was either bracing herself to tell us more or getting ready to toss us out. It was difficult to tell.

"In answer to your earlier question about my daughter's mature appearance," she began.

Relieved, I glanced at Greg. He was leaning slightly forward in his chair, ready to listen.

"Yes, she did appear to be a much older girl. She was so beautiful, and men just couldn't help themselves. They stared at her everywhere. It was one of the reasons I had her in an all-girl school." She swallowed before continuing. "I did know that she flirted with older boys online, but I didn't think she'd ever meet any of them in person. Both my husband and I were very strict and direct with her about rules and boys and things like that. For all his faults, my husband was a good father. But when the police questioned Gabrielle's friends, they found out she'd met several men on the Internet. Unbeknownst to us, of course. Unfortunately, none of her friends knew these men or their names. What information the police found on my daughter's computer led them to dead ends or to people with alibis for the day she was murdered."

"Do you think the Blond Bomber met her online, Debra?" The question came from Greg. "Or do you think she might have met up with him some other way?"

The mother of the dead girl shrugged slightly and pursed her lips. "It's difficult to tell. We knew all her friends, so it seems likely that she met him on the Internet." Debra looked down at the animal resting in her lap. "But with all the lies we discovered she'd been telling, who knows who she was meeting and how."

We were at the door, saying our goodbyes and thanking her, when I just had to ask the million-dollar question. "Debra, who was the decorator who did your home?"

Without hesitating, she answered. "Jane Sharp did both the house *and* my husband." The words came out as deadly as a serrated knife.

"And did you decorate this condo yourself? It's quite lovely, very traditional but with well-blended touches of modern decor."

"Thank you, but no, I didn't. It was done by Mason Bell."

"Mason Bell. Didn't he work for Jane Sharp?"

"He apprenticed with Sharp Design for a number of years and was her assistant on our house. Soon after, he left her and started Mason Bell Interiors. He's a rising star, and I understand he's lured quite a few clients away from Jane Sharp."

Debra Kerr gave us a smug smile. "And I'm doing my best to make sure he does."

TWENTY-TWO

I DIDN'T PLAN ON liking Jane Sharp. With all the things I'd heard about her, my mind was set to judge her as a vain, calculating, cold-hearted power grabber with hot pants. And she might have been all those things, but like her husband, I found her appealing in a sad and tragic way.

About half past one, I had showed up unannounced at Lil's, clutching a large bouquet of flowers. I've discovered that when you bring flowers, people generally forgive you for intruding. Either that or they're too polite to bring up the gate crashing in the face of gifts. Upon ringing the doorbell, Lil opened the door to me with a look of haggard surprise.

"I know you're meeting your daughter-in-law this afternoon, Lil." I spoke in a rush, trying to hide my buttinski presence with grace and lies. "Since I was in the area on business, I thought these would be a nice touch for your tea party later today." I knew darn well she was meeting Jane at one but pretended it was at two.

"Jane's here now, Odelia." She looked at the flowers and her face brightened a bit. "But thank you for being so thoughtful." Her graciousness made me feel guilty, but sometimes a person had to be a heel to get things done.

"Please come in."

"I don't want to intrude." But, of course, I did. One day, I knew, I would pull this stunt and someone would say *okay, then goodbye*, and shut the door in my face. I just hoped that day wouldn't be today.

"Don't be silly, Jane and I were talking family business, but we've just finished." As her lips moved, Lil's eyes implored me to stay. I wondered what was up and was glad I had butted in on their meeting. Obviously, her invitation to join them went beyond good manners.

Lil showed me into the dining room and introduced me. Then she excused herself to put the flowers in water, leaving me face to face with Jane Sharp.

The first thing that struck me odd was Jane's hair. It wasn't long and blond like in the photos on the website, but chin-length and a light red strawberry blond. Her body was spectacular, and I wondered if her boobs were real or from her hubby's catalog. Considering what Steele had told me, I was guessing they came from someone's catalog. She was wearing an exquisite outfit with every detail attended to, from her nail polish to high heels that matched her nearby handbag. Everything about her was chic and expensive, but not over the top. Tasteful with a capital *T*.

And Steele was right. Jane Sharp was incredibly beautiful and did seem rather cold and aloof. Her eyes were like two deep wells that held sad secrets. Her mouth was generous but her smile strictly professional. I took a chair across from her. In front of Jane and at Lil's place were china dishes with half-eaten salads. Goblets held what looked like iced tea.

Breaking the silence, I said, "I believe you know my boss."

Jane Sharp looked at me with polite interest.

"Michael Steele," I continued. "You decorated his condo a few years back. Did a terrific job."

She looked puzzled, and her eyes rolled upward as she dug into her memory bank.

"Laguna Beach," I prodded. "On Blue Lagoon Lane."

She directed her eyes back to me. The corners of her mouth turned upward with a hint of amusement. "Oh, yes. The obnoxious attorney. Drives a Porsche, plays a lot of tennis."

"You nailed it at obnoxious."

This prompted a nearly genuine smile. "But aren't they all, Odelia?"

"Attorneys or men in general?"

The smile blossomed into a slight chuckle. Jane Sharp looked at me, openly taking stock. I felt like a pair of drapes that didn't quite measure up.

Her decision about me made, she dabbed at the corners of her mouth with a linen napkin. "Odd that you should show up, Odelia. Lil just mentioned to me the favor you're doing for her. Something involving my husband."

"Umm." The comment took me by surprise. Obviously, Lil had said something to Jane, but how much? Did she actually tell her daughter-in-law that she suspected her own son of being the Blond Bomber? I had to tread lightly, something I wasn't physically or emotionally prone to doing. But I needn't have worried. Jane helped me out by answering my unspoken question.

"Lil told me everything—how she suspected Brian of being the serial killer and how she asked you to look into it."

I sighed in relief. Still, where in the hell was Lil? It shouldn't take this long to stick a bunch of flowers in a vase unless she was hand-blowing the glass.

"Did she also tell you that I don't think Brian is the killer? I know for certain that he didn't kill Laurie Luke, the nurse from Hoag Hospital."

"No?" Jane's eyes widened in surprise.

I shook my head from side to side. "No. The police are pretty sure that whoever did it made it look like the Blond Bomber."

Jane didn't look convinced. "But even if Brian didn't kill that unfortunate woman, there are still the others, including Amber."

Had Lil also told Jane about Perfect4u and her online dalliance with Knotdead? I leaned forward slightly, "Are you telling me that you also think Brian is the Blond Bomber?"

Jane Sharp remained as still as a Greek statue, her beauty, tinged with tragedy, only enhancing the similarity. She focused her blue eyes on my green ones.

"Yes, I've suspected it for some time, actually." She paused. "And I think he's doing it to get back at me."

Again, the question Greg and I discussed came to mind. "If that's true, Jane, why didn't he kill you? Why take out his anger on innocent women who looked a lot like you, at least physically?"

Jane Sharp looked genuinely pained. "You, or maybe the police, will have to ask him that."

I was about to say something when Lil popped back in bearing a crystal vase with the flowers. She placed the vase on the small antique table and disappeared back into the kitchen without a word. Again, I started to say something to Jane, and again Lil came into the room, this time bearing a tray with two glasses of ice and a pitcher of iced tea. Geez, at the exact time when I didn't want her around, she decides to play gracious hostess.

"Odelia, I know how much you enjoy iced tea, so I made a fresh pitcher for you. I brought you a fresh glass, too, Jane." She placed the tray down on the table. "You girls help yourselves while I clear the lunch dishes."

"Sit down, Lil." Jane put her hand gently on Lil's arm. "You and I can clear them after we speak with Odelia."

"Thank you, dear. But the truth is, I'm too nervous to sit." She started clearing their luncheon plates. "I'll be back and forth and can hear most of what you're saying. If you have any questions, just stop me and ask."

Jane tried to protest once more, and again Lil waved her off. Just then my cell phone rang. Pulling it out of my tote bag, I saw that it was Dev.

"Please excuse me," I said to the ladies, "but I have to take this call."

I got up and moved into the living room for privacy. Dev informed me that the hospital would be releasing Lisa after three thirty. A glance at my watch told me I'd have plenty of time to finish up my chat with Lil and Jane and get to the hospital. When I asked Dev if he had any more information on either Laurie or Amber, he reminded me that my job was to take care of Lisa, nothing more, nothing less.

When I returned to the table, I found all the lunch dishes cleared and my glass filled with tea. I took a long, refreshing drink. I was parched, and the discussion ahead was going to be a scorcher. I also wasn't sure I wanted Lil around for this conversation. Although she was a seasoned woman, I was worried that Jane might not be totally candid around her mother-in-law. I needn't have worried.

"One of the reasons I asked Lil to meet with me today, Odelia, was to tell her that Brian and I are getting a divorce."

So, I thought, *Knotdead was telling Perfect4u the truth when he told her about the divorce.*

"We probably should have done it years ago, but we thought it best for the children." She paused. "I also think we both hoped we could make it work. After all, it started out so well."

"What do you think went wrong?"

Jane turned to look out the large window. Beyond it, manicured green grass rolled like a soft blanket.

"Probably our two demanding careers. If I had to pinpoint any one thing as the beginning of the end, it was when my company, Sharp Design, started taking off." She turned back to look at me as she spoke. "Don't get me wrong, Odelia, Brian is very proud of my accomplishments, but as my company grew and so did his practice, we spent less and less time together. And when we did, it was all about the kids. Now, with the children grown and about to leave the nest, we're not sure we want to stay together. And now this Blond Bomber thing..." Her voice drifted off.

I wanted to ask her about the cheating, but how does one do that in a polite fashion? And how does one ask that question in front of the mother-in-law? But in my usual dogged way, I pushed on. After all, it wasn't like Lil was some innocent babe in the woods, considering her shenanigans online.

"Do you suspect Brian of having an affair? Now or in the past?"

As soon as the question was asked, Lil scooted into the room. She moved slightly behind Jane and stared at me, her eyes wide and frightened. She shook her head back and forth in quick, slight movements. It was a gesture that clearly let me know Lil had not disclosed her online persona to Jane.

"I know he's had a couple in the past several years. And he's been discreet, until now."

"Now?"

Jane sighed. "Not too long ago, he started having a fling with his tarty assistant—Amber, the last Blond Bomber victim."

"How do you know?"

She gave a slight catty chuckle. "Because the little bitch called me up and told me. Said he was going to marry her." She took a drink of her iced tea before continuing. "I told her she could have him. I told him the same thing." Jane cast her eyes downward. "And now she's dead."

"Is that why you think your husband is the Blond Bomber? Because Amber's now dead?"

She shook her head. "As I told you, I've suspected for a while. Same as Lil."

"Think about it, Jane. Do you really believe your husband is capable of killing those women?"

"The man I married, no. But there are just too many connections."

"Is it because the dead women resemble you or because you are connected business-wise to some of the victims?"

That got her attention.

"You know about that?"

"I know that you decorated Crystal Lee Harper's ex-husband's condo and Gabby Kerr's home. What was the connection with Elaine Epps, the first victim?"

Jane cast her eyes downward again. "I decorated the home of her boss. Elaine was very involved with the project and worked closely with me on it."

"And did you sleep with Elaine's boss, as well?"

Her head snapped up so fast you could almost hear it. Her eyes searched my face, trying to pry into my brain to see what else I knew. A moment later, she looked away, deflated and sad. "I slept with them all."

"Even Gordon Harper?"

She nodded. "Every male client for the past six years—though there were a few who declined my advances."

Lil left the room, but not before I noticed that she was crying.

Leaning forward, I asked softly, "What happened, Jane? What happened six years ago?"

Jane Sharp got up from the table and retrieved her handbag, which was on the floor next to the small antique table a few feet away. Pulling from it a linen handkerchief, she began dabbing at her eyes. She turned to look out once again over the expanse of rolling green. A few minutes later, after a huge sigh, she returned to the table. Lil had not reappeared.

"Seven years ago, Brian started accusing me of having an affair with my assistant."

186

I ran that tidbit across the data bank in my brain. "With Mason Bell?"

She nodded. "Yes. We were spending long hours together getting the company up and running. I assured my husband that nothing was going on, but he didn't believe it, no matter what I said. Until then, I'd been totally faithful to him. I later found out that his accusations stemmed from a guilty conscience. It turned out he had been having an affair with one of his former patients."

"So you got back at him for his affair."

"It's stupid and juvenile, I know."

"Did you sleep with Mason?"

She shook her head. "No. I thought about it, but it seemed too complicated to involve him. He was young and my employee—and, it turns out, gay. It was easier to follow my husband's example and sleep with clients." She swallowed hard. "At least until now. I ended my last affair as soon as I realized that all the victims had ties to me and my business."

"All except Laurie Luke?"

"No." She dabbed her eyes with her hankie again. "Even the Luke girl is connected. I was in the middle of decorating her future in-laws' home when she was murdered."

"Are you still working for the Thomases?"

"I couldn't. I turned the remainder of the project over to Mason. He has his own design company now, and I knew he would finish the job to their satisfaction." She smiled tightly. "I'm not in the habit of giving work away to competitors, but I knew I could trust Mason's work."

Running a finger up and down the cool glass in front of me, I processed this new information, blending it with what Steele had told me about Jane's past. A possibility crossed my mind and I went for it, not caring if it upset Jane or not.

"Were you one of Brian's patients once upon a time? Is that how you met?"

Jane Sharp's eyes widened, then narrowed, going from surprise to anger without a blink in between.

"How I met my husband is none of your business."

I laughed lightly. "Jane, none of this is my business, and frankly, I'd rather not know about your extensive sexual activities. But Lil asked me for a favor, and getting to the bottom of things is part of that favor."

I narrowed my own eyes back at her. "My guess is that you were a patient and somewhere along the line had an affair with Dr. Eddy, eventually marrying him. Was he already married at the time?"

She looked horrified at the question, but in a fake how-dare-you way.

I continued. "Six years ago, he may have had an affair with a patient, but it wasn't the first time, was it? Maybe you were afraid he was shopping for wife number two, so you started shopping for a backup yourself?"

Jane looked towards the door to the kitchen, but Lil was nowhere in sight. Seeing that we were alone, she sat back down at the table and leaned forward. Her tragic appearance was gone. In its place was the cold and calculating predator Steele had observed.

"It's true. Brian did do my surgery and, yes, we did end up getting married. But he was single and so was I. I started sleeping around to get back at him, that's all it was." She quickly dropped her eyes and started up the waterworks again. "I'm so ashamed."

"I heard you were quite a party girl back in college—that you specialized in high-profile jocks and married professors. What was your motivation for that behavior?"

Before I knew what had happened, my face was soaked with iced tea.

Okay, maybe I deserved that.

I grabbed napkins Lil had left on the table and started blotting my face and clothing. Fortunately, Jane's glass had been nearly empty when she tossed its contents at me.

Jane Sharp and I stared at each other—she with open hate, me with curiosity. I had obviously struck a nerve, making it worth getting soaked with tea. But whatever her reasons were for sleeping with every Tom, Dick, and Mike Steele, I honestly didn't think it had anything to do with Brian Eddy being or not being the Blond Bomber, or even with his prior indiscretions.

Finished with my mop-up, I headed in another direction with my probing. "Maybe instead of looking to your husband as the killer, you should be looking at your competition."

"You really believe Mason Bell would do such a thing?" Her voice was tight, but at least she was still talking to me.

"I don't know Mason Bell, but anything and anyone is a possibility. All of the murdered women had ties to you or your business, but only Amber and Crystal Lee Harper had ties to Brian that I know of."

Jane didn't say anything more, and she was a hard read. I could tell she was tossing information around inside her beautiful but crazier-than-batshit head, but I couldn't tell which way she leaned theory-wise.

"Whoever the killer is, Jane, *you* seem to be the common denominator."

TWENTY-THREE

WITH A CLEAR AND definite connection between Jane Sharp and the Blond Bomber, more possibilities came to light. The killer could be a competitor, such as Mason Bell, or a spurned lover. And there were still good reasons to suspect Brian Eddy. He might have a bone to pick with his wife's promiscuity, hence the word *whore* written across the bodies. Or he could very well be jealous of her growing business and the time it took away from him and was trying to sabotage it. And he admitted to Perfect4u knowing a couple of the victims from being online. Although no connection between Sharp Design and the murders had yet been made public, if it ever was, Jane's company would be poisoned. I wondered if this connection was one of the things the police were keeping out of the media. I'd have to ask Dev.

And then there was Amber. Amber had no decorating connection to Jane that I knew of. She was Dr. Eddy's employee and his mistress. The pattern of killing women attached in some way to

Sharp Design was broken with her death, except that she did know Jane personally.

Mentally, I fanned out the information about the victims and their connections to the possible suspects like a dealt hand of cards and began moving them around. I discarded Laurie Luke because although she had a connection to Jane, I was almost positive she'd been killed by Gordon Harper.

If Amber wasn't killed by Dr. Eddy, then I'll bet whoever killed her knew she was his nurse. She'd been carefully selected either to discredit the doctor or to send a message to his wife, or both, whereas the others seemed only to be targeting Jane.

Before leaving Lil's, I asked Jane if Dr. Eddy knew that Amber had called her.

"Yes, I told him." She'd set her jaw as she spoke. "I also told him that while I knew he'd been having affairs, same as I had, that sleeping with that office tramp was the height of indiscretion. That he should choose his bedmates better." She got up and went to the window again, where she paced nervously. "He said he never told Amber he was going to marry her and was planning on ending it. That was a couple of days ago. That same night, we decided we couldn't go on like this and should get a divorce. It was the only civil thing to do."

"Did Amber have any involvement with your company? Or was she only connected to your husband's work?"

"Amber never had anything to do with Sharp Design." Jane stopped abruptly and raised an elegant hand to her mouth. "Except that I redecorated my husband's office shortly after she was hired. But that was two years ago, maybe more."

A thoughtful silence fell over us as we considered this information. Lil slipped back into the room and leaned against the door to the kitchen, quiet as a mouse. Her eyes were red. If she noticed my hair, face, and clothing being damp, she didn't say anything.

Jane looked at her mother-in-law. "I told Brian that I would tell Lil about the divorce. She and I are quite close." She paused. "Although he loves her very much," she emphasized the words for Lil's benefit, "Brian can sometimes be rigid with his mother." Jane gave Lil a small, sad smile. Turning back to me, she continued. "Because of Amber's death, however, we've decided not to make our separation public just yet. We don't want any unnecessary suspicion cast on Brian."

"But I thought you believed him to be the killer."

"I do have my own suspicions, yes. But if Brian is not the killer, and I pray he's not, then I don't want him or his business suffering needlessly. The police questioned him extensively about Amber. If they decide he's a suspect, let them be the ones to ruin him, not me."

Jane looked suddenly small and defeated. Her elegant clothing appearing suddenly rumpled and too large, as if the confession and spent anger had shrunken her frame, leaving behind a delicate shell.

"In spite of everything, I still love my husband." She began crying softly. Lil moved to her side and began gently stroking her hair.

Her hair.

"Jane, why did you change your hair? It was long and blond, like the victims', in photos on your website."

"I changed it for exactly that reason, Odelia. It was spooking me that the victims looked so similar to me and were connected to clients. So about two weeks ago, I changed my look. The physical similarity was one of the reasons I suspected Brian."

"Lil told me once that Brian was out of town when most of the victims were killed. Is that true?"

She nodded. "It's the thread of hope I cling to as evidence that he's innocent. I've double-checked his calendar, but I don't have all the information. On the downside, I do know that most of those trips were within California and didn't cover the entire time the women were missing."

Without her saying, I knew what Jane was thinking. Travel within the state meant that it was possible he could have done the killing and still had time to get wherever he was going, within reason, or go there, come back to kill, and return to wherever he was on business. The police would spot the holes instantly and would look into them.

"Jane, I could be wrong, and I could be very naïve about this, but I still don't think your husband is the Blond Bomber. As for the Luke woman, the police are pretty positive that whoever killed her was not the killer of the other women."

I thought briefly about telling Jane and Lil that I had proof of who killed Laurie Luke, but something made me hold my tongue. If Jane had been sleeping with Kirk's father during the decorating of the Thomas home, I didn't want to run the risk of her going back to Mr. Thomas with information that might be premature and interfere with the police investigation.

I left Lil and Jane huddled together for support and started my journey back to Newport Beach. It was time to collect Lisa from the hospital and get her settled in our home in Seal Beach. Another half-day shot for Woobie. But at least I'd be home a little early and could make something decent for Lisa's first dinner with us. One way or another, I was determined to make a home-cooked meal this week. In my murder-sodden brain, it seemed imperative to have that touch of normalcy in our lives.

I was almost on the ramp to the freeway when my cell phone rang. It was Greg.

"Where are you?" His question came as soon as I said hello.

"In Laguna Hills, about to head to Hoag Hospital to pick up Lisa. Why?"

"Pull over, sweetheart. I don't want you driving while we talk."

"Greg, what's happened?" Worry coursed through me like an electrical current.

"Pull over and stop the car. We don't need you getting into an accident."

I obeyed, pulling into the parking lot of a strip mall near the entrance to the freeway.

"Okay, I'm parked." I felt my stomach tense.

"Horten's at Memorial."

My heart stopped on a dime. "My father's in the hospital?"

"He's going to be okay, Odelia. He fell and hit his head and is going to need a few stitches. The doctor's running some tests to make sure the fall wasn't caused by a stroke or blackout or something like that."

"Did Dad call you?"

"The hospital called me. They found an emergency card in his wallet."

Both Greg and I were listed as my father's emergency contacts. Even though I was the daughter, Greg's name was first because his office was closer to my father's home geographically.

"In his wallet?" I felt my blood pressure rising. "Didn't Gigi or someone go with him to the hospital?" My stepmother, Gigi, was an evil ditz, a woman who could have given the Wicked Witch and her horde of flying monkeys a run for their money. Her loser son, JJ, lived with Gigi and my dad.

"The hospital said no one came in with Horten. Apparently, he walked in through the ambulance entry and passed out as soon as he stepped over the threshold. I'm the only one here with him."

"How did he get there? By cab?"

"No one seems to know."

I was about to pass out myself. "I'll be right there, Greg."

"Sweetheart, calm down. Take a deep breath, and sit still for a minute or two. I don't want you driving all worked up."

"But he could have been killed, Greg."

"I know that, Odelia, but he wasn't. He has a nasty gash and possibly a concussion, but he seems to be fine otherwise. Let's wait for the test results before panicking."

Greg was right. But it wasn't my father's accident that had me in a lather. It was the fact that although my father lived with Gigi and JJ, neither of whom worked, and Gigi's daughter Dee was close by, my dad had arrived at the emergency room alone.

Taking Greg's advice, I tried to calm down. A fast-food restaurant was located at the edge of the strip mall. I ducked into their ladies' room to use the toilet and to press a cold wet towel to my forehead, cheeks, and the back of my neck. It helped.

My father is in his eighties; stuff like this is bound to happen. Right after Greg and I were married, he'd had a heart attack scare. It wasn't his heart, but it put us all on pins and needles. I wanted him to come live with us, at least until he felt better. I know Gigi doesn't look after him, and JJ just adds to his anxiety. But as Greg often tells me, my father is a grown man with all his faculties. He knows if he ever wants to leave Gigi that we would welcome him, but it has to be his decision. And Greg is right, of course. It's just that I've wanted Dad to leave Gigi for thirty years, ever since I left his house and struck out on my own at eighteen. But that's not Dad's style. My father's one glaring fault is his passivity. Maybe that's why I'm such a bull in a china shop. I watched my mother verbally abuse him until she kicked him out, and now I watch Gigi and her brood do the same. My father just doesn't seem to have any *cojones* when it comes to women.

Before pulling out of the parking lot and heading for Memorial Hospital, I called Zee and told her about my dad. Immediately, she wanted to go with me, but instead I asked her for another favor. She agreed to pick up Lisa Luke and take her to my house. Next, I called Dev and told him about the change in plans. He told me not to worry about Lisa, he and Zee would make sure she was safe.

The last call I made was to the office. I spoke to both Jill and Tina Swanson, explaining about my father. I told them I'd let them know if I needed to take the next day off. Jill was assigned the enviable task of alerting Steele.

TWENTY-FOUR

MEMORIAL WAS A MUCH older hospital than Hoag and was situated in a less affluent area. Yet, from the smell you couldn't tell the facilities apart. Both gave off that unmistakable and unmatchable odor of antiseptic, illness, and fear, a fragrance dedicated to failing health and helplessness. No matter how modern and shiny the hospital, stepping inside one always gave me the willies. The emergency room was the same, just intensified.

"How is he?" I asked Greg as soon as I located him in the emergency waiting room.

"He's resting. The doctor wants to keep him overnight as a precaution, but I asked him to wait to explain everything until you got here."

"Any sign of Gigi and her no-good spawn yet?"

"Not a word. I called the house a few times but there's no response." Greg paused, measuring his words before he spoke. "You know, Odelia, Gigi and JJ might have been out of the house when Horten fell. Let's not be too quick to blame them or wonder why they're not here. You know Gigi never turns on the cell phone you gave them. They simply might not know about your dad's accident."

As usual, my husband was the voice of reason in contrast to my knee-jerk nastiness.

"You're probably right." I sighed. "Dad didn't say anything about how he got here?"

"I asked him, but he was too drugged on painkillers to say. They've stitched his head wound up."

The doctor called us in and explained why he wanted to keep Dad overnight. Besides the gash on his head, his injuries included a tweaked back, a few bruises, and a slight concussion. Other than that and his usual blood pressure issues, my father seemed to be in pretty good condition. But because of his age, the doctor wanted him kept for observation. Dad had told the doctor that he had slipped in the kitchen and hit his head on the corner of the table before falling to the floor.

While they prepped Dad to take him to a room, I answered questions for his admission paperwork. Greg went back to the waiting area to call Gigi again. We were almost done when a nurse rushed in and asked me to help with a problem.

Dashing into the waiting room, I found Greg and JJ in a heated verbal exchange. Gigi stood nearby, telling Greg to leave her poor JJ alone. JJ is in his sixties, of average build but with a big potbelly from years of beer drinking and inactivity. He was dressed in his usual attire of khaki shorts, a tee shirt, and flip-flops. Over the tee shirt, he wore an open, loose short-sleeved shirt. He looked like he hadn't shaved in several days, but on him it wasn't trendy. Gigi was in her usual uniform of prickly polyester pants and a stretchy top, both in Day-Glo colors. Her beehive hairdo looked pinker and shinier than usual. Hooked over her right arm was a large, floppy purse made of quilted fabric in pastels.

The other people in the waiting room moved away from my family. I didn't blame them one bit.

I stepped between JJ and Greg. "What's going on?"

"The crip is in my face," whined JJ. "Tell him to heel."

I glared at my stepbrother before turning to Greg. My husband's face was the color of borscht, even his ears. Generally, Greg is pretty even-tempered. It takes a lot to push his buttons, which is one of the things I like best about him. But once activated, look out. And this current look was beyond anger. It was even beyond being pissed off. Greg was outraged, and I was pretty sure it wasn't about being called a *crip*.

"Tell Odelia what you just told me," Greg said to JJ.

JJ looked at me. "Why don't you just mind your own goddamn business, both of you?"

Greg persisted. "Tell Odelia how her father got to the hospital." The words were delivered through clenched teeth.

"Yes, mind your own G. D. business," chimed Gigi. "Horten's my husband. As his wife, he's *my* responsibility, not yours."

Greg turned on my stepmother. "You should be ashamed of yourself, treating that sweet old guy that way."

The nurse stepped forward. "Please, folks, be quiet, or I'll have to ask you to leave."

"I want to see my husband," Gigi demanded. "When's he gonna be done so we can go home?"

"Dad's being admitted," I told her.

"For a little bump on the head? That's ridiculous."

That got my attention. "So you *knew* he'd fallen and hurt his head?" Gigi and JJ looked at each other but didn't say anything.

Greg wheeled in closer to JJ. "Tell her, JJ. Tell Odelia how you and Gigi dumped Horten at the hospital and then went on your merry way."

"What?" I couldn't believe what I was hearing.

"That's right, sweetheart. They dumped him off on his own. Gigi had a hair appointment. JJ drove her there and waited to bring her home." Greg looked disgusted. "From the smell of him, I'd say he waited in a bar."

"It's not my fault Horten slipped." JJ looked at his mother for support.

"Your father's always whining about something," Gigi added. "After he got up, I gave him a towel for his head and told him to go sit down. But he kept going on and on about how much it hurt and about the bleeding. About drove me nuts. So I told JJ to drop him off here on our way to the beauty shop. We'd come back for him afterwards. And here we are, just like we promised Horten. Don't know why he called you at all."

"Dad didn't call us. The hospital did."

I was livid and thought my head would explode. I wanted to hit Gigi—knock her on her skinny, hateful ass, not caring one whit that she was in her eighties. Instead, I tried to pull myself together and behave civilly.

"My father has a concussion and pulled back muscle. The doctor wants him to stay here tonight. They're taking him to his room now." I looked Gigi in the eye. "I'm sure as soon as he's settled, you can see him."

She seemed to be making a decision. "He's not going anywhere. We'll be back after supper." She turned to go. "Come on, JJ, take me home where I can get some peace and quiet."

JJ started past me and Greg. "Next time he falls, maybe he won't get up. Then we'll all get some peace."

Faster than a coiled snake, Greg reached up and grabbed the front of JJ's shirt with both hands. With a mighty grunt, he threw JJ into a group of empty plastic chairs lined up against the wall. JJ hit the chairs and landed sprawled across the floor.

"If you ever speak to my wife like that again or mistreat Horten in any way, I'll show you just how able-bodied this *crip* can be."

Applause broke out from the other folks in the waiting room.

It was nearly eight o'clock when I finally made it home. I'd sent Greg ahead of me hours before to make sure Lisa was getting along okay, then I stayed next to my father's bed. I seemed to be spending a lot of time next to hospital beds these days and hoped it was not going to become a habit. I left when Gigi and JJ returned.

Coming through the back door, I was greeted by meows and a wagging tail from the three four-legged kids. I went through the petting ritual, which now included Muffin. I was also greeted by three humans—Greg, Seth, and Zee.

I sniffed the air. "Do I smell Zee's famous chicken and dumpling casserole?"

"That you do, sweetheart." Greg gave me a big kiss, which was followed by hugs and kisses from Seth and Zee.

"After the day you've had, I wanted to make sure you had a hot meal." Zee winked and headed for the kitchen. "The food's ready. Just sit down and relax."

Numb with exhaustion, I obeyed, sitting at the dining table, which was set for dinner. Zee brought out a big salad bowl filled with greens. Greg followed with a basket of warm bread.

Seth handed me a large filled wine glass. "How's your dad?"

I took a big gulp of the wine before answering, holding the soothing and tasty alcohol in my mouth before letting it trickle down the back of my throat. "He's going to be fine. Doctor said the overnight is just a precaution."

Zee returned to the table holding the large, steaming casserole dish. She placed it on a trivet on the table. "Come on, everyone, let's eat while it's hot."

I glanced around the table, counting the place settings. "There are only four places." I turned my head, looking around, listening for evidence of our houseguest. "Where's Lisa?"

TWENTY-FIVE

"She's *where*?"

Before anyone could tell me again, I took another big swig of wine, this time draining half the glass.

"In Compton. At my Aunt Miriam's." Zee sat in the chair next to mine, smiling, dishing out the food and passing plates around like we were in a Norman Rockwell painting. "She'll be perfectly safe there."

"Compton?" I polished off the rest of my wine and looked around the table for the bottle.

Compton, California, is primarily black and known for its high concentration of street gangs and homicides. It can be a very dangerous place, even lethal, if you don't know your way around its neighborhoods.

Zee stopped serving and fixed me with a stern look. "I grew up in Compton, and I'm fine."

"I don't notice you living there now. In fact, I've heard you say you'd never let your own children go there, not even to visit Miriam."

Seth refilled my glass. "Odelia does have a point, Zee." Zee shot her husband an even sterner look.

"The idea was to hide Lisa for a while. How in the world is a white, blond, depressed woman going to go unnoticed in Compton?"

"It's not like she's strolling the streets, Odelia. And besides, Dev thought it was a good idea. Of course, Lisa didn't like it at all. She wanted to come here, as planned, but Dev convinced her. Finally, she gave in and left the hospital with us."

"Dev knows about this?"

She nodded.

"Actually, sweetheart, it's quite a clever plan."

I looked across the table at Greg. "You know about it, too?"

"They told me when I got home. Just let Zee explain."

"Can we at least talk about it while we eat?" Seth asked.

He held out a hand to me and one to Greg on his other side. Following his lead, we each took the hand of the person on either side of us while Seth said grace. Then we dug into our food while Zee gave me a rundown of her plan.

Not wanting to see Lisa hiding out in my home any more than I wanted Lisa to go back to her apartment, Zee put on her thinking cap. When she arrived at the hospital to pick up Lisa, she ran it past Dev, who said it might be worth a try. In a nutshell, using wigs, makeup, and an old-fashioned housedress, Zee dressed up Lisa as an elderly black woman. Quickly, they spirited her out of the hospital and into Seth's waiting car, and from there drove Lisa to Compton. Lisa never removed her disguise until she was safely inside Miriam's house.

"So now, instead of just Greg and me being involved, we're all involved." I turned to Seth. "Even you?"

He shrugged as he ate. "What can I say, I was beginning to feel left out. Besides, I didn't want Zee going alone, in case the bad guys did follow her."

Even though I still had my reservations, it did seem like a pretty good plan. After all, who would think of looking for Lisa Luke in Compton, and it did free me up to look in on my father and work more on the Brian Eddy issue. My brain was like a closet stuffed to the rafters with odds and ends. One less item to jam in there would certainly be a relief. And Lisa and Zee's Aunt Miriam should get along fine. Miriam would mother Lisa to death, and no one needed more motherly care right now than Lisa Luke. One taste of Miriam's sweet potato pie and Lisa might even consider staying in Compton.

After Zee and Seth left, Greg and I tidied up in the kitchen, then headed to bed. I was exhausted, and he didn't look too perky himself.

"By the way, Steele called." Greg was sitting up in bed, reading and waiting for the eleven o'clock news to begin.

I popped my head out of the bathroom. "Steele? When?"

"Shortly before you got home. I forgot to tell you. He said he didn't want to call your cell in case you were still at the hospital."

"What did he want?"

"Just checking on your father's condition."

I ducked my head back into the bathroom to apply my nightly moisturizer. Finished, I shut off the light and crawled into bed.

"That's it?"

"Pretty much. I told him Horten was going to be okay, but I wasn't sure you'd be in tomorrow." Greg looked at me. "I don't think you should go in. Take the day off, sweetheart. Look in on your father, try to relax a bit. It's a Friday, and you could use a nice long weekend. Besides, you really need to touch base with Dev tomorrow about everything Jane Sharp told you."

Greg was right. While working in the kitchen, I filled him in on what I'd learned from Jane and about the connection between the victims and her clients. Whether the Blond Bomber was Brian Eddy or not, both Greg and I agreed the killer was somehow tied to Jane.

"You're right. I'll call Dev first thing in the morning before I go to see Dad. Then I'll pop in on Lisa."

Greg shot me a warning look. "Don't worry about Lisa. She's going to be fine at Miriam's. And Laurie Luke's murder is in Dev's hands now, not yours. Besides, just in case Harper is watching, you might lead him to her. You wouldn't want that."

Again, my smart hubby was right. I nudged Muffin over a few inches with a knee. She was scratching around her collar but still managed to squeak out a protest.

"Steele did say one thing, though." Greg grinned. "He said to tell you that if you do take Friday off, not to worry about it being on your tab."

"What a prince."

Once again, I notice Muffin digging around her neck. "That collar is really bothering her. I wonder if it's too tight."

"I've noticed her scratching at it off and on." Greg joined me in watching her. "It's an odd collar for a cat. Maybe it's too heavy for her."

I reached over, plucked Muffin to me, and undid the rolled-leather collar. As I rubbed the freed fur around her neck, she went into a state of kitty nirvana and started purring like a outboard motor. When I released her, she curled up in her place by my legs, a satisfied customer.

I held up the collar. "It looks handmade and fairly new, but it is a bit heavy for a young cat." Opening the drawer of the nightstand, I stashed it inside. I would return it to Lisa when she reclaimed Muffin.

The news came on just as I kissed Greg goodnight and scooted low under the covers. I'd had enough drama for the day and didn't need to watch any more. I closed my eyes and half listened, knowing I'd be asleep before the first commercial break.

"Our top story tonight: did the Blond Bomber kill again on the heels of his last alleged victim?" I heard the anchor announce. My ears perked up, expecting to hear a recap of Amber's murder.

"Late this afternoon," the male anchor continued, "just hours after the discovery of the body of Amber Jorgensen, hikers in Laguna Canyon discovered the body of a woman who might be another victim of the Blond Bomber, the serial killer currently plaguing Southern California."

I shot up out of bed. With all the worry about my dad, I hadn't seen the news since Amber's body was found. Greg, too, was watching the screen, the book on his lap forgotten.

"The body of twenty-nine-year-old Madeline Sparks was found in Laguna Canyon late this afternoon." The camera switched to an on-scene reporter who was interviewing a rugged-looking young man.

"My girlfriend and I were hiking," he explained, "when my dog starting going nuts, barking and running back and forth. We followed him and found the girl tied to a tree. She was already dead." It was clear the guy was starting to choke up. "There was writing on her body."

The screen switched back to the newsroom, where a photo of a woman was now shown in the upper right-hand corner. Ignoring the protests of both Muffin and Seamus, I scooted on my knees closer to the TV for a better look. Madeline Sparks had been lovely, with clear, smooth skin, bright eyes, and pretty hair.

"Oh my gawd, Greg!"

"What, sweetheart? What's the matter?"

I jumped off the bed and ran to the kitchen, where I'd dropped my tote bag, returning with my cell phone. "I have to call Dev."

"Right now? It's after eleven."

"Right now. Right this minute." I pointed at the TV screen, which was now displaying a commercial. "Did you see that girl's hair? The one in the photo, the latest victim?"

"Yes, of course. And it wasn't blond. Maybe it's another copycat?"

I shook my head as I fumbled with the phone. All thumbs in my agitation, I had trouble locating Dev's cell number on speed dial.

"It's not a copycat, but it is proof that the Blond Bomber is connected to Jane Sharp." Finally, Dev's cell was ringing. "Look for more news, Greg."

He grabbed the remote and began clicking through the major stations, looking for more late-night news. Finally, he found one showing the same photo and talking about the murder.

"There, see?" I pointed at the screen.

"Not really."

Then I remembered that I'd forgotten to tell him.

"Jane's hair isn't long and blond anymore. It's now short and red, just like hers."

TWENTY-SIX

IT WAS OBVIOUS TO me that the Blond Bomber was after Jane Sharp in one way or another. Maybe it was Brian Eddy trying to get payback for his wife's indiscretions, or maybe it was someone else with an axe to grind, such as one of her many jilted lovers, but there was no way now not to miss the connection between Jane and the victims. Before, the Blond Bomber was going after women with long blond hair. Now, he had targeted a woman with bobbed light red hair. If this was a coincidence, I'm a size 2 and my stepmother is Glinda, the Good Witch of the North.

It was seven thirty on Friday morning. After listening to me rant and rave last night on the phone about hair color and serial killer theories, Dev said he'd come by our house early in the morning. I told him I'd have coffee and a hot breakfast waiting for him. I was finally getting to cook a meal.

"You've been investigating Dr. Brian Eddy all this time?" Dev asked in a semi-cranky voice.

"Yes, sort of." I looked to Greg for support. He was feeding Wainwright and gave me a look of encouragement. "Mostly, Greg and I have talked to a few of the victims' families. I was trying to find a link, or more accurately to *not* find a link, between Dr. Eddy and the victims. That's what we were doing when I stumbled upon Gordon Harper's connection to Laurie Luke's murder."

I pulled an egg, spinach, and sausage casserole out of the oven and placed it on a trivet on the table. Earlier, I had walked down to the bakery and bought some fresh cinnamon bread. Pops was there. As soon as he saw me, he started mumbling again about the van. I bought him a coffee and another egg and cheese breakfast sandwich.

Dev gripped his coffee mug while I dished up eggs for all of us. "Odelia, you have to end this right now. You too, Greg." He sighed. "I used to just worry about Odelia. Now the two of you are running around pretending you're Nick and Nora Charles. It's got to stop."

Dropping the serving spoon with a clunk, I sat my butt down in my chair and stared at Dev. "What do you mean it's got to stop? Dev, because of us you know who killed Laurie Luke. And what about the connection between Jane Sharp and the Blond Bomber victims? You didn't know about that until we told you."

Dev turned in his chair to look me square in the eye. "The Laurie Luke murder may get turned over to the feds. Except for a minor role, I'm off it. And you two need to stay out of it."

"The feds? But why?" Greg asked.

Dev shoved a forkful of eggs into his mouth. He chewed before answering. "Smuggling is a federal offense. Since Laurie Luke's murder may be entangled in those activities, they may start calling the shots, or at least try to."

"You're not involved at all?"

He shook his head. "Only as called upon."

Greg took a drink of orange juice and stared at me over the rim of his glass. I could tell he was churning information around in his head. Finally, he asked, "What about Kirk Thomas and Gordon Harper? Have they brought them in yet?"

Dev took a few more bites of eggs. He shook his head. "Kirk has disappeared."

"Wasn't he supposed to leave for Africa today?" I pushed eggs around my plate, unable to eat.

"According to Lisa, yes, but there's no indication that he's left the country, at least not yet. He had reservations for a red-eye flight that he never made. The feds have alerted all the airlines and Customs to be on the lookout for him."

Greg also started eating and passed the cinnamon bread to Dev. "Great breakfast, Odelia," Dev said as he took two slices of bread.

The men stuffed their faces as if it was just a normal, casual brunch. I'm convinced that no matter what their ages or occupations, nothing comes between a man and his stomach.

My eggs forgotten, I cleared my tight throat with a gulp of coffee. "And Harper? What about him?"

"Without Thomas, we have nothing to directly connect him to Laurie's murder and the smuggling."

"But I heard them talking. I saw and heard Harper threaten Kirk and Lisa."

Dev wiped his mouth with a napkin and leaned back in his chair. "I know, Odelia, and that information was very helpful. The feds have been watching Gordon Harper for a long time—another reason why we're taking a step back—but he's slippery, and they have never been able to grab him and keep him. When they nab him this time, it will be with evidence that will nail his coffin shut. Kirk Thomas is the key. They need to find him and get him to spill his guts." Dev took a big swallow of coffee. "From the way you described his emotional state when you last saw him, it shouldn't take much to get him to cave once he's found."

It flashed across my mind that Kirk might be dead. "And if they don't find Kirk?"

"The feds will handle it as they see fit, Odelia. They may just continue to watch Harper, waiting for a slip-up that will bring him down." Dev paused and once more looked me straight in the eye. "You need to butt out." He turned to Greg. "Both of you."

"And Lisa?" Under the table, my left foot was tapping the floor tile in annoyance. I steadied it before the noise became obvious.

"Lisa is to stay where she is for the time being. I told the feds that I have her in a safe house, and they were cool with that. Kami and I will remain the contacts with regard to her."

I let out a laugh that sounded more like a snort. "Who'd ever have thought that Compton would be considered a safe haven?" Then another thought occurred to me. "What if they don't find Kirk and can't nail Harper? What about Lisa then? How long is she supposed to hide out?"

"I talked to Lisa late last night. She's antsy to get home and get on with her life, especially now that she realizes she didn't have anything to do with her sister's murder. I really drilled home to her that she's in danger. She's gotten a leave from work and is willing to stay put for a few more days. If nothing turns up by then, we'll have to rethink it." Another pause. "She also said to thank you for all your help."

"Can I talk to her?"

"It's best that you don't, especially since Harper knows you know her. You may inadvertently lead him to her, one way or another."

I nodded in understanding, but my lower lip was definitely in pout mode.

Dev chuckled. "Don't worry about Lisa, she's fine. Zee's taking her some clothes today and will spend time with her. She's well cared for."

The three of us went back to our meal, eating in silence for a few moments. My eggs were almost cold, but I ate them anyway, taking bites and chewing on autopilot while I thought over the recent turn of events. The federal government was now involved. This was, indeed, way over my stumpy little head.

Greg changed the topic. "Dev, what about Brian Eddy? Do you think he could be the Blond Bomber?"

Dev looked from Greg to me. "Dr. Eddy has a tight alibi for the Amber Jorgensen murder. As for the others, I'm sure the Laguna Beach Police will be happy to learn of the connection between Jane Sharp and the victims. I have no doubt they will look more closely at her husband and at all her past affairs and business associates."

"Why the Laguna Beach Police?" Greg pushed away his plate and waited for the explanation.

"The Laguna Beach Police have taken the lead from the beginning. The victims were from all over Southern California, but the bodies were found in Laguna Canyon. Three different agencies have jurisdiction over various parts of that area, but the bodies were all dumped in the part of the canyon under the jurisdiction of the Laguna Beach PD. Kami and I were working with them on the Luke murder because she lived in and disappeared from Newport Beach. Several of the detectives down there are buddies of mine. So I will, of course, help out whenever and however they need me."

As I digested this along with my eggs, Steele crossed my mind. "Mike Steele was one of Jane Sharp's clients. Will he be questioned? It was four or five years ago."

"He might be. Depends on how far back they go."

After both men left for their respective workplaces, I cleared the table, unloaded the dishwasher of clean dishes, and put in the dirty ones. It felt odd to be home alone on a weekday, even if it was a Friday. I made a quick call to the office to let them know I wouldn't be in and then another to Memorial Hospital to check on Dad. The nurse said he was resting comfortably and that the doctor had already been by to see him. They expected him to go home later in the afternoon. The nurse transferred me to his room. Dad is very hard of hearing, and I hoped he had his hearing aid in so he could pick up the phone and talk to me. I was in luck.

"Hi, honey," the warm, familiar voice said after realizing who was calling.

"Hi, Dad. How do you feel today?"

"Not bad for an old man who took a tumble."

"How's your head and back?"

"Both still ache a bit, but nothing I can't live with. Doc came by and said they want to take one more test this morning. If all is well, I'll be home in time to watch Judge Judy."

"I'll stop by later, then, and wait until you can go home."

"Don't bother, honey. I know you're busy. JJ can pick me up and cart me home. He's much closer than you to the hospital."

"JJ will probably make you walk home, Dad. Or at the very least, charge you for gas."

There was a pause, and I wondered if Dad had fallen asleep.

"Odelia, I know you dislike Gigi and her kids and have good reason, but you have to understand something."

I waited, my nose twitching with annoyance.

"They're not really bad people, honey, just ignorant. It's how Gigi was raised and how she raised JJ and Dee. True, they're selfish, but they're my family. Same as you." Dad paused, letting what he said sink into my hard head.

"Will you do your old man a favor? Will you try to get along with them better? Take the high road, no matter what happens. They're not capable of that, but you are. Both you and Greg."

"I suppose they told you about the fight between JJ and Greg. And I'm sure they claim Greg started it."

"I know JJ, and I know Greg. I have no doubt who really started it." He chuckled. "I just wish I'd been there to see it."

Dad suggested that instead of coming to the hospital, I wait and visit him at home either tomorrow or Sunday. He said a few days would cool things down in the family. He also asked me to bring Wainwright when I visited. My father loved the goofy yellow dog almost as much as he loved Greg and me.

After making the bed and straightening up, I began to think about going into the office. Things seemed to be tied up, or as least tied up enough for the authorities to step in and unravel the players and who did what to whom. But it nagged at me that I still hadn't finished what I'd set out to do for Lil. I hadn't proved yet that Brian Eddy was not the Blond Bomber, and it wasn't clear that he was, either. Dev even admitted this morning that with the obvious ties to Jane Sharp, the Blond Bomber could be almost anyone who'd had contact with her and her business. It didn't leave her husband out, but forced him to step aside and make room for other possible suspects, like the dozens of men she'd slept with in the past six years, including Mike Steele. Picking up the phone, I called Steele's direct line.

"Steele here."

"Hey, it's me."

"How's your dad?"

"Fine, thanks. Just bumps and bruises from the fall and a nasty cut on his head. He's going home this afternoon."

"That's good news. I heard you weren't coming in today."

"Actually, I might be in later, especially with Dad doing so well."

"What, no Murders'R'Us today?"

Hmmm. "Actually, that's why I'm calling." I paused for dramatic effect. "Steele, are you the Blond Bomber?"

"What?" His voice raised and caught in his throat, as if he'd swallowed a fishhook.

"That's the question the police might be asking you soon—and your friend Stuart."

"Why in the hell would they ask us that?"

I gave Steele a rundown of what I'd learned about Jane Sharp.

"So the police are going to question all of her past lovers? That could take a long time."

"More on point, they might be questioning all of her clients in the past several years, and considering the bodies were all dumped just a few miles from where you live, they might start with you."

"Do you really think that I'm the Blond Bomber?"

Again, I paused for effect.

"Damn it, Grey!"

I let loose with an evil chuckle. "No, Steele, I don't. The only way you'd ever put that much time, thought, and effort into something is if you could bill for it."

"Damn straight."

Although tweaking Steele's nose was fun, it wasn't the reason why I'd called him.

"Steele, when Jane Sharp was decorating your place, did she have an assistant named Mason Bell?"

There was silence while Steele foraged around in his memory bank. Even over the phone, I could hear a faint *squeak ... squeak* as he swiveled in his chair.

"I do remember her having an assistant. A young guy. Not sure of his name though. He was mostly in the background doing the leg work."

"Do you remember what he looked like?"

There was a long moment when all I heard was Steele's chair. "If my memory's correct, he was average height and on the slim side. One of those guys you aren't quite sure if he's gay or straight. Know what I mean?"

"That's all you remember? Was he attractive? What color hair did he have? Any distinguishing marks, tattoos, things like that? Did he speak with any particular accent?"

Another long pause. "I do remember one specific thing, now that you mention it. It was something about his face, not sure which side, but he had a scar—a thin one extending from his side-burn area over his jaw and slightly down his neck. I remember noticing it when he was bending close to me, fussing over swatches. Otherwise, I might not have seen it."

Paul Milholland crossed my mind. "Do you recall seeing anyone else working with them? A delivery guy or someone like that?"

"Hmmm, no, no one else. But I was staying with a friend while the bulk of the work was being done."

"Thanks, Steele."

"So, you coming in or not?"

"Not sure yet. I'll let you know."

"Now that your dad's better, Grey, your tab's running."

"And you say hello to the police for me when they come to question you about your sex life."

TWENTY-SEVEN

THE JANE SHARP/BLOND BOMBER connection nagged at me while I threw a load of towels into the washer. I still wasn't sure if I was going into the office today or not, but decided if I did, it would be this afternoon—that I'd take the morning for myself and try to sort out my mind unencumbered with office work.

As soon as the washer started, I sat down at the dining table with a large sheet of brown paper torn from a roll kept in our home office. With a marker, at the top I wrote *Blond Bomber, Jane, Brian.* To the left, down a column, I wrote the names of the murdered women. With this grid in place, I started checking off any connections between the victims and the three at the top of the sheet.

Elaine Epps was connected to both the Blond Bomber and Jane, but I didn't know if she had ever known or seen Brian Eddy. A check across from her name went under both the Blond Bomber's and Jane's columns. A question mark went into Brian's column.

Crystal Lee Harper received checks in all three columns; Gabby Kerr in only the first two. Laurie Luke went only in Jane's column.

Amber received checks in only the Blond Bomber's column and Dr. Eddy's. But what about Madeline Sparks, the latest victim? Except for her hair color, what connection did she have with the people across the top of the chart? For now, I just checked the column under the serial killer.

I thought about Jane Sharp and Madeline Sparks, and wondered what was going through Jane's head right now. Did she know Madeline? It must be scaring the snot out of her that the latest victim had hair similar to her new hairdo. I made a separate note to try and reach Jane later.

Under the names of the murdered women, I also listed Kirk Thomas and Gordon Harper. Kirk received checks in the first two columns, while Harper received them in all three.

I didn't know if this chart meant anything or would be of any help, but it certainly did help clear my mind to take what was in my head and lay it all out. There were definitely more checks in Jane's column than Brian's. It still didn't prove Dr. Eddy wasn't the killer, but it looked more orderly all spread out across the sheet, even if the ties were a mess in reality.

Another thing that caught my attention was that the murders were happening more often, with less time between them. Looking back over the chart, I jotted down the approximate dates of the earlier murders. The first three happened approximately three months apart. Laurie Luke's murder, had she been one of the Blond Bomber's victims, would have been right on schedule as the fourth victim. It made me wonder if Amber had been prescheduled as the fourth victim before Laurie's murder—in the killer's sick mind, was she just an expendable note, no more valuable than a Post-It, jotted to the police? Madeline, the latest victim, had been right on the heels of Amber, with virtually no cool-off time between the two. What did that mean? And no matter what the pecking order, whoever was killing these women knew that Jane had changed her hairstyle, so it was someone who had seen her in the past month.

From the kitchen table, I went into our home office and looked up Mason Bell's company on the computer. Mason Bell Interiors was located in Los Angeles on Olympic Boulevard off of La Cienega. As with Sharp Design, Mason Bell Interior had an online portfolio with photos from several projects. I recognized Debra Kerr's living room, with its marriage of traditional and modern styles, among them. But because he'd not been in business very long, his client list was short. With a click of the mouse, I opened his bio page and came face to face with Mason Bell himself.

Although as stylish as Jane Sharp, Mason Bell was much more hip and happening. His clothing was tasteful, trendy, and full of pizzazz all at the same time. He had a nice face, neither handsome nor ugly but far from plain, behind a close-cropped beard. His hair was also worn cropped very close. I saw no sign of the scar Steele remembered, but the headshots weren't close-ups and the beard would have covered much of it. From the photos, it was easy to see that Mason worked out a lot. His body was tight and buffed, and the clothing he wore accentuated it.

If the Blond Bomber was a competitor, Mason Bell would be a good candidate. After all, he was inheriting a lot of her clients, including the Thomases. And Mason knew her well enough to plan such a heinous thing. He knew who her clients were and would probably know Brian. Maybe Mason, either in an attempt to ruin Jane's business or in the role of frustrated suitor, had marked the look-alike clients for death.

I picked up the phone, called Mason Bell Interiors, and asked to speak with the man himself. When the receptionist asked what it was about, I gave him my name and told him it was about Jane Sharp. For several minutes, I listened to easy-listening music until someone came on the line.

"Hello, this is Mason Bell." His voice was refined and a bit dramatic, as if he were bored with the call already.

"Thank you for speaking with me, Mr. Bell. I'd like to ask you a few questions, if I may."

"About Jane?"

"Yes. It's important."

"Are you looking for a review or comment on her work?"

"No, nothing like that."

"Then I'm really very busy."

Sensing he was about to say goodbye and hang up, I laid it on the line. I had to say something to shock him into paying attention and want to hear more.

"It's about her connection to the Blond Bomber."

"Her *what*?" His voice went almost shrill.

"Her connection to the Blond Bomber—you know, the serial killer."

He laughed. "Don't tell me she's sleeping with *him* now."

I looked at the photos on the computer screen in front of me. Steele said that years ago he couldn't tell if Mason Bell was gay or straight. But looking at his photos and listening to his voice and tone, I would bet my collection of Elton John CDs that Mason Bell was gay, even if Jane Sharp hadn't said anything. Somewhere along the line, he must have openly embraced the rainbow within him.

All the victims had been sexually assaulted. I found it difficult to believe that a gay man would do such a thing to a woman, but it certainly would not be impossible. A closeted, frustrated homosexual maybe, but not an openly gay man. It just wouldn't make sense.

"You were her assistant until recently, when you started your own company, were you not?"

He stopped chuckling. "What did you say your name was?"

"Odelia Grey."

There was a pause. Unlike before, I didn't get the sense he was going to hang up, but was measuring his words carefully.

"Yes, I was, for a number of years. Jane employed me right out of design school."

"So, like her, you knew all of the women killed by the Blond Bomber?"

"Are you a cop? Or a journalist?"

"I'm not with the police or the media, but I am personally looking into the connection between the slain women and Sharp Design. By the way, you can expect the police to be knocking on your door very soon and asking the same questions. They've figured out the connection, too."

"Excuse me a minute, I need to take this in my office."

Another long pause while I was put on hold, followed by Mason coming back on the line. He took a deep breath before speaking.

"I've been following the news, and yes, I knew all the women killed, except one. I'd never met the Luke woman. I knew who she was but never met her in person. I started working on the Thomas home after she was killed."

I decided to let him think that Laurie was part of the Blond Bomber death stable, or at least let him think I believed that myself.

"Are you still doing work at the Thomas home? I understand Jane turned that project over to you after Laurie Luke was killed."

"Actually, Mr. and Mrs. Thomas have put the rest of the project on hold. I just finished up what Jane was working on when their son's fiancée was killed."

"What about Madeline Sparks? Did you know her?"

"Madeline Sparks? What does she have to do with this?"

"Didn't you see the news last night or this morning?"

He laughed. "I was at wrap party last night. The only thing I saw this morning was a pot of hot coffee."

"Madeline Sparks was found dead last night in Laguna Canyon, just like the others."

"Oh no!" He sounded shocked and upset, but without seeing him in person it would be difficult to tell if it was genuine. "She was such a nice person."

"Who was she, Mason? How is she connected to Jane?"

"She was a client of Sharp Design—or at least her sugar daddy was. About two years ago, some old guy hired Jane to decorate this adorable little beach house for his mistress."

"Madeline Sparks?"

"Yes. She was going to grad school at the time and he was putting her through."

"And do you know if Jane slept with Madeline's ... um ... benefactor?"

"Of course she did. She slept with them all. For a while, I was sure he was going to dump Madeline and put Jane up in the beach house." He laughed lightly. "I don't know what old Janie girl did in bed, but some of the guys became obsessed and did not want to let go. Almost made me want to turn straight for an afternoon and have a go."

My ears perked up. "I heard that Jane's husband suspected you and his wife of having an affair."

"Dr. Brian? No way. He knew I was gay from the get-go. In fact, I even went to him to have a little work done. And just last year, he removed a facial scar I'd had since childhood. I've also referred him to many of my friends."

Was Jane lying about the fact that her husband thought she was having an affair with Mason Bell? And if so, why? Was she trying to make it look like her husband had a motive for murder?

"You said some of the clients didn't want to let go. Did any of her past clients cause trouble once she ended it sexually?"

"Some of them dogged her for a while, then gave up. Some showered her with gifts and promises, especially that idiot Harold Kerr, but she was strictly a do 'em and dump 'em kind of girl. As soon as she cashed the final check for the job, the guys were given the boot. And what could they do about it? Most were married. They weren't about to cause a fuss."

"Were there any that might have done more than just pursue her? Any that might have stalked her?"

"You mean were any crazy enough to start killing to get back at her?"

"Yes, that's exactly what I mean. All the victims looked like her."

"Madeline didn't. She had red hair the last time I saw her. Short red hair."

"Jane Sharp's hair is now short and red."

There was a sharp intake of breath on the other end of the line, then a moment of silence.

"You mean the killer is killing women who look like Jane and whom Jane knows? Are you sure about that?"

"Looks that way to me, but I could be wrong." I backtracked a bit with my line of questioning. "As far as you know, would Mr. Thomas be the last client she might have had a fling with?"

Mason paused again before speaking. "The Thomas gig was a bit different. Jane wasn't sleeping with Mr. Thomas—not that she didn't try, but he wouldn't have any of it. Politely turned down her advances."

"How do you know this? You weren't still working with her, were you?"

"It's a small community, Ms. Grey. Employees love to gossip. Although word on the grapevine is that she did finally get a Thomas, just not the lord of the manor. After the old man turned her down, Jane set her sights on the son and nailed him." He made a clicking sound. "Another notch on her belt."

Son? I remembered Lisa talking about Kirk's family, but I didn't recall her talking specifically about his brothers and sisters, or that he had any.

I took a stab in the dark. "Which son did she finally nail?"

"Kirk, of course. The other boy's only fourteen or fifteen. Even Jane Sharp has her morals."

At the time of Laurie Luke's death, Jane Sharp was sleeping with Kirk Thomas? If the gossip were true, then Kirk was toting around enough guilt to last several lifetimes. It made me wonder if Jane knew about the smuggling.

"Mr. Bell, if you'd be so kind as to answer one last question." When he didn't respond, I ploughed ahead. "You've known both Jane Sharp and Dr. Eddy for several years. Do you think Brian Eddy is capable of killing?"

"You think Jane's husband is behind the killings?"

"You never know. After all, it's no secret that his wife was sleeping around. She didn't try to hide it. Misplaced rage. Symbolic killings. Maybe he was sending some sort of sick message to her."

"I don't know about that. Dr. Brian's a pretty nice guy. Rather mellow and humble for all his talent and fame. She'd been cheating on him for years. Seems like he would have flipped long before now, doesn't it?"

"Thank you for your time, Mr. Bell. I appreciate it."

"Then again," he continued, ignoring my goodbye, "they always say it's the quiet ones."

After my talk with Mason Bell, I placed a call to Paul Milholland. Might as well pick his brain while I was on a roll. I only reached a mechanical voice mail. After leaving a short message to call me, I took a quick shower, applied my makeup, and got dressed in a pair of khaki trousers and a lavender sweater set. I stuck my feet into some cute new open-toed shoes with a nice heel, but on second thought threw on some socks and a pair of rubber-soled flats, sacrificing style for comfort. Who knew where the day would take me, and it was hard to think when breaking in new shoes.

I was about to call Jane Sharp's office and see if I could talk to her about Madeline when my cell phone rang. The display said it was Lil. *Great*, I thought. She might be able to give me a direct line for Jane instead of going through her office. I also braced myself for hysterics about last night's murder.

"Hi, Lil." I tried to keep my voice upbeat, but my effort went unnoticed.

"Jane's disappeared."

TWENTY-EIGHT

IMMEDIATELY, IT OCCURRED TO me that the Blond Bomber had tired of playing his little game and had gone after his main target: Jane herself. Not wanting to put ideas in Lil's head, I kept my theory to myself. I need not have bothered.

"Oh, dear, Odelia, what if the Blond Bomber finally came for her? I was getting worried that she was in danger—the children too—I wished I had said something sooner."

I noted that she didn't say Brian came for Jane, just the Blond Bomber.

"Slow down, Lil, and tell me what's happened."

Lil took a couple of deep breaths before answering. "Brian called me this morning and told me that when he and the children got up this morning, Jane was gone."

"*Gone* gone, as in vanished without a trace? Or gone as in packed her bags and moved out?"

"Hard to say. My granddaughter was the first to notice her mother was gone."

"Not Brian?"

"Brian and Jane have not shared a bedroom in quite a while, and usually Brian leaves very early to do rounds at the hospital before going to his office. This morning, he was running late."

"What else did Brian tell you?"

She took another breath. "He said Jane didn't come home for dinner last night, so he took the children out to eat and later to a movie. He told me when they got home, which was after ten, Jane was sitting in the dark in the den drinking a glass of wine. She didn't talk to any of them much beyond saying good night. When they went to bed, she was still in the den drinking. But this morning, she was gone, and there was no note. Brian said that some of her clothes are missing, too."

"Sounds like Jane just decided to leave, Lil. You knew that she and Brian were separating."

"That's what Brian thinks, Odelia. In fact, he called to see if she might have shown up on my doorstep." There was a short silence before Lil continued. "But what if she didn't? What if that monster finally came after her? You heard about that poor girl from yesterday, didn't you? Her hair was the same as Jane's is now."

"Lil, I seriously doubt that if the Blond Bomber came for Jane, he'd give her time to pack a bag."

"You're right, of course." She let loose a nervous chuckle. "I'm probably overreacting. It's just that she was so frightened yesterday after talking with you. And then that girl yesterday must have put her right over the edge."

"Did you speak with Jane about Madeline Sparks? You know, the dead girl with the short red hair?"

"No, I did not. I didn't hear the news until early this morning. I was going to call her, but Brian called me first."

"I spoke to Mason Bell just a little while ago. Jane decorated a home the Sparks woman was living in."

Lil gasped. "Just like the others."

"Yes, just like the others."

Immediately, a thought hit me. If Jane had not cut and colored her hair, would Madeline Sparks have been spared? Did the killer have someone else in mind, only to have his plans change when he noticed Jane had altered her look? Jane said that she had changed her hair only about two weeks ago. Whoever was killing the look-alikes was either someone she saw regularly or someone who was stalking her. A lot of women complain that their husbands or boyfriends never notice when they make changes to their appearance, yet here was one man who was paying attention—deadly attention.

"Lil, do you still think Brian might be the Blond Bomber?"

"No, not anymore, Odelia." There was a long pause on her end.

"Lil, you still there?"

When Lil answered, she spoke barely above a whisper, as if the two of us were sharing secrets in a crowded room. "There's something else about Jane and the Blond Bomber."

I waited, but Lil said nothing further. I prodded. "Yes?"

"Jane asked me not to tell anyone, especially Brian, but I think it's okay to tell you."

On the other side of the phone, I was dancing a jig of impatience. *Come on, out with it.*

With a sigh, Lil reluctantly let loose with the information. "Jane called me last night. I didn't tell Brian when he called this morning, because she didn't say anything about leaving and specifically asked me not to tell him about the call. She said it was for their safety—Brian and the children."

The hair stood up on my arms. Something told me this might pop the doozy meter enough to send it to the moon. "And?"

"Jane called about nine thirty last night. It was late for her to be calling me, so I knew it had to be important."

"And?" I prodded again, ready to bust a gut.

"Odelia, Jane said she now knows who the Blond Bomber is, and it's definitely not Brian."

The hair standing at attention on my arms was nothing compared to the scary tingle that shot up and down my spine. "Did she tell you who she suspected?"

"I asked, but she wouldn't tell me. I'm very worried about her, Odelia."

Now so was I.

"Maybe, Lil, Jane is running from the Blond Bomber. By leaving the house, maybe she thought she could remove the danger from her family."

"Or maybe he already has her."

"I think you should tell the police, Lil. Right now, as soon as we hang up. Under these circumstances, they need to be looking for Jane. And you need to tell Brian everything."

"But I can't, Odelia. I can't tell him his own mother suspected him. Or why."

"Would it be better to have Jane found dead and tied to a tree?"

Silence.

I made the decision for her. "I'm hanging up and calling the police myself, Lil. You do what you need to do, but I have to do what I have to do."

After disconnecting the call, I placed one to Dev Frye. I gave him the details and answered any questions he had as best I could. There really wasn't much more to go on beyond what I'd told him this morning, but the fact that Jane Sharp had flown the coop right after telling Lil that she knew who the Blond Bomber was might help in some way. I also knew if he felt the information important and helpful, he would make sure it got put to good use. And, in a way, it was my way of washing my hands of the scary mess.

If Brian Eddy wasn't the Blond Bomber, then mission accomplished. I could walk away, right? *Right?* I asked myself again with more oomph. I could go back to being a middle-aged newlywed, where my biggest problem would be picking up warm cinnamon buns in the morning and working off my time debt to Mike Steele. After all, I had promised everyone that I was only trying to prove that Brian Eddy wasn't the Blond Bomber. Now that that was pretty much a done deal, I had to fulfill my promise to my loved ones and butt out.

I called Greg and gave him the update. Immediately, his brain went to the obvious.

"So, you're out of the murder business now, right?"

"Looks that way. Dev has the new lowdown on the Blond Bomber. The feds and the Laguna Beach Police are handling Harper and the Luke murder. Lisa Luke is in good hands. Even my father is doing fine and said not to visit until this weekend."

"Great. So what are your plans for today?"

"I'm not sure. I could go into the office." I looked at my watch. It wasn't even eleven, yet I felt like it should be four in the afternoon. "I have work to do, but nothing that has to be done today."

"I think you should take the day off, sweetheart. Relax. Go shopping. Sleep. Whatever you want. Then tonight, I'll take you out for a nice romantic evening. How's that sound?"

I felt a purr start to rise from my chest. Plans for a facial, manicure, and even a massage danced around in my brain.

"Sounds heavenly. Maybe I'll even go to the mall and get some new candles for the bedroom."

Greg chuckled. "Too bad that hot outfit isn't ready."

In spite of that scary thought, a smile came to my lips. "I'm sure I can come up with something suitable to wear after dinner."

TWENTY-NINE

AFTER GIVING GREG A sloppy phone kiss, I transferred the clean towels to the dryer and placed a call to the office to tell them I would be taking a vacation day. At least that way I wouldn't be running up the tab with Steele. Then I dialed Zee's house. I knew she was heading to Compton to see Lisa today, but maybe later she'd have time to come with me for a little pampering.

When I got the answering machine at the Washington's, I called Zee's cell. She answered on the third ring.

"Odelia! I'm so glad you called." Her voice sounded anxious, not pleased.

"What's wrong?"

"Is Lisa with you?"

My heart stopped. "No, why would she be?"

"We hoped maybe she called you, and you picked her up."

I didn't like the sound of the word *hoped*. "Are you saying she's not at Miriam's?"

"That's exactly what I'm saying. When she didn't get up this morning, Miriam thought she was just sleeping late. Later, when Lisa still didn't stir, Miriam checked the bed and found pillows under the covers."

As my plans for a relaxing day of girly stuff sailed away into the horizon without me, I wondered what in the hell Lisa was thinking by leaving Miriam's without telling anyone.

"Why, Odelia, would Lisa pull a fast one on us?"

"I have no idea, Zee, but I intend to find out. When was the last time Miriam saw her?"

"Last night about nine thirty. Miriam said Lisa was sitting up reading when she went to bed. She didn't check the bed until just after nine this morning. That's when she called me. I dashed up here as soon as I got the call." I heard Zee talking to someone before coming back on the line with me. "Miriam just told me that Lisa seemed nervous last night, but she attributed that to everything she's been through."

"Dev was here this morning. He also said Lisa seemed antsy last night. Said she told him she wanted to get back to her life."

"Doesn't she realize the danger she's in?"

"Dev said he really pushed her to understand that, and she seemed willing to wait it out a couple of days. She even got a leave from work." I paused a moment. "Speaking of Dev, did you call him about this yet?"

"No, I wanted to check with you first. It was a long shot, but I really hoped she was with you."

"Why don't you stay at Miriam's for a bit, just in case she turns up there?" Another long shot in my mind, but you never know. "I'll call Dev and also drive down to Lisa's place to see if she returned home."

Compton's about a forty-five minute to an hour drive from Newport Beach with good traffic. If Lisa did return home, how in the world did she manage it? She didn't have a car. Did she call someone to come pick her up? Compton is definitely not the sort of place to wander around late at night, especially if you don't belong there in the first place.

"Zee, did Lisa have her purse at the hospital, and a cell phone? I can't remember."

"She did have her purse. I remember because she told me how thoughtful Kirk had been in remembering to take it to the hospital for her insurance information. I don't recall seeing a cell phone though." I heard Zee talking to someone again, probably her Aunt Miriam.

If a woman has a cell phone, chances are it's kept in her purse. Many purses now even have separate compartments for them. Unless Lisa left it on a table at home and it was overlooked when the paramedics came, I was pretty sure she'd have it with her.

"Odelia, Miriam confirmed that Lisa has her cell phone with her. She said Lisa got two calls on it last night. She knows one call was from Detective Frye because he also spoke a minute or two to Miriam, to thank her for her help. She's not sure about the other call or whether or not Lisa received or made any after she went to bed."

"Did Lisa ever call you while she was in the hospital? If so, and she used her cell phone, her number might be stored on your phone."

There was a pause while Zee tried to remember. "No, sorry. I coordinated everything with Detective Frye."

"The only way Lisa could have gotten out of Compton last night without us knowing was to have called a cab or called someone to pick her up." I paused. "Or she could have taken a bus. Do busses run late at night in that area?"

"I'm not sure, but there's not a bus stop near Miriam's. So if Lisa left the house on foot to catch a bus, she wouldn't have any idea where to go to get one or where it was headed."

I started pacing the kitchen floor, trying to piece all the probabilities together. Something was fishy. Lisa was obviously dead set on going back home, if that's where she went after leaving Miriam's. And she was willing to risk her life to do it.

"I think she called someone or someone called her. But just to be safe, Zee, why don't you call the cab companies that serve Compton and ask if anyone picked her up last night and where they took her—if they'll even tell you."

I grabbed my tote bag. "I'm on my way to Newport Beach," I told Zee as I left out the back door and headed for the garage.

I was in the car, ready to back out of the garage, when I remembered the laundry.

"Hey, Odelia, where ya going?"

The question came from Silas. He was standing by our garage door, holding onto his bike.

"Just running an errand, Silas."

"Can I come?"

"Actually, I'm heading to a friend's place in Newport Beach. And I'm in an awful hurry. Besides, you should be in school."

"Teacher conferences today, so no school. And Billy's home with a cold. I'm bored."

"Sorry, sweetie, maybe next time. Okay?"

I scooted back inside and checked the towels in the dryer. They were far from dry, so I reset the timer and hit the start button. A moment later, I was back in the car and hitting the road.

There were two calls I had to make ASAP: one was to Dev and one to Greg. I had promised Greg I would keep him informed, and I intended to keep that promise. Once in the car, I dialed Greg first, knowing that call might take less time than the one to Dev. As soon as Greg came to the phone, I filled him in. He wasn't pleased that I was heading to Lisa's.

"I don't like it, Odelia. Harper could be watching the place. You could be heading right into danger."

"I'm calling Dev right now, Greg. Either he'll be there or he'll send someone long before I arrive."

Greg was silent for a moment. "Do you have keys to Lisa's place?"

"No, of course not. I'm just going to see if she's there and she's all right, that's all. I'm thinking that maybe she called a friend to take her home."

"Good. Then make the call to Dev, pronto. If you insist on going, then just wait outside until he arrives, preferably in your car with the engine running. Although I'd prefer you to just call Dev and keep your nose out of it altogether."

"I just want to make sure Lisa's okay."

"Sweetheart, Lisa made her choice to leave Miriam's. If she's in danger, she did that to herself. It doesn't mean you have to follow her into the land of stupidity."

240

My nose twitched, not because what he said offended me, but because I knew Greg was right. Lisa did make this choice on her own and without my involvement.

"As soon as I see whether or not she's there, I'll turn everything over to Dev. How's that? It's just that I'd feel better knowing myself. And if she is there, Dev might be able to convince her to leave. Maybe she just wanted to go home and pack a few things. Maybe there's something very personal she needed, and then she was going to go back to Compton."

"Do you really believe that, Odelia?"

"Not for a New York minute, but I have to know, Greg. As of this morning, both Jane Sharp and Lisa Luke have disappeared. I don't know if they're connected or even know each other, but it would drive me crazy to sit home."

He gave me a big, exaggerated sigh.

Just as I was about to say something more, there was a loud noise, followed by my car acting funny. I pulled over to the curb.

"Greg, I think I have a flat tire. Hold on."

I got out of the car and checked. Sure enough, my rear right tire was blown. But at least it blew on a surface street and not while I was sailing along on the freeway.

"Honey, I have a flat—the back right tire."

"I'll be right there."

"No, don't bother, it's no biggie. I'll call the Auto Club. They'll send someone. That's why we have them."

"Okay. Damn, I knew those tires were getting bad. First thing tomorrow, we're taking your car in and having all four replaced." He laughed. "Someone must be watching out for you, sweetheart.

At least the flat will keep you out of trouble for a while and give Dev time to get to Lisa's."

My nose twitched again, because again Greg was right.

After hanging up from Greg, I dug out my AAA membership card and called them. The dispatcher said they were very busy and it might be about twenty minutes before the service truck came. Nuts.

I was about to climb back into my car and call Dev when a vehicle pulled up—a white van I didn't recognize. Although it was broad daylight and I was on a busy street, my natural instinct as a woman alone was to dash back into my car and lock the doors. Then the driver got out and asked if I needed help. I gave a sigh of relief. It was Paul Milholland, Jane Sharp's delivery man.

"Hi," he said, standing by the front of his van. "I thought I recognized you when I drove by, so I made a U-turn and came back. Can I give you a lift somewhere?"

"Thanks, but it's just a flat tire. I called the Auto Club."

"There's a nasty tie-up on the 405. Four or five vehicles playing bumper cars. Might be awhile before a tow truck gets to you."

"They warned me when I called."

He ran a hand through his sandy hair. "If you have a spare, I'll change it for you. Hate to see a woman stranded."

"I couldn't impose."

"Not a problem. Why don't you pop your trunk so I can get to work while you call the Auto Club back and let them know you've been rescued?"

It certainly sounded like a great plan to me and would save me a lot of time. "Are you sure?"

"Absolutely." He made a gesture for me to open the trunk. After thanking him, I returned to the driver's side of the car, reached inside, and pulled the trunk release.

Back standing on the curb near the front of my car, I called the Auto Club and cancelled my service call. Then I called Dev but only got his voice mail. I left him a message letting him know that Lisa was missing and I was heading to her place to see if she was there. I asked him to call me if he knew anything about her where-abouts.

Finished with my calls, I walked to the back of the car and watched Paul work. He had the spare out of the trunk and the car up on the jack, and was working on releasing the lug nuts. He worked efficiently, handling the wrench with tanned, muscled arms and work-worn hands. In spite of the slight breeze, he was dressed in just a tee shirt and jeans. On his feet were heavy work boots. At Lil's I hadn't noticed that his face was lined beyond his years.

"You have such a deep tan for so early in the year—do you work outside a lot?"

He shook his head. "Nope, actually spend most of my workday inside or driving." He glanced at me and gave me a smile. "But I do love to surf. I do it almost every morning. When I'm not working, I spend most of my time at the beach."

"My husband and I live less than a mile from here, just a few blocks from the beach. Sometimes we go to Sunset Beach on week-ends to watch the surfers before breakfast."

"You ever surf?"

"No, but my husband does on occasion. He's in a wheelchair, a paraplegic, and very athletic. But his big sport is basketball."

"Amazing what guys in chairs can do, isn't it?"

I gave Paul a big smile. "He's absolutely amazing."

The last time I had a chance to talk to Paul Milholland, I was in a rush. I really needed to ask him some questions, so maybe the flat tire was a blessing in disguise.

"I left you a voice mail earlier today," I told him.

"You did? Sorry I missed your call. I'm always missing calls when I'm in and out of the van, then forget to check for messages." He looked up from his work for a quick moment. "What's on your mind? Was it about that job you might have for me?"

"Actually, I wanted to ask you about Jane Sharp. Have you worked for her long?"

"Several years now."

"Was she in this morning? I had hoped to give her a call about something, a surprise for Lillian." There I go again, lying my fat ass off.

"Sorry, wouldn't know. I don't work directly out of Sharp Design. In fact, I'm a contractor and work for several designers, as well as other folks. I like the independence."

"Mason Bell, too? I heard he left Sharp Design and started his own company."

Paul nodded. He had the flat tire off and was putting on the spare. "Yes, Mason's doing quite well. Lately, I've been doing more work for him than for Jane."

"Is Jane's business going through a slow period? I thought she was the hottest of the hot."

He tightened the lug nuts as he answered. "It's a fickle business. One day people are waiting six months just to meet you, and the next day someone else is the darling of upholstery and wallpaper."

244

I was trying to figure out how to ask Paul about possible stalkers but wasn't sure how to do it. And if he didn't work day in and day out with Jane, he might not know anything.

"Paul, during your time with Jane, have you ever noticed anything odd with her clients, like maybe one who might have had a thing for her?" When he gave me an odd look, I added a quick lie. "Lil mentioned something to me about how Jane has had problems with some of her prior clients—that some of them have almost stalked her. She is very beautiful, so I can see how that might happen."

With a grunt, he gave the lug nuts a final twist. "That should hold you until you replace the spare with a new tire."

Without addressing my question, he put the damaged tire into my trunk along with the jack. I was sure he was going to ignore my query. But after he closed the trunk, he turned to me.

"Honestly, I've never seen anything like that. I know over the years Jane has become close to some of her clients, but nothing unusual."

Either Paul was unobservant or clamming up for some reason, maybe even out of decency. Mason Bell and even Steele had made it sound like everyone who knew Jane knew she diddled her male clients. But Paul Milholland didn't strike me as the sort of person I could push to talk. Better I get down the road to Newport Beach and see what was happening with Lisa.

I held out my hand to him. "Thanks so much, Paul, for helping me out." He took my hand and shook it, but didn't release it.

"Well, I'm off to deliver a couple of antiques. Some real beauties. Want to see them?"

I really didn't have time to window shop and was about to decline, but it was obvious that Paul was eager to show them to me.

I extracted my hand. "I loved that table you brought to Lil's, but I'm kind of in a rush."

"If you liked that table, then you'd really love these." He chuckled. "One of them cost more money than I make in a year."

The man had done me a huge favor, and I didn't want to seem rude. "Well, a quick peek won't hurt."

When we approached the side of the van, I noticed that Paul moved to stand behind me and was very close. Then I felt his hand on the small of my back. It was an intimate gesture and one I didn't appreciate. At that point, my cell phone rang. Happy for the interruption, I excused myself to Paul and deftly put some space between us.

When I answered, I couldn't believe my ears. "Where are you?" I asked the caller. I listened for a few seconds before interrupting. "Hold on, hold on. Just a minute."

I turned to Paul. "I'm sorry, Paul, but this is a very important call. Perhaps another time." I started for my car as I talked. "Thanks for everything. You have no idea what a huge help you were today."

With a smile and a salute, Paul Milholland climbed into his van and took off before I was even settled into my own vehicle.

I went back to my call. "Okay, Lisa, now tell me where you are and why you ran away from Miriam's."

THIRTY

ACCORDING TO LISA, SHE left Miriam's because she wanted to go home, pack, and leave town for a few days. She couldn't stand the thought of being cooped up like a hostage, not even for her own good and with such a nice lady as Zee's Aunt Miriam. She said she snuck out because she knew we'd try to stop her. Then she remembered Muffin and decided to take the cat with her.

Listening to her explanation, my gut—which was correct, by the way, about Dr. Eddy—told me something wasn't right. A few days ago, Lisa couldn't stand the sight of Muffin, and now she couldn't leave town for a few days without the animal? Maybe now that Lisa realized she had nothing to do with Laurie's death, she wanted to be near something that her sister had loved. But if she was only going to be gone for a few days, why take the cat? Cats aren't good travelers even under the best of circumstances, so why uproot an animal from a stable environment just to drag it around to who knows where? It just didn't make sense.

I agreed to meet her, and I agreed to bring Muffin. And yet again I lied my ass off. I had no intention of bringing Muffin to the rendezvous. Instead, my plan was to talk some sense into the girl and/or find out if she was involved in any way with Kirk and the smuggling. And with Jane Sharp's connection with Kirk, I was now wondering if Jane was involved. After all, she also had connections to Gordon Harper and was now missing. Maybe Jane wasn't running from the Blond Bomber, maybe she was running from Harper. Whichever—it didn't matter. Jane Sharp had two big targets pinned to her designer outfit. We still weren't sure what Kirk was bringing into the States for Harper, but according to Dev the consensus was pretty much diamonds. It was the number one illegal export from the continent of Africa and easily transportable.

With my spare tire securely in place, I flew down the 405 Freeway towards Newport Beach. Along the way, I saw the remnants of the accident Paul had alerted me about. The cars involved, tow trucks, and police cars were lined up along the right shoulder, and the only slowdown now was caused by lookey-loos.

Arriving at Lisa's condominium complex, I turned cautiously into the guest parking area, keeping my eyes peeled for signs of Harper's silver Mercedes or any other suspicious vehicles. I also didn't see Dev's car or any sign of police.

After parking my car, I made my way cautiously towards Lisa's unit. It was on the end, conveniently located to the parking lot. I knocked gently. After a moment's hesitation, during which I'm sure Lisa was making good use of the peephole, the door quickly opened to allow me inside. Just as quickly, it closed behind me.

Unlike my last visit, this time the condo was dark, the drapes drawn. Although it still looked the same, it felt abandoned—no longer a warm, welcoming home but an empty shell. As soon as my eyes adjusted, I noticed two bags near the door—a small suitcase on wheels and a matching overnight bag. I also noticed that many of the photographs that once sat on the credenza were gone.

I turned to Lisa, who was standing by the door dressed in jeans and a blue sweatshirt, her long blond hair pulled back in a ponytail.

"You leaving until this blows over or for good?"

"Where's Muffin?" Lisa didn't look at me when she spoke.

I ignored her question and asked my own. "How did you get here from Compton?" When she didn't respond, I asked another. "Did Kirk come get you?"

This time she nodded but still didn't look up. "I appreciate everything you've done for me, Odelia. Both you and Zee. But Kirk thought it best to get me out of town, and I agree."

"You do realize that Kirk is responsible for Laurie's death, even though it was only indirectly."

She nodded again. "Yes, he told me everything."

"Everything? Even about the smuggling and his deal with Gordon Harper? And what about the smuggling? Was it diamonds?"

"Yes. It was just as you and Detective Frye said. He was smuggling diamonds. That Harper guy killed Laurie to teach Kirk a lesson, to get him to do what he wanted."

"And now the two of you are going away together?"

"No." Lisa jerked her head up. "I mean, yes. We are going away, but not as a couple. Kirk just wants to make sure I'm safe. He says if I stay, that guy will kill me."

"He's probably right. That's why you were staying in Compton. You took a big risk coming here."

"Then give me Muffin and I'll be going. The sooner the better."

"I didn't bring Muffin."

"What?" Lisa's eyes went huge and her face paled. "But I told you I wanted her back."

"And you can have her back, as soon as everything settles down and you're safe again. If you're running, an animal will only slow you down. Cats aren't dogs. You can't use them for protection."

"That's not fair. She's mine."

"I'm doing what's right for both of you. I'd hate to see Muffin abandoned or you get bogged down with her when things get tough, and they will get tough if you're dodging a scumbag like Harper."

"But you don't understand," Lisa whined. "She's all I have left of Laurie."

Her eyes started to tear, and I allowed her emotion to tug at my heart, but just for a moment. Then I straightened my shoulders, ready to get to the bottom of things.

"I do understand. The police are on to Harper. Hopefully, they'll nab him soon. In the meantime, Muffin will be safe with us. When all this blows over, we'll gladly hand her back."

I indicated the bags. "Although I think running is stupid, you'd better get going. Every minute you spend here is dangerous. Are you meeting Kirk somewhere, or is he coming here to get you?"

"But I can't go without Muffin!"

I studied Lisa with a suspicious eye. I couldn't see Lisa becoming an animal lover overnight. There was definitely something special about Muffin, but what? She'd been with us a couple of days and so far seemed like a normal, healthy feline.

"A few days ago, you couldn't get rid of the animal fast enough. Now you're willing to risk your neck for her. I don't buy it. What's up?"

Although Lisa was facing me, her eyes shifted from side to side, as if she expected someone to jump out from behind the curtains or from the next room. Her skittishness was as infectious as the flu.

"Nothing's up, Odelia. Kirk and I just want the damn cat, especially Kirk. It's all we have of Laurie. Why can't you understand that?"

I was about to say *bullshit* when a slight noise came from the closed door to Laurie's room. This time it wasn't a cat crying for attention. Already pale, Lisa's face drained of all color, leaving her as white-faced as a mime.

"Leave, Odelia," Lisa whispered to me. "Go now."

"Who's there, Lisa?" I whispered back. She didn't answer but the fear in her eyes was loud and clear.

I turned my head as nonchalantly as possible in the direction of the front door, gauging how fast the two of us could make it out and to my car. A successful escape would depend on who was behind the door and whether or not they had a gun. I made a slight motion with my hand like I was holding a gun. Lisa took note of it and nodded, confirming what I feared. The next question was whether it was male or female, followed by how many, but it would be difficult to play charades without the unknown assailant catching on.

I gave Lisa an exaggerated shrug and sighed. "Muffin's out in the car."

"She is?" Lisa sounded surprised and relieved.

I nodded. "Yes. I didn't bring her in because I'd hoped to reason with you to let her stay with us until things calmed down for you."

"Muffin will be fine with me." When I made no move for the door, she added, "Why don't you get her so I can go."

I bent over and picked up Lisa's overnight bag. "Come on," I said to her, hoping my voice sounded resigned. "I'll walk you out to your car. Then we can transfer Muffin at the same time." I widened my eyes at Lisa, hoping she'd catch on to my plan. "I have her other stuff, too. You know, her cat box and dishes."

Lisa stood as still as a rock. "But ... but," she stammered for a moment. "No, that's okay. I still have some more things to pack."

"Fine." I tried to keep my voice casual with overtones of annoyance. The annoyance part wasn't a difficult stretch. "Suit yourself. But the least you can do is come with me and get the stuff so I don't have to make two trips. Then I'm washing my hands of you. If you won't listen to reason, there's nothing more I can do."

Maybe, if we really did look like we were going to my car to get the absent Muffin, whoever was in the other room would let us do it, thinking we'd return in just a couple of minutes. Then we could hop in the car and leave. Providing, of course, Lisa was in sync with my desire to skedaddle. I still wasn't sure if she was part of the smuggling or just someone who got dragged into the drama by her proximity to Kirk and her sister. My hope was pinned to the latter.

I started for the door, trying to be as normal as possible. However, the best laid plans of mice, men, and stumpy-headed paralegals was not to be.

"That's far enough, Ms. Grey."

The familiar voice wasn't Lisa's, nor did it belong to Gordon Harper. With caution, I turned around to find a gun pointed in my direction. Holding the gun was Maria Santiago.

THIRTY-ONE

"Seems your duties at Seventh Veil extend far beyond managing the costume business."

While she ignored my comment, I studied the woman standing before me, the gun in her hand contrasting sharply with her tasteful pantsuit, conservative makeup, and Coach shoulder bag. I'd been held at gunpoint before by women, but they'd all been nut jobs and often looked the part. There was something truly disturbing about being threatened by a woman who looked like she should be shoe shopping at Nordstrom's.

Maria Santiago didn't seem at all surprised to see me at Lisa's. With confidence, she ignored my comment and pointed the gun at my stomach.

"Why don't we all go down to the parking lot together? And I wouldn't advise trying anything foolish."

Like ducklings crossing a busy street, the three of us left the condo single file and started down the path to the parking lot. I was in the lead, with Lisa sandwiched in the middle—the only thing between me and the gun. I would have preferred being directly in front of Mrs. Santiago. If I came up with a plan of escape, it would be too difficult to implement it with Lisa as a buffer. And Lisa seemed too shell-shocked to think of anything clever on her own.

"I thought you said Kirk picked you up last night," I said to Lisa over my shoulder.

"Actually, it was very early this morning."

"You should have just left, Lisa. You'd be far away from here by now if you'd forgotten about Muffin."

"Enough!" Mrs. Santiago barked.

As we made our way into the parking lot, I looked around. There was not a soul in sight. Not surprising, considering it was a workday, even for a Friday.

"Which car is yours?" Mrs. Santiago asked. I pointed in the direction of my sturdy old Camry, and she steered us in that direction.

Of course, Muffin was not in the car. The little cat was at home, probably snoozing in a ball on our bed, happy to have it all to herself. I had no idea what I was going to do once we reached my car and Muffin's absence became apparent. My mind worked faster than a Weedwacker as it went through possibilities and cut them down as too harebrained and dangerous.

As soon as we approached my car, I noticed a black SUV start to pull out of a parking space not very far away. Maybe I could somehow flag it down without getting us shot. I quickly judged my position. Maybe I would throw myself at Maria Santiago and knock her sideways before she could get off a properly aimed shot. A gun blast would certainly get the attention we needed, as long as it didn't hit one of us. I had to act fast, and I had to act now.

Once at the car, I went to the back door on the passenger's side. Maria told Lisa to go to the back and put her hands on the trunk where she could see them while I retrieved Muffin—the cat who wasn't there. "Remember," Maria said to me, "nothing foolish."

As soon as I opened the back door, I knew something wasn't right. The blanket I keep in the car to cover the back seat when Wainwright rides with me was sprawled on the floor. And it looked lumpy. Positioning my body so that Maria couldn't see into the vehicle, I cautiously pulled back a corner of the blanket and found myself eye to eye with a hot and sweaty Silas. He was scrunched up, his small body molding as best it could to the contours of the floor and the small space between the front and back seats. He looked at me wide-eyed and fearful and, thankfully, kept silent.

Doing my best not to let out the shriek of surprise that hovered on my lips, I mouthed a *shhh* to him and replaced the corner of the blanket. Then I turned back to Maria.

"Where's the cat?" she asked me, still holding the gun on Lisa.

"She's not here. I lied. I never brought her."

Lisa's eyes begged me to say it wasn't so. I glanced at her and looked away. I didn't want Lisa shot, but I didn't want Silas found either. I didn't know if Maria would shoot a child, but I wasn't about to take that chance. Though, heaven knows, I wanted to strangle the kid myself for stowing away and complicating matters. *Just wait until we get out of this mess*, I promised him silently. *If* we get out of this mess.

When Maria looked skeptical, I made a motion to get out of the way. "See for yourself."

It was a bluff move. I was praying she wouldn't call me on it and search the car, but I knew if I tried to keep her from searching, she'd do it for sure.

I also was stalling, praying that the damn SUV would get moving and finally drive by. It had to pass us to leave the complex. If the driver was even paying a modicum of attention, he or she would see Lisa and me being held at gunpoint. But the vehicle seemed to be taking forever to back out. I glanced quickly in its direction. Its backup lights were lit and it had pulled out slightly, but not all the way. What the hell was it waiting for, gas to go back down to two dollars a gallon?

Then, like a Louisville Slugger to my skull, it hit me. Maria was totally unconcerned about the driver of the SUV. The SUV was waiting—waiting for us. Or a least for Maria Santiago.

Questions peppered my brain like buckshot. Had I brought Muffin to Lisa, would Lisa have gone off with them as soon as I left? Would I have been *allowed* to leave? Would Lisa have lived after handing the cat over to Maria? And what about the cat? What was so special about that scrawny little furball? I needed time to dissect each question, to play with the facts and the suppositions and see what presented itself to me in living color. But I didn't have time. Whatever conclusions I decided upon would have to come to me fast and furious and be able to stop on a dime.

My thoughts were interrupted by Maria aiming the gun at me. "So where's the cat?"

I held one hand up and slowly closed the car door. I might as well face the music. Chances are Maria was going to kill me as soon as I handed over Muffin, so maybe not having her would buy me and Lisa some time—and keep her from discovering Silas.

"You said you had her and now you don't? Which is it?"

"I told you, I lied." I glanced at Lisa, who was listening and watching in fear. "I told Lisa I had the cat to get her outside."

"So where is the cat?"

"At the vet." I looked at Lisa, hoping she wouldn't see through my new lie. "I'm sorry, Lisa. But Muffin and our cat got into a pretty bad scuffle this morning. Muffin's going to be okay, but she'll be at the vet for another day or so. I was hoping you wouldn't have to know just yet. That's why I wanted to convince you to leave without her."

If Lisa was concerned about Muffin's safety, she hid it well. Whatever the reason she wanted the animal, it wasn't to love and cuddle it.

Maria Santiago stepped a bit closer to me. "Guess you'll just have to go pick her up and bring her here."

I shifted from one foot to the other. The movement caused Maria to get a little nervous. She took one step closer to me and positioned the gun at my chest.

"Can't—the vet closes every Friday at noon."

"I don't believe you."

"Check it out for yourself. Seaside Pet Hospital in Huntington Beach."

While still holding the gun on me, Maria motioned with her free hand towards the SUV. It backed out of the space and cruised over to where we were.

As soon as the vehicle was next to us, the driver lowered the window. The driver was Harper's thug, the one who had beat up Kirk in the Seventh Veil parking lot. His eyes darted from me to Lisa as he acknowledged Maria with a jerk of his chin.

"What's the number for the pet hospital?" Maria asked me.

Shrugging, I said, "I don't know, but it's on my cell phone. The phone's in my bag." I indicated my tote bag. It was on the ground next to the car, where I'd placed it before opening the car door. "I can call them if you let me dig out the phone."

Maria stepped back but kept the gun trained on my midsection. "Get the phone, but that's it. Anything else and you're dead."

Slowly, I bent to retrieve the cell phone from the side pocket of my bag. "So, Maria," I said loudly, hoping Silas was keeping his ears open, "why does Gordon Harper want the cat anyway? You going to start using cat fur at Seventh Veil?"

"That's none of your concern." She waved the gun at me. "Use just one hand. Keep the other in the air."

I did what she said and pulled out the phone using only my right hand. "I'll call the hospital for you."

"No." Maria shook her head. "Just read off the number."

She turned to the driver of the van. "You call the number she gives us."

The driver pulled out his phone and readied himself to dial. I scrolled through my speed dial numbers until I found the one for the pet hospital. Generally, the vet was closed on Friday afternoons. On Friday and Saturday they were only open from eight to noon. I prayed that today was no different. I didn't want to think about what would happen if they answered and said Muffin wasn't there.

I read off the number, and the driver pushed the corresponding buttons on his phone. Once done, he listened. After several seconds, he turned his attention to Maria.

"It's a recording. The place is closed until eight tomorrow morning."

"Why not just break into the place and take Muffin?" The question had come from Lisa, still slightly bent over, with her hands flat on the trunk of my car.

Maria Santiago and Harper's muscle exchanged quick glances, weighing the plan amongst themselves as a possibility. As for me, I wanted to back the car over Lisa's foot. She obviously didn't understand that all they wanted was Muffin, and that once they had the cat, she and I would be as expendable as used tissues. Call me cranky, but as much as I love animals, I wasn't about to trade my life for a cat I've known for only a few days. Once I put my life in danger for Seamus, but he and I go back a few years.

Thinking about Seamus made me wonder yet again about the value of Muffin. Seamus had once been catnapped, but that had been to use him as leverage to get something of value. He hadn't been the prize but the bartering chip. Was Muffin being used in the same fashion? It seemed unlikely. Seamus had been valuable because of the love I felt for him. The catnapper knew I would turn over the item in exchange for his safety. That wasn't the case here. Lisa hadn't displayed any affection for Muffin, so it was unlikely that she would trade her for anything of value.

Once again, I needed time to think about the connection between Muffin, Kirk, Harper, and Lisa, and possibly even Laurie Luke's death. But time to sit and think wasn't a luxury I had right now. I was too busy surviving. If keeping Muffin out of the paws of these creeps kept me and Silas alive, there was no way I was giving her up.

While I pondered killers and cats, the goon made another call. Attempts to hear what he was saying were fruitless. Finally, he snapped the phone shut and turned his attention back to us.

"The chief said to bring them back to the shop."

"What about the cat?" Maria asked.

"He said no break-in, just bring these two to him. He'll find out a way to use them to get the animal."

THIRTY-TWO

THE GOON GOT OUT of the SUV and opened the back hatch. The back seats had been removed to provide maximum cargo space. Maria motioned with the gun for Lisa and me to climb in. Obviously, wherever we were heading, we were going steerage. Lisa had other ideas. Just as I was about to climb into the cargo area of the vehicle, she made a break for it, running like hell in the direction of the public street. And she might have made it, had the street not been so far away and the henchman so fit. Quickly, the big man covered the distance she'd traveled and brought her down like a lion bringing down a slow-moving wildebeest. When Lisa started to fuss, he slammed a meaty fist into her head to quiet her and dragged her back.

Lisa was half unconscious when the two of them returned to the vehicle. He threw her hard against the bed of the back of the SUV, where she lay sprawled and moaning while he retrieved something from the front seat.

During all the commotion, Maria Santiago never let the gun drift from my gut. And during the commotion, I never let loose of my phone. With as little movement as possible, I let a finger slide over the buttons, hoping it would find redial. Greg's cell phone had been the last number called. I gently pushed down with my finger, praying it was the redial button and not the off button, which would give off a telltale chime.

When the goon returned to the back of the vehicle, he was holding a large roll of duct tape. With a deftness that came from experience, he taped Lisa's mouth and bound her wrists. Next, he turned to me, indicating for me to hold out my wrists.

"There's no need," I told him. "I won't do anything stupid."

"Damn right you won't," he growled. "The chief said to be particularly careful of you. He wants you delivered safe and sound."

As much as I liked the sound of *safe*, I wasn't so sure about the concept of being delivered. When I hesitated, the creep grabbed my cell phone from me and flung it to the ground, then he proceeded to tape my wrists. Right before he slapped the tape across my mouth, I managed to suck my lips inward, determined that when, or if, the tape was ever removed, my lips wouldn't be ripped off with it.

"Aren't you going to wrap their ankles, too?" The question came from Maria, who still held watch with the gun.

The henchman shook his head. "If their ankles are taped, they can't walk. You want to carry these heifers once we get to the shop?" Maria laughed and relaxed the gun a bit.

The guy roughly helped me climb into the back of the vehicle.

"Lay down," he ordered. "And keep your head down until we say so, got it?"

I nodded in understanding.

As soon as I was settled on my back with my head facing the front of the vehicle and my legs straight out towards the rear, Lisa started whimpering. She was alert now, and her eyes were wide as saucers and wet with tears. With my own eyes, I tried to relay comfort. I nodded, hoping to convey a confidence I didn't feel. We were in deep shit, no doubt about it, but I sure didn't need a hysterical partner should any hope of escape present itself.

Soon, we were on our way. I wasn't sure, but my guess was that we were heading to rendezvous with Harper at Seventh Veil. As much as I didn't relish being transported like a side of meat to the market, I was thankful we were moving away from my car and Silas. Dev or the police should be here soon and would find the boy. Silas, if he was paying attention, might be able to give them some information.

I had wanted time to think through what was going on, and now I had it. From Lisa's place, it was a forty-five minute to an hour drive to Seventh Veil Costuming, providing traffic moved at a reasonable rate. Although my brain would have worked better sitting at my kitchen table unfettered by duct tape, beggars couldn't be choosers.

What was it about that damn cat? In my brain, I methodically ran down what I knew, or thought I knew. Kirk was smuggling diamonds for Harper. Laurie had been killed by Harper, held by him in order to strong-arm Kirk into fulfilling his commitment. Kirk had given the cat to Laurie as a gift, and now Harper and his minions wanted the animal. The first thing I'd done as soon as Muffin had come into our home was check her over for fleas using a special comb. I'd found nothing unusual about her. She was healthy, her limbs sound, her fur sleek and flea free. Until Laurie died, she'd been very well cared for, loved and regularly groomed.

Riding like a sack of potatoes in the back of the SUV, I went over every possibility, from the obvious to the ridiculous. A groan tried to escape my taped lips as I realized an oversight on my part. Maybe it wasn't the cat everyone was hunting for, but the cat's collar—the heavy, handmade leather collar. The collar that seemed unusual for a young cat and that bothered the animal so much we finally took it off of her. The collar that now resided in the nightstand drawer next to our bed. I wasn't sure about my theory that the collar held the missing diamonds, but I was fresh out of other ideas and it seemed plausible, though pretty stupid. If Muffin had gotten outside and disappeared, so would the diamonds. Would someone really be so lame as to hide diamonds on something attached to four swift feet?

I mentally put a star next to the collar idea and moved on to other thoughts. If I could stumble upon some other solid connections, maybe I could use them to bargain for our lives. Knowledge is power, and right now all I had were a lot of semi-connected dots.

Supposing Kirk had hidden diamonds in the cat's collar, my next question was whether or not he had acted alone. Did Laurie know about it? Lisa didn't seem to think so. Then again, maybe Lisa was in on it and had been from the start. Maybe she had a reason to feel guilty about her sister's death other than flashing her photo around the Internet. The next suspect to float across my brain as it bounced along on the floor of the vehicle was Jane Sharp. Jane had been having an affair with Kirk Thomas, and Jane also knew Gordon Harper. Had Jane been the link between Kirk and Harper? Had she been the one to link up the two men in the first place? That was a distinct possibility. And, if so, and she was on the run, she might be running from Gordon Harper and not the Blond Bomber. Maybe even both.

It was likely that the Blond Bomber was being used as a convenient pawn in this whole matter. Laurie's death had mimicked the style of the Blond Bomber's except for some details. And the Blond Bomber had let the world know specifically that her body was not his handiwork when he scrawled his message across Amber's corpse. Call me crazy, but it didn't seem smart to piss off a serial killer.

I glanced over at Lisa. Her eyes were closed, and she was very still. I couldn't tell if she was asleep or unconscious. She had received a nasty blow to her head and might have a concussion. I gently nudged her. When I received no response, I kicked her again a little harder. The second kick reaped a muffled groan from behind her taped mouth, and her eyes began to flutter. I nudged her leg again with one of my feet, and her eyes came open and stayed open. After a few seconds, they focused on my eyes. Eye to eye, I willed her to stay awake.

I strained to hear any conversation from the front seat, but there was none that I could make out. Maria Santiago and Harper's hired gun had little, if anything, to say to each other. Eventually, I felt the SUV slow down, followed by the vehicle taking a wide curve to the right. We must be taking an off-ramp. As much as I wanted to try to lift myself up and flag down help, I knew it would be fruitless. The windows of the SUV were tinted so that no one could see inside. From my position, I could see sky dotted with power lines and trees passing by through the side and hatch windows.

Turning and twisting my wrists, I tried to loosen the tape. It gave a little, but not much. I needed something sharp to rub the tape against, but saw nothing convenient. It crossed my mind to scrunch down close to the hatch opening and kick out as soon as the door was opened. But I doubted I could kick hard enough to do any damage and was pretty sure Maria would still be holding a gun on us when we exited. Instead, I just continued to twist and turn my wrists, hoping to loosen the tape even further.

It wasn't long before I felt the vehicle turn again, then stop. A moment later, it continued on its way. There were a few successive stops and starts, which I was pretty sure indicated intersections with stop signs or signals. Eventually, the vehicle made a slow right turn, then traveled very slowly past a building. From my vantage point, the building looked a lot like the one that housed Seventh Veil.

I felt the SUV turn slightly, then stop before backing up. As it backed up, more of the building came into view. We were in the belly of the U-shaped parking area of the building, the area where deliveries were made and where I saw Kirk Thomas being shoved around. With some effort, I raised myself enough to look out the window and confirm that we were in the parking area at the costume factory. Before dropping back down to my back, I glimpsed Harper's Mercedes.

Lisa had drifted off again. I kicked her softly, and her eyes opened. She'd been crying, and her eyes and nose were runny. She closed her eyes again, and I knew that she'd given up hope of coming out of this alive. But I hadn't, not until a bullet pierced my brain or my neck was snapped in two.

When the hatch opened, the goon grabbed my ankles and pulled me out of the vehicle halfway, then he grabbed my taped wrists and yanked me to my feet. Immediately, I collapsed to my knees on the pavement, supported like a tripod by my taped hands. Lisa was hauled out next in the same fashion. She also fell to the ground but landed prone, facedown on the asphalt.

I was pulled to a standing position first and ordered to stay standing. Lisa was grabbed by the collar of her sweatshirt and pulled up next to me. Her nose was bloody from her fall, her cheek scraped by gravel. As soon as she was on her feet, she slid to the ground again, her eyes closed.

While Maria Santiago stood guard over us with the gun, the henchman disappeared through a side door positioned next to the roll-type delivery door on the loading dock. He returned almost immediately with a cart, a long platform on four wheels generally used for hauling several boxes at a time. He dumped the half-conscious Lisa onto the cart and started pushing it through the door. Maria told me to follow. She and the gun brought up the rear.

Inside, we were greeted with an eerie silence. We were in the factory part of Seventh Veil, but the hum of industry I'd heard during my earlier visit was absent. The lights were on but the place was empty of workers. Colorful costumes in various stages of completion hung in clusters here and there at various stations throughout the large, cluttered area. To my right, I saw a couple of commercial pressing machines. Over to my left, a row of sewing machines, each one with a rack of garments next to it. Feathers and rolls of cloth and boxes containing other materials were in another corner of the large area near worktables. More rolls of fabric were against the back wall. Scraps of fabric littered the floor.

Our little parade made its way through various aisles. Along the way, I kept my eyes peeled for possible escape routes. Except for a few very distinct aisles, the place was as confusing as a rabbit warren. We halted in front of a large elevator. Next to it was a staircase going up. The muscle hit a button, and the doors opened. He indicated for me to enter. As soon as I was inside, he pushed Lisa and the cart in, trapping me against the back wall. Maria Santiago was the last to enter. There were only two buttons on the panel, one for the first floor and a button for the second. Maria put a key into a lock on the panel and pushed the button for the second floor. The doors closed, and the lift started to rise.

As soon as the elevator doors opened, a different scene presented itself. Instead of a cluttered work area, the four of us faced a large apartment. It was decorated simply and fashionably, using soothing colors and fabrics and elegant, comfortable-looking furniture. The elevator opened up onto a great room, with a living room to the left and a large open kitchen to the right. The living room had two very large windows that looked out over the back parking lot. Directly across from the elevator, on the other side of the room, was an open door leading to a hallway, and no doubt the sleeping quarters. This had to be Crystal Lee's personal apartment that Effie had mentioned.

"Welcome, ladies."

THIRTY-THREE

At the sound of Gordon Harper's squeaky voice, my stomach knotted up. I didn't see him until he lifted himself out of a deep armchair. As soon as we filed out of the elevator, Harper came over to take stock of his captives.

He jerked his head towards the hallway. "Take Miss Luke to the spare room and put her on the bed," he said to his hired gun. "Leave her bound and stay with her. I'll tend to her later." Without a word, the big man wheeled the moaning Lisa through the door and disappeared.

Gordon Harper watched them go before turning to me. "You, my dear, should take a seat."

With a gallant gesture, Harper indicated the chair he had just vacated. I walked over to it and plopped myself down. Maria stood sentry nearby, the gun steady and pointed at my chest.

Harper walked over to where I was sitting. With one quick movement, he ripped the tape from my mouth. My lips thanked me for having the good sense to pull them in before the tape was placed. I breathed through my mouth several times before I ran my tongue around my lips and rubbed them together.

"Well, Odelia," Harper began. He pulled a chair close to me and sat down. "You're quite a busy bee, aren't you?"

I just looked at him, keeping my mouth shut as if it were still taped.

"Did you ever find out who the Blond Bomber is?"

"You mean it's not you?" I looked him directly in the eye. "I know you killed Laurie Luke."

I was ninety-nine percent sure Gordon Harper wasn't the serial killer, but maybe he knew who was and my question would prod him into telling me.

He raised an eyebrow in my direction, then it dropped, and suddenly he looked sad. "Beautiful woman, the Luke girl. She looked so much like my Crystal. Her death was actually an accident."

"An accident? I thought you grabbed her as an incentive for Kirk Thomas—to make him do what you needed."

In a flash, the sadness was gone, replaced by amusement. "That I did, though I'm surprised and very impressed that you know that much. It's also a pity you do." He paused and looked me over. "Because I like you. You and your husband seem like nice people. Too bad you couldn't keep your nose out of my business." He squeaked out a chuckle. "It's also too bad you won't be wearing that costume you ordered."

"You going to palm off my death on the Blond Bomber, like you did Laurie's? I'm hardly his type."

"Ah-ha." Harper's face lit up with interest. "So you *do* know that I'm not the serial killer."

I nodded. "I'm pretty sure that's one thing you're not. You might be a killer and a crook, but you're not the Blond Bomber."

"And did you find out who is?" When I said nothing, he leaned forward in his chair. "Telling me his identity will buy you your freedom."

"You'll let me go if I tell you?"

"Yes, I will—providing, of course, you also fulfill other requirements."

I didn't like the sound of his addendum. I looked over at Maria Santiago but her face was a blank, her eyes trained on my face, the gun on my chest.

I gave Gordon Harper a tight smile. "Like any contract, yours comes with small print." It was a statement, not a question.

He laughed his squeaky laugh. On any other man, it would have come out as a hearty bark.

"This *is* a business transaction, Odelia. You have something I need. Two somethings, actually. And I have something *you* need: your life."

"So how much is my life going to cost me?"

Harper leaned back in his chair and studied me before answering. "The name of the Blond Bomber and the cat."

"Sure you don't mean the Blond Bomber and the cat's *collar*? Or more to the point, the Blond Bomber and the diamonds?"

Harper gave me a broad smile. "That's exactly the price of your life right now. Can you pay it? Think quick before the price goes up."

Right—like this gangster would let me go, knowing what I know about him and his dealings. I didn't trust him to make good on his end of the bargain. I had to stall.

"The Blond Bomber and the diamonds for my life and Lisa's."

Harper laughed again. He turned to Maria. "Her life is in the balance and she's negotiating for a package deal. Now that's *chutzpah*." He turned back to me. "Or stupidity."

I twitched my nose. I might be behaving in a stupid manner, but I was running out of options.

"I understand about the diamonds, but why do you want to know who the Blond Bomber is?"

Gordon Harper rose from his chair and paced across the carpet. He finally stopped, coming to rest behind the chair he had vacated. He gripped the back of the chair, his face flushed and splotchy.

"Because when I find the bastard who took Crystal from me, I'm going to draw and quarter him and tie *him* to a tree in Laguna Canyon."

"Personally, I don't think that's such a bad idea."

He gave me a tight-lipped conspiratorial grin.

"But what makes you think I know who the killer is?"

Still smiling, Harper gently shook a meaty finger in my direction. "Because I've been keeping my eye on you. You've been nosing around, talking to people. If you don't know who the bastard is, you have an idea."

"Actually, I'm clueless." I hoped my honesty didn't get me killed on the spot, but I was fresh out of bluffs. "All my suspicions have met dead ends. One thing, though—I know who it's not."

Harper's smile vanished. "Don't screw with me, Odelia."

"I'm not, Gordon. Whoever the Blond Bomber is, he's connected somehow to Jane Sharp, the decorator. That's all I know."

"Jane Sharp?"

I nodded. "Yes, all of the victims looked like her and all of them were connected with her in some fashion, mostly through jobs she'd done."

He stared at me in disbelief.

"Did you see the news about the last victim, Madeline Sparks?"

He nodded. I continued.

"Madeline had short red hair. Jane recently cut her hair and dyed it red. Whoever the killer is, he's ultimately after Jane. The sicko's toying with her and enjoying it."

Harper didn't say anything. He just stood glued to the carpet while he processed the information I just spilled. I twisted my hands slightly, trying to loosen my bonds.

"I need to pee," I announced.

Maria just stood there, shifting her weight from one foot to the other. The gun must have been getting heavy in her outstretched hand because she was using her other hand now to balance it. Her eyes shifted from me to Harper and back to me.

"Gordon." I tried to get him to refocus on me. "I said, I need to go to the bathroom."

He came out of his thoughts and looked at me. Without saying a word, he retrieved a small knife from the kitchen and cut the tape around my wrists. It felt good to have two hands again. I rubbed my wrists and flexed them.

"The bathroom is down the hall." He turned to Maria. "Go with her."

Maria came with me every step of the way. The bathroom was down a hallway on the left. Across from the bathroom was an open door, and through it I could see a king-size bed, dresser, and chair. The room was decorated as simply as the living room. It looked like the master bedroom. Glancing in, I saw it was empty. At the end of the hall was a closed door. I guessed it to be another bedroom and probably where the goon had taken Lisa.

The bathroom was large but seemed like a cell when Maria pushed her way in behind me.

I turned to her. "Is this really necessary?"

In response, she narrowed her eyes at me. Sheesh, I don't even pee in front of Greg, and I'm supposed to do my business in front of a stranger?

Although I did need to use the bathroom, I was also hoping it would buy me time to think and devise a plan. I had to get to Lisa and find a way out. Maria had used an elevator key to get to this floor, but usually elevators only need the key to open the doors to a particular floor, not to leave one. At the office, our security cards will open the elevator on the floors occupied by Woobie after hours, but we don't need the card to leave. I was hoping it was the same in this case.

As discreetly as possible, I undid the front of my pants and got down to emptying my bladder, dawdling as best I could and avoiding eye contact with my guard. The Santiago woman didn't seem like the type who could be swayed to chat about her boss, but it was worth a try. I turned my head to look at her and the gun.

"So, you come here often?" I kept my voice low so as not to carry the sound through the door.

"Hurry up," she ordered, not keeping her voice down.

"Why? So I can get to the business of dying sooner?"

She remained silent.

I finished up and moved to the sink to wash my hands, again taking my time. My eyes discreetly scanned the room, looking for something of use but found nothing. I would have liked to have rummaged through the vanity drawers and the medicine cabinet. Maybe there were scissors or even a container of hairspray I could use as a weapon, but I didn't think Maria would give me the opportunity to hunt. As I dried my hands, I spotted a container of hand cream with a pump. I reached for it.

"Don't be foolish," Maria cautioned.

I looked in the mirror over the sink. She was standing behind me. I studied her face. She studied mine.

"Relax, Maria. I'm just getting some hand lotion. One pump of the bottle, that's it. Wouldn't want the coroner to see me with rough, dry skin."

Putting one hand under the spout, I gave it a pump with the other hand. I massaged the lotion into my hands and over my chafed wrists. Except for relieving myself, the trip to the potty seemed a bust. Then I felt Maria step closer behind me.

"Don't do anything stupid and you might live." Her whisper was warm as it gently hit my ear from behind.

I studied her again in the mirror. Her eyes locked onto mine as she whispered more. "If there's any trouble, stick by me."

"Why would you help me?" My own words were barely more than a light breath.

"Just trust me."

THIRTY-FOUR

IN SPITE OF MARIA Santiago's words, I didn't leave the bathroom any more assured than when I entered it. Maria was offering me protection, but how and why? And what about Lisa? If Maria had a plan, how would I know when it kicked into action?

Back in the living room, we found Gordon talking with his hired gun.

"Where's Lisa?" I asked.

Gordon turned and smiled at me. The goon glowered.

"She's fine, Odelia, don't worry. Charles here says she's resting."

"She might have a concussion."

"Don't worry about the girl. We gave her something to relax her."

"The same drug you gave her sister?" As soon as I said the words, I wanted them back. I was letting them know how much I knew.

Gordon looked momentarily surprised, then his face relaxed. "Oh, that's right. You're good friends with a cop in Newport Beach. Did he give you a rundown on Laurie Luke's autopsy?"

Now it was my turn to show surprise. Charles grinned. Maria remained as stone-faced as ever. Harper shook his head and pursed his lips in a condescending manner. I wanted to slap him.

"Don't be so surprised, dear lady. I told you that I've been watching you."

The reality of that comment ran through me like cold water through copper tubing. Dev had been concerned about that, and he'd been right. It also meant Gordon Harper probably knew where we lived.

"Then why all the drama? Why didn't you just come get the cat, preferably when no one was home?"

"Honestly, I didn't know you had the diamonds until today." Gordon flashed me one of his grins. "I was following you, hoping you'd lead me to the Blond Bomber. When the Luke woman's sister reappeared, she told us you had them—at least you have the ones stolen from me."

"From one of the prior jobs Kirk did for you, correct?" I slapped a hand over my mouth. I just couldn't seem to help myself.

"I'm more impressed with you by the minute, my dear."

"I'm honored."

"And you do make me chuckle. Too bad we won't have time for you to model an outfit for me." His eyes dropped down, visiting my chest before returning to my face.

"I won't lie to you, Gordon. I do have the cat's collar, though until today I had no idea what was hidden in it. But I really don't know who the Blond Bomber is. Does that mean your offer of letting me go is off the table?"

"You willing to give me the collar?"

"In a flash. The only diamond I want is already on my hand." I held up my left hand and wiggled the finger with my wedding and engagement rings.

Harper motioned for me to take my seat, which I did. He paced a few steps, then came to rest on the sofa positioned a few feet from me under the large windows. When Harper ordered Maria into the kitchen to make coffee for us, Charles the thug pulled a sizeable gun from a shoulder holster and took over the cover job. They seemed to be waiting for something.

I didn't move a muscle, at least for a few seconds. I still had questions and wanted answers, and my nervous tendency to babble got the best of me.

"Do you know where Jane Sharp is?" I asked Harper.

Harper hesitated, looking me over before answering. "No, why should I?"

I shrugged. "Well, this morning she disappeared. I figure she's either running from the Blond Bomber or running from you."

"Why me?"

"My guess is she's the one who hooked you and Kirk Thomas up. She knew both of you. Slept with both of you."

"Is your theory just a guess?"

I was playing with fire and had to choose my words carefully or get burned beyond recognition. "Call it the result of connecting the dots."

Again, he shook an amused finger at me. "You're good."

He leaned forward and retrieved something from a wooden box on the coffee table. It was a cigar. He went through the ritual of lighting it up, using a lighter he pulled from his pocket.

"I hope you don't mind cigars, Odelia, but I find they relax me." He replaced the lighter while he took a few initiating puffs.

I wrinkled my nose. "It's your place, not mine. Or should I say, Crystal Lee's place?"

He looked around the fresh, pleasant room. "Yes, this was Crystal Lee's home. So different from the offices downstairs, huh?" He smiled to himself. "I offered to buy her something much nicer, but she loved being above the shop. I've kept it exactly as she did. Being here is also relaxing for me."

"You never answered my question, Gordon."

He took a puff on the cigar and looked at me, waiting. I repeated my earlier question.

"Do you know where Jane Sharp is?"

"Not at this moment, but I know where I want her to be."

I raised my eyebrows in encouragement for him to continue.

"Dead is where I'd like her to be."

He took another puff. The pungent smoke of the cigar teased my nose.

"You were right, Odelia. Jane Sharp is the connection between me and Kirk Thomas. She's been helping me out here and there with some of my more, let's say, *exotic* endeavors, ever since we met. When she met Kirk Thomas, she knew he might be right for the African job. He took some convincing but enough money turned his righteous head."

Speaking of heads, Gordon turned his towards the kitchen. "Maria, where's the damn coffee?"

"In a minute," came the reply from the other room.

With a flourish of impatience, Gordon took another puff from his cigar.

"Are we waiting on something or someone?" I asked, once I had his attention again.

"Why? You in a rush to die?"

Yikes!

"Not really." My response came out calmly, in direct contrast to what I was feeling inside.

I thought about Silas and hoped that somehow he'd made contact with someone by now, preferably the police, and repeated to them what I'd said at the car. The precocious kid might be my only chance of survival.

"As a matter of fact, Odelia, we're waiting for the cat."

"Muffin?"

"If that's the animal's name, then yes. At least we're waiting for its collar."

"But I thought you weren't going to break into the vet's office."

Gordon Harper eyed me again with amusement. If this kept up, I was going to ask for a contract for three shows a week.

"We're not." He stretched one thick arm out across the back of the sofa and adjusted his bulk. "You see, I don't believe for a minute that the animal's there. And even if it is, I doubt it's still wearing the collar. The vet would have taken off the collar to care for its wounds." He paused to wink at me. "I've had lots of pets over the years. I know the drill."

Maria Santiago came in with a tray. On it were two colorful mugs, along with a coffee carafe and sugar and creamer made from porcelain.

Maria poured two cups of coffee. She picked up the creamer and looked at me.

"I take mine black, thanks," I told her.

She handed me a mug and went on to pour cream and add one sugar to the other mug, which she handed to her boss.

"How civil," I quipped. "You always serve coffee to people before you whack them?"

Gordon Harper surveyed me over the rim of his mug. "Only the ones I like."

It crossed my mind to throw the hot coffee at him, but it wouldn't do any real damage and would get me shot in the bargain. Instead, I took a sip. It was rich and comforting and made me wish I had a few cookies to go with it. If I was going to die soon, it didn't seem right to do it on an empty stomach. The coffee also seemed to clear my head momentarily.

"Since we're waiting for the collar to arrive, I guess you already know where we live."

Gordon nodded.

"Then you know we have a dog—a mean attack dog."

He put his coffee down on the table and took a puff of his cigar. "What you have is a charming golden retriever who plays Frisbee with the neighborhood kids and who goes to work every day with your husband."

"You've been watching us that closely?" My stomach did a somersault.

"I've had you tailed ever since we met. But if I'd known you had the Luke woman's cat and the cat had the diamonds, I might have done more than just observe."

He shook his head in what appeared to be disgust. "I can't believe that imbecile hid those diamonds in a cat's collar." He said it more to himself than to any of us. "Who in their right mind hides valuables with something that can run away?"

I was still waiting to hear the logic behind that myself.

"So who's ransacking my home while I sit here and sip coffee?"

"None other than the imbecile himself."

Great. Kirk Thomas might be a very talented wildlife photographer, but he was hardly a genius when it came to criminal activities. I didn't even want to think about what my house would look like when I got home.

If I got home.

"Why don't I save you some trouble and tell you where the collar is? That way Kirk won't have to destroy our home."

"Very sensible of you." Harper tossed a look at Charles. "Get Thomas on the phone." Then he turned back to me, awaiting further instructions.

"Tell Kirk it's in the master bedroom, in a nightstand drawer. My nightstand, the one on the right. The collar was bothering the cat, so we took it off her."

Harper looked back to Charles, who still had the phone to his ear. After a few moments, he ended the call.

"I got voice mail," he reported.

"Try again," Harper ordered, impatience coloring his voice like a thick Crayola.

Charles dialed again. After what seemed like an eternity, he closed the phone. "Voice mail again."

"Call Jane."

That caught my attention. "But I thought you didn't know where Jane was?"

Harper put his cigar in the ashtray and hoisted his thick body up from the sofa. "I don't." Then to Charles, "Wait, don't call from your phone."

Gordon came to stand over me. "Why don't you call her, Odelia? She might respond to a friendly call from you."

"My phone and purse were left behind when these two grabbed me."

Harper rolled his eyes. He looked at Charles, then walked over to Maria. "Why didn't you two just send up flares announcing the abduction?"

"You told us to hurry," Maria started to explain. "We didn't think—"

Faster than a cartoon roadrunner, Gordon Harper swung out his right arm and slapped Maria Santiago backhanded, sending her backwards against the door next to the elevator. I jumped in my chair.

Harper glowered at her as she rubbed her cheek.

"That's the problem: you don't think." He shot a scowl at Charles. "Neither of you."

If this was any evidence of how Harper treated Maria in general, no wonder she was up to something. It also made me wonder how she could protect me if she couldn't protect herself.

Harper walked back to the coffee table, picked up his cigar, and took several quick puffs. His back was to us as he gazed out the window. He'd just belted one of his underlings, then had the guts to turn his back on her. I wondered if he'd be just as confident if Charles wasn't nearby.

I glanced back at Maria. She was still crouched against the door, but I could have sworn I saw her fiddling with the door knob. Maybe she was going to make a run for it—get away from Harper before he really got down to beating her.

Shortly, he turned around and barked a command at Maria. "Get Crystal Lee's phone. Maybe the bitch will pick up if she doesn't recognize the number."

Maria left the door and retrieved a cordless phone from the kitchen. Using the display on Charles's cell as a directory, she dialed Jane's number on the cordless and listened.

"No answer, Gordon," she reported. "Just kicks into voice mail."

"Damn it!"

Coming from him, the expletive lost some of its intended juice, sounding more like a Munchkin who'd tripped on the Yellow Brick Road than a crime boss ready to blow a fuse. Gordon's entire head flushed in agitation. He turned and looked back out the window.

"If those two grabbed the shit and took off, I will hunt them down personally." He spun back around and gave me a hard look. The amusement of earlier was gone. "Right after I have some fun with you and the other broad."

Fighting back tears, I willed myself to think straight. He couldn't kill me; I'd just found love and happiness. And my father needed me. And what about Zee? Who'd aggravate her to distraction? I didn't even care how much time I owed Steele, as long as I could be around to fulfill our bargain.

"Give me the damn phone," Harper barked. At the same time, both Charles and Maria held out the phones in their hands. Harper snatched the cell.

"Paul's number on this damn thing?" he asked Charles.

Paul? He couldn't mean Paul Milholland, could he? But then, why not? If Jane was involved with the smuggling, maybe Paul was, too. Given Gordon's mood, I didn't think I should ask *Paul who?*

"Yeah, boss. Just scroll down."

This call didn't go into voice mail.

"It's me," Harper snapped into the phone. "I need you to do something." He listened. His face flushed again. "I don't give a flying fuck if you're busy. Go by the Stevens' place. See if Kirk's there. If he is, put him on the phone to me pronto." A pause. "Give me a call either way. Got it?"

I stole a glance at my watch. The movement caught Harper's attention.

"What? You got a bus to catch?"

"Just a nervous gesture, that's all."

Although it felt like it'd been hours and hours since we'd left Newport Beach, it had only been just over two hours. I wondered if Dev had gotten my voice mail yet and whether or not he and the police had gone to Lisa's place. They'd find my abandoned car and tote bag, unless they'd been stolen. They might even find a kid babbling about guns and missing cats. I hoped Silas was okay. If I ever got out of here, he was going to get a stern lecture about sneaking into people's cars.

I peeked at my watch again, this time breathing a sigh of relief. It was too early for Greg to be home. At this point, I didn't care if the creeps ransacked my house, as long as no one got hurt in the process. I thought about the two cats. I didn't know what Muffin would do, but Seamus would go into hiding as soon as he smelled a stranger. I hoped the younger cat would take her cue from him.

Harper ordered Maria to pour coffee all around and then check on Lisa. She returned to report that Lisa was sleeping. Harper's face and skull returned to its normal pale.

Time dripped by, ticking in beat with the painful pulse growing inside my skull. We sat in Crystal Lee's living room sipping coffee as companionably as old friends awaiting the arrival of good news.

Charles sneezed. Two of us said *bless you*.

THIRTY-FIVE

THE CALL CAME AFTER the coffee was gone and my captors had each taken turns strolling down the hall. I'd even asked permission to tinkle and again Maria Santiago was sent to keep watch. And yet again I had to perform at gunpoint.

This time, she'd remained silent. Even when I asked about her face and if she was okay, she merely stared at me with dead eyes, as if she couldn't hear a word I said. On this trip to the potty there were no promises to help me live. It was almost enough to make my bladder seize.

Gordon Harper had placed the cell phone on the coffee table. When the call came in, it didn't ring but instead vibrated, sending the same hum of dread through my body as a dental drill. Had Kirk been found? Was Jane with him? Had the diamonds disappeared? Were my home and pets intact? Inquiring and terrified minds wanted to know.

Harper picked up the phone and studied the display before answering. "Yeah."

He listened for quite a while, saying nothing. But again his face and bald head turned scarlet.

"Are you shitting me?" he yelled into the phone. He listened some more, then said, "Any sign of Jane Sharp?" More listening. "Okay. Get the hell out of there. Just go about your business. I'll be in touch, but I'm not sure when."

After he hung up, Gordon tossed the cell on the table and paced. I'm sure I wasn't the only one in the room curious about what had happened to Kirk. Finally, Charles broke the silence.

"What's up, chief?"

In reply, Gordon Harper grabbed the coffee tray, mugs and all, and flung it against the wall. The pieces hit, breaking into a cacophony of crashing, jagged porcelain. I ducked my head and covered it with my arms as soon as the tray went airborne.

I didn't know what was going on, but it couldn't be good. For any of us.

"That stupid piece of shit got himself arrested for breaking and entering." Harper glared at me. "Seems some old local bum takes his neighborhood watch seriously and called the police."

My mind did an internal scan of the names and faces of our neighbors, and none fit the description of *bum*. Then I thought about Pops. Our house was just a few blocks from the beach, his usual haunt. I didn't think he knew which house was ours, but maybe he did. Or maybe he was strolling the nearby area and simply saw Kirk and reported it. It wouldn't have been difficult. The police station was almost spitting distance to everything. Although we weren't sure where Pops spent his nights, everyone in the area knew he was pretty territorial about Seal Beach and its inhabitants. He knew who belonged and who didn't.

"Was the Sharp woman with him?" It was Maria, daring to ask for further information.

Harper shook his egg-shaped head. "No. Paul just saw Kirk being led away in cuffs and asked some of the locals what was going on."

I just had to confirm the suspicion nagging at me like a hang nail. "So Paul Milholland works for you, too, huh?"

Harper stood in front of me, hands on his chunky hips, his barrel chest less than a foot away. He looked to be studying me but his eyes were active, displaying the plotting and planning going on behind them.

"Who in the hell do you think was tailing you?"

It took a moment before clarity sunk in. When it did, I wanted to slap myself upside the head. The van. Those mornings at the bakery. Pops wasn't babbling about Greg's van, he was trying to warn me that a van was following me. A van that didn't belong.

"What now, boss?" asked Charles.

"We need to get the hell out of here," Gordon announced. "Pronto. The fool's probably spilling his guts right now."

Charles jerked his chin in my direction. "What about her and the other one? Do them here or someplace else?"

"Why kill them at all?" Maria interjected.

The men looked at her as if she'd lost her mind.

She shrugged. "They don't know where we're going or any real details. Anything this one knows," she indicated me, "Kirk Thomas knows more, and he's the one who's going to talk."

Sounded like a reasonable argument to me.

Charles looked disappointed. Gordon scowled. He went to a nearby desk, opened a drawer, and pulled out a good-sized handgun.

This was it. Since I wasn't being offered a blindfold, I scrunched my eyes closed.

"Leave the other broad," Gordon ordered. He reached down and grabbed me roughly by the arm, yanking me to my feet. "This one's coming with me for insurance."

I didn't relish the idea of another road trip, especially with this bunch, but at least it meant I could live a bit longer.

We were about to pile into the service elevator when a loud noise came from outside, from above. It grew louder by the second. Charles stepped quickly to the window and looked out. Immediately, he scooted to the side of the window, with his back to the wall.

"It's a chopper. Cops. Right overhead."

"Can't be," Gordon shouted. "They've barely had time to get Thomas to the station."

Gordon Harper moved to the window and looked up, then down, before he also moved away from the window. "The place is crawling with cops."

"Grab the other broad," he yelled to Charles, "and bring her in here. We have hostages. The cops won't do anything stupid. If we have to, we'll use the two of them as shields to get out of here."

I felt like I was center stage in a rerun episode of *S.W.A.T.*

As Charles took off down the hall to get Lisa, the cell phone on the table vibrated. My heart about stopped. Gordon picked it up and looked at the display. His puzzled look made me think he didn't know who was on the other end. He handed the phone to Maria.

"You answer it," he ordered.

Maria took the phone and said a tentative hello. She listened, then said to Harper, "It's the police. Downstairs."

After a short pause, he took the phone from her. "What?" he shouted into it.

He listened briefly before shouting again into the phone. "They're alive now, but they won't be for long unless you clear out!" He snapped the phone shut.

Charles came back half-dragging a groggy Lisa Luke. He tossed her on the sofa. Lisa stirred and moaned.

"She's too out of it to drag around," he announced.

The phone vibrated again. Gordon looked at Charles, then Maria. "It's not just LAPD downstairs, it's the feds."

"How'd they get this number?" Charles asked.

"Who gives a shit!" Gordon yelled at him. "They got it."

He picked up the phone. "Yeah?" A short pause. "No, *you* listen to *me*. I'm getting out of here, and you're letting me. Otherwise both of these women will be shot and dumped out the window. You want that?" He listened some more. "That's more like it. I'm coming down. I'll have the Stevens woman with me. When I get downstairs, I'm getting into my car and driving away. It's that simple. Otherwise, she gets a bullet to the brain. Got it?" He hung up.

Bullet to the brain. I felt as green as Kermit the Frog.

Gordon Harper stuck the phone into his shirt pocket. We piled into the service elevator and started the trip to the ground floor, leaving Lisa behind. Gordon kept me directly in front of him and had a steel grip on my arm. The others were posted on either side of us. When the doors of the elevator opened, the hair on the back of my neck stood up. The place looked the same but my personal radar was picking up on something, almost like the air in the place

291

was charged. Gordon must have felt it, too, because behind me he stiffened and tightened his grip. Yet ahead of us, everything looked the same as when I'd arrived earlier.

We moved quickly in a single file through the maze of sewing machines, fabric presses, and rolls of material towards the small door next to the large delivery door. Charles led the way, his gun poised and ready. I followed with Gordon close behind me, still attached to my arm with a death grip. Behind him was Maria Santiago.

Gordon gave final instructions. They were to take the SUV. We'd go in the Mercedes. He said they'd rendezvous in the usual place. I didn't know if the final rendezvous plans included me or not.

At the door, Charles unlocked it and pulled it open.

That's when things changed.

Instead of pushing me forward behind Charles, Gordon yanked me to the side and gave Charles a shove from behind with a foot to his backside. He stumbled out the door alone. Gordon then slammed the door shut and locked it, leaving Charles virtually naked in front of the armed police squad.

I pictured Charles with his hands up, surrendering, but knew that wasn't the case when we heard gunshots, many of them. They hit the other side of the door and wall where we were standing fast and furious, like raindrops on steroids. The three of us instinctively took a dive to the floor.

When the shooting stopped, I felt myself being tugged and pulled. It was Maria Santiago. Without a word, she gestured for me to stay down and crawl away from the door, in the direction of the front office. I didn't know whether I should do it or not, but I sure didn't want to stay where I was. I thought about sneaking off towards the stairs and going back to the apartment. Thoughts of barricading myself in the back bedroom with Lisa until everything was over entered my brain. But Lisa was now passed out on the couch, and by the time I moved her to safety, Gordon would have gunned us both down.

I felt Maria push me from behind. She was on her feet and had her gun still drawn, but it was not aimed at me. It was aimed at Gordon Harper, who was just now getting to his feet and hadn't noticed it yet.

That was enough to get me moving. As Maria had directed, I started crawling off on my hands and knees, trying to get behind a nearby machine for cover as fast as I could.

"Federal agent," I heard her say.

I poked my head up just enough to see what was going on. Maria had moved behind some large boxes, her gun still trained on Gordon Harper. "It's over, Harper."

Maria Santiago was a fed? An undercover federal agent?

Gordon Harper was standing up now, leaning against the wall near a panel of switches.

"You're shitting me. You?" The disbelief in his voice was thick and mocking. "I was sure the snitch was Charles."

"Drop the gun and put your hands on your head." Maria's voice was even and controlled.

At this point, I expected Gordon to yell *you'll never take me alive, copper,* and start shooting. Instead, he started to raise his hands above his head, one still holding the gun.

"Drop the gun," Maria ordered again.

Instead, with the same speed as the earlier backhand to her face, Gordon simultaneously hit several switches on the panel, plunging the factory into darkness save for a few low-level security lights scattered throughout the place. The security lights were about as effective as the nightlight in our bathroom.

At the same time, Gordon fired his gun towards Maria. The gunshot flashed in the darkened space. She fired back. I shrunk in fright so intense I thought my hair would fall out. From Gordon's direction came more shots, this time scattered. One of the bullets hit a box next to the machine I was behind, and I nearly fainted.

I'd been shot at before, but it's something you never quite get used to.

Shouts from outside could be heard when the shots died down.

I didn't know how many shots had been fired, or if any in the short barrage had come from Maria. But even if I had counted the bullets, I had no idea what type of weapons were being used. To my gun-ignorant mind, Gordon could have none, two, or one hundred bullets left.

I peeked out to see if I could make out a silhouette of Harper against the wall, but I saw none. I heard slow movement among the aisles but had no idea if it was Gordon Harper or Maria Santiago. I wasn't about to open my mouth to find out.

Then I heard Gordon talking. "I don't care if he's dead. I still have the Stevens woman and that skank agent." He must have been talking into the cell phone to the people outside.

I didn't think the police would bust into the place as long as they thought Gordon had hostages. If they couldn't get to me, I had to get to them, or at least to Maria. But if Maria was still near Harper and the door, there was no way I was going in that direction.

I tried to get my bearings. From the door, I knew the elevator and stairs leading to the next floor were back to my left. Based on that, I determined that the office and fitting areas of Seventh Veil would be behind me to my right. I turned on my hands and knees and headed that way, shuffling quietly along the floor as fast as the low visibility would allow, hoping the noise outside would hide any sounds I made.

The other two both knew the layout better than I did. But Maria was focused on nailing Harper, and Harper was determined to save his neck. I hoped the two of them forgot about little ol' me until I was safely out of range.

With reduced vision, I continued my tedious way on my hands and knees, not daring to raise my head. I moved slowly in and among boxes and various garment-making equipment, often meeting dead ends and having to awkwardly turn around in the narrow spaces. The building wasn't huge, but it wasn't small either, and neither was I. From this position, in the semi-dark, with the outside noise and two guns behind me, I felt like I was crawling to Palm Springs by way of hell.

After reaching another spot that caused me to change directions, I had an idea. I groped around for something small and solid, but found nothing on the floor. I raised my hand to the surface above me, which seemed to be a small worktable, and found a heavy bottle of some kind. It felt sticky. I curled my fingers around it and brought it down to me. My nose confirmed it was glue or some type of adhesive.

Taking a deep breath, I straightened on my knees and hurled the container as far as I could in the opposite direction. It hit something with a loud bang. Although I expected knee-jerk gunfire from Gordon, all that followed was some shuffling, and again, I couldn't tell if it was from Maria or Gordon.

I didn't know if I was getting closer to the office area or still weaving my way through the guts of the place, and I was too scared to raise my head to find out. In the semi-darkness and confusion of the maze of aisles, it was possible that I'd gotten totally turned around and was heading back towards where I'd started, which wouldn't be good at all.

Instead of moving farther, I tucked myself up under the small worktable, deciding to stay put for a bit. Until I knew for sure I was heading to safety and not doom, I didn't want to proceed. There were two small boxes nearby. I pulled them in front of me as camouflage in case Harper went by on his own way out.

Except for the noise outside, which was considerable, it was deathly quiet, making me wonder if Maria had been hit in the gun battle. I strained my ears to block out the noise beyond the doors and listened for sounds of the other two.

Nothing.

THIRTY-SIX

I smelled it before I saw it.

Then I saw the glow of light. Small at first, but growing. Flickering against the walls and contents of the warehouse, the fire lit the darkened area.

Moving aside the boxes, I crawled from under the protective table. Even without raising my head, I could tell the fire started near the back wall between where I was squatted and the elevator. It spread rapidly, fed by fabric, glue, and other materials used to construct the elaborate costumes.

And it brought light. There was enough light now for me to peek out and see that I was nowhere near the office area, but had, as I feared, been backtracking or even circling.

Turning my head, I saw movement. It was Maria, crouched low, doing surveillance. I saw her head turn and stop, frozen, as she spotted her prey. Several yards away from her, I could see Gordon Harper's bald pate as he moved, half upright, away from the fire.

He was moving towards the bulk of the security light, in the direction of the office area.

The smoke was starting to sting my eyes and nose, and the flames were growing. With all the fabric and packing material inside the warehouse, it wouldn't take long for the place to become an inferno.

I took a second to consider my options. If Gordon was going towards the office, there was no way I was heading in that direction. But if he was moving that way, then the door next to the loading dock would be uncovered.

I looked again for Maria. This time, she spotted me, and with a jerk of her head confirmed that I should head for the door. She took off through the maze after Harper.

The smoke from the fire was getting thicker, and the air in the close space was growing hot. Half bent over, I started to run for what I hoped would be safety but only succeeded in tripping over something in the aisle. I went sprawling, ricocheting off a heavy sewing machine before landing, one knee first, on the concrete floor. Pain shot through my knee but went ignored as a gunshot rang out and struck something near me.

As I stayed crouched, Lisa, upstairs and unconscious, came to mind. I knew there were police outside but had no idea how many. And by the time I reached them, would there be enough time for someone to get Lisa out? Cautiously, I poked my head up. As I expected, the fire was spreading fast. I estimated that if I kept down, I might be able to make it to the stairs. The elevator was out. It needed a key to open on the top floor, and often elevators shut down during a fire. And probably the door at the top of the stairs was locked.

The door to safety and resuming my wonderful life with Greg was ahead of me. The fire was behind me. Gordon Harper was somewhere to my right, and Lisa was to my left and up the stairs, the farthest away.

Eeny, meeny, miny, moe.

But as much as I wanted to bolt for the outside door, I knew I couldn't make my run for safety without at least trying to help Lisa.

I poked my head back up and saw no one. Maria had vacated her last spot. The smoke was making it difficult to see and breathe, and the fire only lit part of the warehouse. I pulled the neck of my sweater up over my nose and mouth. After taking note again of where the staircase was in relation to the fire, I headed in that direction. I stayed down as best I could, using the light from the fire to make my way and hoping the smoke would cover me.

As soon as I hit the stairs, the overhead sprinklers kicked in. Soon there would be even more smoke.

I ran up the stairs as fast as my chunky legs would carry me. At the top was the door I'd seen next to the elevator upstairs—the one Maria had been fiddling with. I tried it; it was unlocked.

I dashed inside but Lisa was not on the sofa where she'd been left. Going down the hall, I found her slumped in the bathroom. I tried to get her to her feet, but she was too heavy. I dragged her into the stall shower and turned on the cold water. Aiming the shower nozzle, I hit her smack on the face with it. It roused her. Her eyes blinked several times but kept closing. I left her in the shower with the water on her and headed back into the hallway.

The smoke wasn't as bad upstairs, but I knew it soon would be. I closed the door to the stairwell to help stem the smoke's progress.

The fire was big enough and spreading so fast that I doubted the sprinklers alone would put it out. And there was a lot of flammable material downstairs—enough to feed a family of four fires.

Unlike the warehouse, the apartment had windows. Going into the back bedroom first, I opened the sliding window. I pushed hard against the screen and kept pushing until I succeeded in pushing it out.

I yanked my sweater away from my mouth and gulped in the air. I coughed several times. Even the outside air was full of smoke.

"Help!" I yelled out the window. "Help! We're up here."

I grabbed a pillow off the bed and ripped the case off it. Returning back to the window, I stuck it out the window and waved and yelled. I could hear the sound of the crackling blaze.

Next, I dashed into the master bedroom and did the same. But its window didn't overlook the large delivery area where the police were gathered.

Before going into the living room, I checked on Lisa. She was coming around, but slowly.

"Come on, Lisa. Wake up!" I shouted. I shook her and slapped her cheeks lightly. "We gotta get out of here!"

She moaned, but this time when her eyelids flickered, they stayed open. I looked directly into her glazed eyes and willed her to focus.

"Can you get up?"

She nodded, then slumped in the shower. She tried to get up again. While she did that, I went into the living room and opened the windows. Again, I shouted and waved my makeshift flag to the crowd below.

"Help! Up here! Help!"

Then I spotted the cordless phone. Maria must have dropped it on the coffee table after Gordon didn't choose it. At this minute, there was only one number I wanted to call. I punched furiously at the dial pad. It was picked up on the first ring. I didn't even wait for him to say hello.

"Greg! It's me!"

"Odelia! I'm at Seventh Veil. Where the hell are you?"

"In the apartment on the second floor. There's a fire on the ground floor."

"We know." Then I heard Greg shout to someone. "It's my wife! She's on the second floor!

"Is anyone with you, Odelia?" he asked, coming back to me.

"Just Lisa, but she's drugged and can't walk." I coughed before continuing. "Harper's still on the ground floor and so is a federal agent. They both have guns."

"Stay where you are, we're sending help."

Suddenly, there was a commotion and someone else got on the line.

"Mrs. Stevens," said an unfamiliar male voice. "This is Federal Agent Mark Hardiman. Can you get out on your own?"

"Where's Greg?"

"Your husband's right here, Mrs. Stevens. Don't worry."

The smoke in the apartment was increasing by the second, in spite of the open windows. And I could still hear the flames.

"Put him back on the line," I demanded. "If I'm going to die, I want his voice to be the last one I hear, not yours."

"But—"

"Now!" I started crying.

There was more fumbling of the phone. The next voice I heard was Greg's.

"Sweetheart, stay calm. We're going to get you out of there. The agent wants to know if you can get out."

"I can. Lisa can't. She's too heavy for me to carry, but I can try to drag her down the stairs. She's been drugged," I repeated. "But she's starting to come around."

"Is Harper with you?"

"No, we're upstairs alone." Coughing stopped my next words.

After conferring with someone, Greg said. "Good. As long as you're not with Harper, they're going to try to go in and get you." More off-line conference talk. "Agent Hardiman said to try to get to the stairs with Lisa. Try to get as far down as you can. They will try to meet you and bring you out the rest of the way."

"Okay."

Gunshots rang out beneath the apartment. Lots of them. More than what would come from two guns low on bullets.

"Greg!"

There was commotion on the phone. "I'm right here, sweetheart." More off-line talk. "Odelia, don't start down the stairs. You hear me? Don't. The police have entered the building, and there's shooting. The firemen are going to try to rescue you from the window."

"Tell them to use the living room window. It's larger, and we can step up on the sofa."

I had to get Lisa from the shower to the living room. Hopefully, the cold water was still doing its trick.

"Greg, how bad is the fire?"

He didn't answer, but I could hear him breathing on the other end of the line.

"Greg?"

"It's bad, sweetheart." His voice sounded choked. "I'm not going to lie to you. It's very bad. But you're going to be okay. Remember that and do what these guys tell you to do. Okay?"

I walked into the bathroom. Lisa was sitting up. She was soaked, but her eyes were open and blinking. It was a start.

"Lisa's doing better," I said into the phone. "I'm going to get her to the living room window."

"Leave the phone on, Odelia. Don't break the connection."

I wouldn't dream of it.

Holding the phone with my left hand, I squatted down and put my right arm under Lisa's left armpit.

"Come on, Lisa. You have to help me out here."

She put her left arm around my shoulders and tried to get to her feet. It was slow going, but she managed to do it. Once on her feet, she had to stand still a minute to stabilize herself.

"That's it, Lisa. You're doing fine."

Grabbing the edge of the shower enclosure with her right hand, Lisa took a few shaky steps. Then a few more. Finally, she let go, and together we shuffled out of the bathroom.

We were almost to the living room when we heard breaking glass and metal. We stopped our progress and waited. Peeking around the corner into the living room, I saw that the firefighters had broken the window out to give us more room to crawl through.

"We're almost there, Lisa." I coaxed her along, step by shaky step.

By the time we'd reached the sofa, a strapping fireman had come through the window to help us. He started to reach for me, but I told him to take Lisa first. He guided her out the window and handed her over to another firefighter who helped her down the ladder to safety. I went back to the phone.

"Honey, the firemen are here, and Lisa's being taken out right now. I'll be right behind her." I sniffed back tears. "I love you, Greg."

"I love you, too, sweetheart."

THIRTY-SEVEN

LISA WAS PARTWAY DOWN the ladder when I heard heavy footsteps on the stairs. Thinking the police or more firemen had made their way through the gunfire and smoke, it didn't concern me until the door was flung open and we were face to face with Gordon Harper.

Gordon's clothing was dirty and torn. His left bicep was bleeding. His face and bald head were sooty, his eyes red and wild. From time to time, he coughed. In his right hand was a gun, but it was a different gun than he'd had earlier.

I raised my hands slightly, including the one with the phone.

"I thought we had a date, Odelia. Not standing me up, are you?"

"Okay, fella, take it easy," said the fireman.

Harper looked at him as if just noticing him for the first time. He smiled at the man standing in his bright yellow suit and shot him. No warning, no threat. Just shot him. The firefighter fell to the floor like an anvil.

I screamed.

From the phone, we could hear Greg shouting.

Gordon held out his hand for the phone. Reluctantly, I handed it to him, then stepped back.

"This is Gordon Harper," he wheezed into the phone. "Who's this?" After listening, Gordon smiled. "Hey, sport. Hope you don't mind if I borrow your wife, but she's my not-so-little ticket out of this mess."

There was a longer pause. Harper appeared to be listening. Finally, he spoke again. "Agent Hardiman, nice to talk to you again."

Harper sneered. From the wild look in his eye, it was clear to see his train had come off the track.

"As I told you before, Hardiman, I'm leaving here with Mrs. Stevens. Any attempts to stop me and she's dead. And this time there will be no playing games." He listened, then exploded. "No, *you* listen to *me*! I'm leaving here in my car. Odelia is driving that car."

At that moment, another fireman raised his head over the windowsill. Harper fired a shot at him but, thankfully, missed. The helmet dropped out of sight.

"You already have one dead fireman. You want more?" Harper shouted into the phone. "I'll pile up the bodies and put Odelia on top as the cherry. How's that?" A long pause. Harper smiled, his teeth very white in his grimy face. "That's what I thought. Good decision."

With the gun, Harper indicated for me to come to him. I hesitated but eventually took a small step forward. He was standing to the side of the staircase, the gun pointed at me from his extended hand.

"We're coming down, Hardiman. Get everyone back if you want to see this lady alive."

What happened next was a blur. A big golden blur.

Just as the gun was being waved at me again, Wainwright came charging up the stairs and launched himself at Gordon Harper, knocking him to the ground. The powerful jaw chomped down on the big man's gun arm without mercy. Both man and animal fell to the floor, wrestling for control. Wainwright's growls and Harper's cries of pain filled the room.

The gun didn't come loose, but the phone did. I grabbed it. "Harper's down," I screamed into the mouthpiece.

That's when I heard the shot and Wainwright's yelp.

My world stood still.

The big yellow dog lay sprawled on top of Gordon Harper. Harper struggled to get out from under the animal. Just as he pushed Wainwright's still body aside, I shook off my shock and horror and kicked into action. Literally.

Rushing to where both lay on the carpet, I starting kicking Gordon Harper in the head before he could get up. I kicked as hard as I could, both his head and face. Had he been a soccer ball, I would have scored the winning goal. His nose gushed blood. His hand let loose the gun. When he tried to protect his head, I assaulted his ribs.

Every kick came from my gut and meant something. I kicked for those who couldn't. I kicked for Greg. I kicked for Seamus. Even for Muffin. But most of all, I kicked for Wainwright.

Gordon Harper had just stolen the heart out of our family, and it was unforgivable.

THIRTY-EIGHT

SUMMER WAS AROUND THE corner. Soon the kids would be out of school and the tourists would flock to Seal Beach in droves. Already, traffic was bad along Pacific Coast Highway.

Temperatures were in the eighties today, with a slight breeze coming in off the ocean. A perfect day for a barbecue. It was the Saturday of Memorial Day weekend, and Casa de Stevens-Grey was alive with activity.

We had rounded up the usual suspects. Zee and Seth Washington, minus their nearly grown children. Jill Bernelli and Sally Kipman. Kelsey and Beau Cavendish. Dev Frye and Beverly. Even a few of Greg's basketball chums and their wives and girlfriends were here. Our house and patio were packed with good friends.

Greg manned the grill. Iced tea, beer, and margaritas flowed happily. The dining table groaned under the weight of all the food. I was in the kitchen putting the finishing touches on a couple of desserts.

While Seamus chose to stay in our bedroom, away from all the hullabaloo, Muffin was the belle of the ball. She hopped from lap to lap, purring and soaking in the adoration as if it were a catnip spa.

Muffin is officially ours now. When the dust settled, Lisa Luke admitted she didn't want her. And, of course, we were thrilled to keep the furry little scamp. Cleared of any allegations, Lisa moved to Dallas two weeks ago. The company she worked for has an office there and was more than happy to give her a transfer. With everything that had happened, she was eager to start fresh somewhere else, and I didn't blame her one bit. We had lunch the day before she left, and I assured her she could call on me or Zee any time she needed to talk.

Things didn't go as easy for Kirk Thomas or Jane Sharp. Both of them are facing federal charges for smuggling. It came out that Jane had been smuggling various items into the country for Gordon Harper for quite a while, hiding the goods in antiques and baubles she used in her decorating business. Shortly after Kirk was arrested, she was found safe but a nervous wreck at Kirk's family's cabin in Big Bear. She and Kirk were going to meet there after Lisa got the cat's collar. They were going to divvy up the diamonds and go their separate ways. Kirk told the police that while Lisa knew about the diamonds, it wasn't until later, after the smuggling, when he needed to get the collar back from us. The police came to the same conclusion.

Dr. Eddy and Jane Sharp are going forward with their divorce. Since Jane's arrest, Lil has been spending more time at her son's home, helping with the running of the household and the children. She called the other day to let me know that she and Brian have been talking more and are growing much closer. Perfect4u has disappeared forever, or so Lil says.

Gordon Harper is in prison awaiting trial for a laundry list of things, including the murder of Laurie Luke and the fireman killed at Seventh Veil. I'm sure I'll be asked to testify when the time comes. I hope he rots in prison—which could happen, considering his age.

My thoughts were interrupted by the stampede of young feet and hungry mouths into my kitchen.

"Odelia, Greg says we can have some ice cream," the boys said as a duet.

I looked from Silas to his brother Billy. "He did, did he? And what about your lunch? The food will be done soon. Wouldn't you rather have a burger or a hot dog first?"

Billy piped up. "We can eat it all!"

I tousled his hair. "I bet you can."

Silas had been one of the heroes of the day, after all. As soon as the SUV carted me and Lisa away, Silas had climbed out of the back seat of my car and searched for the cell phone he'd seen Charles take from me and throw. Silas had located Greg's number on it and made the call for help.

"How about a fruit juice bar instead?" I asked them. "It's better for you."

Silas nodded okay, but Billy had to think it over. In the end, the fruit juice bars were unanimous.

A loud whine broke the air. Behind the boys sat Wainwright, his big tail thumping on the tile. He wanted something, too.

"Can we give Wainwright a snack?" asked Silas.

"Okay," I said, getting out a couple of doggie biscuits, "but don't excite him too much. He still needs his rest."

The boys sat on the floor in the living room next to the thick bed we'd recently bought for Wainwright. With one boy on either side, the dog settled in between them. Together the three munched their snacks, happy as pigs at the trough.

Zee came into the kitchen as the boys left it. "Why don't you go outside and be with your guests?"

"I just have to finish icing this carrot cake, then I'm done. I promise."

I was just about to dip a knife into the cream cheese icing when the doorbell rang. The dog barked a few times and slowly got to his feet.

Wainwright's going to be fine, but it would take time and patience for him to get all his strength back. Still, he keeps his post and protects his family. Injury or no injury, he's still the first to reach the door most of the time.

When Harper had come back to the apartment hell-bent on dragging me off as a hostage for the second time, Greg had sent in his beloved dog to find me—to run into the burning building in his stead and go places and at speeds his wheelchair would not allow him to go himself. Having Wainwright save me had been the same as Greg taking down Harper in person.

"I'll get that," Zee said, as she followed the dog to the front door.

A minute later, Zee returned. "You've got company."

I glanced into the living room to find Michael Steele standing there dressed in tennis togs. Next to him on the floor were two large document boxes. I handed the icing knife to Zee and went to him.

"Well, Steele, this is a surprise."

He shrugged. "I was on my way to a game and thought I'd drop this stuff by."

"This stuff?" I looked down at the boxes. "What's *this stuff*?"

"*This stuff* is the due diligence data for that new deal Woobie just took on. You know, the sale of that restaurant chain. It needs to be sorted and indexed ASAP."

"ASAP? But it's the holiday weekend."

"I'm aware of that, Grey. And a good time for me to call in my marker, don't you think?"

Wainwright busied himself sniffing Steele's sneakers and legs. Steele squatted to look at the animal, snout to snout. "So, this is the big hero." Steele scratched the dog behind the ears. Wainwright wagged his tail and licked his face.

"Traitor," I said to the dog. He just wagged his tail with more enthusiasm.

"But I have guests, Steele."

Steele rose and peeked out towards the patio. "For the entire weekend?"

My nose twitched in annoyance. My plan was to relax all weekend. I looked down at the boxes and up at Steele. "You sure you need this ASAP?"

"I need it by next Monday, and this week is a short workweek because of the holiday."

I sighed. A deal was a deal, especially if made with the devil. "I guess I could get a start on it this weekend."

"Great." He made no move to leave.

"We're having a few friends over, Steele. Would you like to join us?" When he hesitated, I added, "You know some of them."

"Is that Jill?"

"Yes, Jill and Sally are here, as well as Kelsey and her husband." I paused. "But, of course, I wouldn't want to take you away from your tennis date."

Steele whipped out his BlackBerry and punched a button. "Hey, Dodd. Steele here. I'm afraid I can't make it today. Sorry, pal." Steele paused and listened. My guess was that the person on the other line was Marvin Dodd, one of Steele's regular tennis buddies.

Steele chuckled into the phone and winked at me. "Of course, a woman's involved. Isn't there always a woman involved?"

As Steele headed in the direction of the patio, I joined Zee in the kitchen. She'd almost finished icing the carrot cake. Together, we put the last few items out on the food table. As soon as Greg said the meat was ready, we'd yell *come and get it*.

I guess you're wondering about the Blond Bomber. I'm happy to say he has been apprehended, and purely by accident. When I found out his identity, I was equally surprised and not surprised, sprinkled with just a little terror.

The Blond Bomber was none other than Paul Milholland, Jane's longtime jack-of-all-trades. Given the circumstances, it made sense. He knew all of her clients and knew exactly what she looked like all the time, even when she cut and colored her hair. The theory is that because the women knew him from the work done at their homes, they felt comfortable and had no reason to fear him. They had walked into his deadly trap as easily as lambs to slaughter. Once captured, the police learned he was obsessed with Jane Sharp and deeply offended by her sexual promiscuity.

Yet, in his own way, he loved her too much to kill her outright, so he killed her by proxy instead.

When I think about Paul insisting I look into his van, and how close I came to doing it, I get the chilly shakes.

Ironic, isn't it? Gordon Harper was having Paul follow me, hoping I'd lead him to the Blond Bomber so he could kill him in retaliation for his ex-wife's death, and all the time Paul Milholland was the serial killer. The man who'd murdered Crystal Lee Harper was under Gordon's nose the whole time.

During her debriefing, Agent Maria Santiago, who'd been shot by Gordon during the melee, gave the police information on Paul Milholland and his part in the smuggling ring. It was during a search of his home that police uncovered evidence linking him to the deaths of the Blond Bomber victims. They are also checking to see if he might be responsible for the deaths or disappearances of other women in California.

Paul was captured about a week ago, near Santa Barbara. He'd been identified from a photo broadcast on all the news shows. When the police caught up to Paul, he had his latest victim in the back of his vehicle, a different van. Fortunately, she was still alive.

The last Blond Bomber target wasn't a long, lean, and leggy blond. Nor was she a curvy woman with bobbed red hair. The rescued woman was short and fat, with medium-length brown hair.

When I was told, I passed out.

THE END

314

If you like the adventures of Odelia Grey, then you'll love Sue Ann Jaffarian's new paranormal mystery series featuring the ghost of Granny Apples. This cozy series features the amateur sleuth team of modern-day divorced mom Emma Whitecastle and the spirit of her pie-baking great-great-great-grandmother, Granny Apples. Together, they solve mysteries of the past—starting with Granny's own unjust murder rap from more than a century ago.

The first book in the series debuts in September 2009. Sit down with a slice of warm pie and savor this tantalizing preview...

EXCERPT

"Mom went to a séance last night."

As soon as the words were out of Kelly's mouth, Emma White-castle wanted to kick her daughter's leg under the dining table. They were having Sunday dinner at Emma's parents' house. It was Emma's childhood home and where Emma had moved after separating from Grant Whitecastle, Kelly's father, just over a year ago. Instead of a well-landed kick, Emma scowled across the table at her daughter. Kelly was eighteen going on thirty. Graced with the long, elegant legs of a colt and the face of fairy-tale princess, she was both smart and smart-mouthed, and even though Emma would miss her daughter, she was looking forward to when Kelly would leave for Harvard in the fall. The divorce proceedings had been hard on Kelly, and Emma was hoping the move east would help her daughter start a new life without the ugliness of her parents' relationship staring her in the face and from the tabloids. Although she still would not be immune, at least in Boston her daughter might escape the Hollywood sideshow and gossip surrounding the divorce.

"A séance?" Emma's mother, Elizabeth Miller, asked, her knife and fork frozen in midair. She stared at Emma over the top of her glasses, prim and proper, waiting for an answer.

Emma looked at each member of her family seated at the table. Besides her mother and daughter, her father, Paul Miller, a retired heart surgeon, was also waiting to see what her answer would be. She cleared her throat.

"Yes, Mother, a séance." Emma took a drink from her water glass before continuing. "Tracy asked me to go with her. It had to do with research for a class she's giving in the fall."

Tracy Bass was Emma's oldest and dearest friend. They had grown apart during the last years of Emma's marriage to Grant. Tracy never liked Grant and had not liked the way Emma had changed under Grant's influence. And Grant, harboring a similar dislike for Tracy, discouraged Emma from seeing her. Seeing that she lived with Grant and not Tracy, Emma had taken the easier path of acquiescing to her husband's wishes. But in the past six months, with Emma's marriage all but dead, the two women had started mending the fences of their friendship.

Tracy taught full-time at UCLA—the University of California at Los Angeles. She had begged Emma to join her the night before, saying it would be interesting. She enticed her further with the promise of dinner beforehand at one of their favorite restaurants. Tracy had been right. It had been a very interesting evening, but outings with her flamboyant friend usually were. This one, though, had topped the list. Emma couldn't stop thinking about it. It played over and over in her head like an annoying ad jingle.

The table fell into a companionable silence as everyone resumed eating. A few minutes later, Emma asked, "Did someone from our family ever live in or around Julian, California?"

This time, Emma's mother dropped her fork with a loud clunk. All eyes turned to Elizabeth, who dropped her eyes as she retrieved her utensil from the middle of her plate.

"You all right, dear?" Paul asked his wife. His eyes, dark with concern, darted from his wife to his daughter and back to his wife.

"Just a little clumsy, that's all." Elizabeth put her fork back down. "I guess I'm not very hungry."

"Where's Julian?" Kelly asked.

Emma turned to her daughter. "It's a small town in the mountains east of San Diego—a historic gold rush town. I looked it up on the Internet this morning."

"A ghost town?" Kelly asked with rising interest.

"No, it's still a small but thriving community. In fact, it's known for its apples. According to the man who led the séance, we have a black sheep in our family."

"Do tell, Mom."

"Would you believe our family tree harbors a murderer?"

"No way!"

"That's what the man said. A woman who killed her husband. She was then promptly hung."

"That's pretty wild. Is this on Grandma or Grandpa's side?" Her young, eager eyes darted between her grandparents.

"I didn't do it."

In unison, Emma and her mother jerked their heads in the same direction, but saw nothing. Kelly and her grandfather kept eating.

"Did you hear that, Mother? Sounded like someone whispering. How odd."

Abruptly, Elizabeth got up from the table. "Why don't you all have dessert on the patio. It's so lovely outside."

Paul left his place at the table and went to his wife. "Are you sure you're okay, dear?"

Elizabeth patted his arm. "I'm fine, Paul, just tired from the theatre last night, that's all."

"Mother, why don't you rest? Kelly and I will clean up and get the dessert."

"Thank you, Emma. I think I'll go upstairs and read, if you don't mind."

Emma and Kelly were just finishing cleaning the kitchen when Nate Holden, Kelly's boyfriend, dropped by.

"We're going to a movie," Kelly announced.

"You kids want some pie before you go?" Emma cut into an apple pie and placed a slice on a dessert plate.

"No thanks, Mrs. Whitecastle," Nate said politely. "The movie starts soon."

Emma smiled. Nate Holden was a nice young man from a good family and the same age as Kelly. He was tall and slim and wore his brown hair long. They had been dating for almost two years. Emma wondered what would happen to the relationship once Kelly and Nate went their separate ways in the fall. While Kelly was heading to Harvard, Nate was off to Stanford. Seldom did high-school infatuations hold up under long-distance stress and strain.

Kelly had been torn about going to Harvard because of Nate, but in the end knew she couldn't miss the opportunity. As much as Emma liked Nate, she was relieved when Kelly made her decision to go east. She didn't want her daughter to plan her life around a man as she had.

After Nate and Kelly left, Emma carried a tray holding two slices of warm apple pie with vanilla ice cream and two cups of decaf coffee out to where her father was relaxing on the patio. Emma took a seat in a chaise longue next to him. Beyond the patio, the family's black Scottish terrier, Archie, rolled around on the grass.

"Apple pie?" her father asked as he readied to take his first bite. "Where did this come from?"

"I picked it up from the bakery this morning."

Paul studied his daughter with interest. "I didn't think you liked apple pie. Thought you were a lemon meringue kind of gal, like your mother."

Emma shrugged. "Generally, I am." She took a bite and chewed, savoring the homey flavor on her tongue. "It's not that I dislike apple pie. I just never think of having it. Guess it's because we never had it much while I was growing up. This, however, is quite tasty." She took a sip of coffee between bites. "Funny thing, this morning when I was at the grocery store, I got the most intense craving for it." She laughed. "So much so, I'm surprised I didn't stop the car and dig into it on the side of the road like some junkie."

The words startled her father. He stopped eating. "This morning? You got the craving for apple pie this morning?"

"Actually, the craving started last night, during that silly séance. It was quiet, just the leader speaking, and suddenly I could smell apple pie or at least cinnamon." Again she shrugged. "It was probably one of the candles they were burning. Some candles smell good enough to eat."

"Honey, how did Julian come up?"

"Julian, California?" A bit of pie escaped from her fork and landed on her blouse. Emma dabbed at it while she thought about Julian. "It was something Milo said to me."

"Milo?" Paul's graying eyebrows raised like two caterpillars snapping to attention. Milo wasn't a common name, but it was one he'd come across before.

"Yes, Milo, the leader of the séance. He said someone, a spirit, wanted very much to talk to me. Said it was important." She glanced at her father. "How silly is that? Tracy was almost green with envy since no ghosts were speaking with her. Just me and two other folks had that dubious honor." Emma's tone was filled with amusement. "Milo asked me if I had family in Julian. Said the spirit was a woman from there."

"Did he say anything more about the woman? Any details? A name?" Paul tried to hold himself back. He didn't want his daughter to sense how concerned he was, at least not yet.

"Just a woman who'd been hung for murdering her husband."

Emma looked over at her father. He was sitting on the edge of his patio chair watching her, as if she were a child ready to take a nasty spill.

"You don't believe this malarkey, do you, Dad?" When he didn't answer, she continued. "For cripes' sake, you're a doctor, a scientist."

Paul took a big drink of his coffee before responding. "As a doctor, I studied science, Emma. But during my years as a doctor, I witnessed many astonishing things. Unexplainable things. Things having to do with death and dying, and things that happen when people die. The idea that the spirits of people, or ghosts, are among us and are trying to communicate with us is a fascinating one, is it not?"

Emma nodded. "Yes, it is, in theory. But I'm not so sure it's real. Last night, except for me, the other two people Milo said had … well, 'visitors' is how he put it … were desperately looking for that contact. They attended the séance hoping, even praying that someone they loved would speak to them from the grave. It would be easy for them to grasp at any straw held out to them."

"But what about you?"

"What about me?" Emma fidgeted in her seat before answering. "I went to keep Tracy company. For me, it was an evening with a friend, nothing more. Maybe Milo was trying to make a believer out of me, to rope me into his scam. Considering it was fifty-five dollars a head last night, it really is quite a scam."

"Are you sure that's the only reason you went?"

Her father had a knack for digging with questions like some folks worked with shovels. Emma always thought he should have been a psychiatrist instead of a surgeon. When she looked away without responding, he continued.

"Emma, I know things have been very unsettling since you and Grant split up. Your child is about to move away from home. You don't have a career or real purpose in life, and you're floundering a bit. Maybe, in some way, you went along with Tracy to look for answers, perhaps even a focus to your life."

This time, Emma looked directly at her father. "Really, Dad, does that sound like me?"

Paul Miller shrugged with frustration. His daughter had both hardened and softened during her marriage to Grant Whitecastle. She was more cynical these days, but she also lacked the spunky backbone she'd had growing up. He missed the inner strength that used to glow from within her like a candle in a jack-o'-lantern.

"Hard to say, Emma. You used to be much more determined and focused than you are now. I know you're hurting, honey, but it's time to move on."

"You trying to get rid of me, Dad?" Her tone was joking, but in her heart Emma was a bit scared.

"No, honey, far from it. You're welcome to live with us as long as you like. You know that. We love having you here." He paused and studied his daughter before speaking again. "But I think it would be healthier for you to get on with your life. You are far too young to be holed up here with us old folks. Travel. Buy a home. Find a career. As soon as a fair settlement is reached, sign the divorce papers and get on with your life. Kick Grant Whitecastle to the curb like he deserves and be done with him."

"You sound like Tracy."

"Tracy is a smart and charming woman. I'm very glad you two are spending time together again."

Emma laughed lightly. "I'm not so sure Mother agrees with you. I think she's afraid I'll adopt Tracy's bohemian ways." It was true. Elizabeth loved Tracy Bass like a second daughter but didn't understand why Tracy preferred vintage second-hand shops to Saks.

"And I think Tracy rubbing off on you a little wouldn't hurt." He smiled at her. "And that's a doctor's opinion."

Emma and her father sat in silence, enjoying the evening. Archie brought a tennis ball over and dropped it at Paul's feet. He picked it up and tossed it. The dog scampered off in the direction of the throw. The animal brought it back, and Paul threw it again. After another throw, Paul decided it was time to tell his daughter about Ish Reynolds.

"Your ancestors did come from Julian, Emma."

"What?" She looked at her father in disbelief. "Are you kidding me?"

He shook his head as he tossed the ball again for Archie. "No, your mother's people were originally from Kansas but settled in Julian in the mid to late 1800s."

"Is that what agitated Mother at dinner?"

"Partly, yes."

Paul Miller sat forward in his chair and studied his daughter, locking eyes with her. When Archie came back with the ball, Dr. Miller patted the animal and gently ordered the dog to lay down. Archie obeyed.

"How much do you remember about the time following Paulie's death?" he asked his daughter.

Paulie was Paul, Jr., Emma's older brother. He had been hit and killed by a car after dashing into the street to get a wayward ball. It was a tragic accident, both for their family and for the man whose car had struck Paulie. Emma had been nine years old when it happened. Paulie was eleven.

"I remember how difficult it was on Mother—on all of us, but especially Mother." Emma swallowed. "Mother always blamed herself, didn't she?"

Paul nodded. "Yes. That's nonsense, of course. Elizabeth was and is the best of mothers. It just happened so fast. No one could have prevented it except for Paulie. He was old enough to know not to run out into the street."

Emma watched as a gray film covered her father's face like plastic wrap. She knew her parents had never gotten over the death of their son, no matter how many years had passed.

"But what does Julian have to do with Paulie's death?"

"About six or seven months after Paulie died, your mother got it in her head to try and contact him."

"Contact him? You mean Mother went to a séance?"

Paul gave a slight nod. "Your mother went to many séances and spent a great deal of money, most of it on charlatans, trying to reach your brother. She was obsessed with it. Needed to know how he was and to beg for his forgiveness. But nothing happened. Then, almost a year to the date of Paulie's death, she went to someone new—a young man recommended to her by someone she'd met at another meeting."

"Let me guess," Emma said with sarcasm. "Mother found Paulie's spirit there like a pair of sunglasses waiting to be claimed at the lost and found?" Emma snorted softly and got up to clear the dessert dishes. A slight chill wafted through the patio. She was ready to go inside and forget about spirits and séances.

Paul put a hand on his daughter's arm. "Please sit down, Emma," her father gently ordered. "This is important." Emma stopped fussing with the dishes and sat back down.

"Your mother never spoke to Paulie, but she was assured by another spirit that he was fine. It made all the difference to your mother. It brought her back to us."

"Another spirit?"

"Yes. Another spirit."

"And you believe this, Dad?" Emma stared at her father, her mouth hanging open like a marionette with cut strings.

"Like I said, there are a lot of strange things going on in the world, some we can see and explain, some we can't. But I do know that it brought a lot of comfort to your mother and helped us get our lives back on track."

"Well, that's a good thing, no matter how it came about. And did Mother stop going to séances after that?"

"Yes, she did, but according to your mother, the spirit who helped her did not go away. She came to your mother over and over, following Elizabeth and speaking to her."

Emma's eyes grew large. "Dad, that's scary. That's psychotic."

"Certainly could be taken that way." Paul sighed. "Finally, months later, I went to the man who had run the séance, a man named Milo." He emphasized the name and watched as his daughter's blue eyes widened further in disbelief. "I asked him to intercede in whatever way he could. We ended up having a private session, just he and I, during which he asked the spirit to leave your mother alone. And apparently it worked, or seemed to. Elizabeth's never had a problem since, but she's very sensitive about it, as you saw at dinner."

Emma's mind buzzed with this new information, whining and whirring until her ears hurt. Her mother had had a spirit, or ghost, following her around? Her father had gone to a séance to ask the ghost to stop? Her parents were two of the most grounded and intelligent people she knew. It hardly seemed possible. And what did Milo have to do with this? There was no way he could have known who her parents were. Maybe it wasn't the same Milo, though she knew it had to be.

Emma cleared her throat and rolled her eyes, a habit of Kelly's she hated. "So who was this ghost, Dad? Did you get her business card?"

Paul let out another tired sigh. It was difficult to tell his daughter about this, but he knew she'd have to know, especially now. Whether she believed it or not would be up to her. "The spirit who helped your mother with Paulie was from Julian. An ancestor, supposedly Elizabeth's great-great-grandmother."

"Are you kidding me?"

Paul shook his head and pushed on. "Her name was Ish Reynolds. She was hung for killing her husband around the turn of the century."

Emma didn't know what to think or believe. It would take time to digest it all and come to a rational conclusion. There had to be a logical explanation. Lost in her thoughts, she ran a finger around her dessert plate. She raised the finger to her mouth and licked the crumbs off while she processed everything her father had just told her.

"One more thing, honey." Her father got up to leave. "Ish, the ghost from Julian? Her nickname was Granny Apples. She was famous for her pie." He winked at his daughter. "Guess which kind?"

WWW.MIDNIGHTINKBOOKS.COM

From the gritty streets of New York City to sacred tombs in the Middle East, it's always midnight somewhere. Join us online at any hour for fresh new voices in mystery fiction.

At midnightinkbooks.com you'll also find our author blog, new and upcoming books, events, book club questions, excerpts, mystery resources, and more.

MIDNIGHT INK ORDERING INFORMATION

Order Online:
• Visit our website www.midnightinkbooks.com, select your books, and order them on our secure server.

Order by Phone:
• Call toll-free within the U.S. and Canada at 1-888-NITE-INK (1-888-648-3465)
• We accept VISA, MasterCard, and American Express

Order by Mail:
Send the full price of your order (MN residents add 6.5% sales tax) in U.S. funds, plus postage & handling to:

> Midnight Ink
> 2143 Wooddale Drive
> Woodbury, MN 55125-2989

Postage & Handling:

Standard (U.S., Mexico & Canada). If your order is:
> $24.99 and under, add $3.00
> $25.00 and over, FREE STANDARD SHIPPING

AK, HI, PR: $15.00 for one book plus $1.00 for each additional book.

International Orders (airmail only):
> $16.00 for one book plus $3.00 for each additional book

Orders are processed within 2 business days. Please allow for normal shipping time.
Postage and handling rates subject to change.

ABOUT THE AUTHOR

LIKE THE CHARACTER ODELIA Grey, Sue Ann Jaffarian is a middle-aged, plus-size paralegal. In addition to the Odelia Grey mystery series, she is the author of a new paranormal mystery series that is due for release from Midnight Ink beginning in September 2009, and writes general fiction and short stories. Sue Ann is also nationally sought after as a motivational and humorous speaker. She lives and works in Los Angeles, California.

Visit Sue Ann on the Internet at

WWW.SUEANNJAFFARIAN.COM

and

WWW.SUEANNJAFFARIAN.BLOGSPOT.COM